# The Next 167 Hours

## Christa Hickcox

Copyright © 2023 by Christa Hickcox

All rights reserved.

No part of this publication may be reproduced, distributed, or transmitted in any form or by any means, including photocopying, recording, or other electronic or mechanical methods, without the prior written permission of the publisher, except as permitted by U.S. copyright law. For permission requests, contact Christa Hickcox at christacps@gmail.com

The story, all names, characters, and incidents portrayed in this production are fictitious. No identification with actual persons (living or deceased), places, buildings, and products is intended or should be inferred.

Book Cover by Sarah Earnhart

First edition 2023

For my family
My wife Jenny, who always encourages me to follow my dreams
My wombmate, Susan, forever my biggest fan
To the rest of my family, thank you for always believing in me, even when it was hard

# Chapter One

I tossed another book on the growing mountain of magazines that I had read throughout the night; "Food and Wine," my favorite queer read, "Curve," and a random crocheting magazine, "Happily Hooked," that my mother must have left here the other day. I looked over at the clock beside the TV. 8:00 a.m.

"That confirms it. I slept less than three hours again last night." I said to the empty space that continued to create this hollowness inside of me. I looked down at the pile, shrugged my shoulders and thought to myself, *Welp, at least if I ever get into another relationship, I will be able to prepare a romantic dinner, satisfy my partner in the bedroom, and make an unlimited number of doilies for our apartment.*

*I guess I can't stay on this couch forever.* "Come on Stormy, it's time to get up buddy," I grumbled as I nudged my French bulldog with my foot. I could tell he heard me by the two little thumps of his tail I felt against on the couch, but instead of coming to the surface, he just burrowed even deeper under the blanket. His poor little body was sensitive to the cold air that drifted through the apartment, especially after being snuggled under my heated blanket all night. I guess it was also possible he didn't want to get up because he was just sad, like me.

I sighed. "I know buddy, I miss her too..." When he still didn't budge after another tap from my foot, I attempted another coaxing method that typically worked. I lifted the blanket so he could see my face and started to tease him with some of his most beloved things. With an emphasis on his favorite words, I said, "Do you wanna go for a *walk*? Go to the *park*? I promise we can stop by the *bakery* and get you a *pup cakeeee*."

Now the morning zoomies began. Stormy flew out from under the blanket, superman leaped off the couch, raced down the hall, jumped back onto the couch, jumped off the couch, then ran back down the hall again. He repeated this boisterous charade until his little heart couldn't take it any longer and he finally collapsed on my chest, panting and snorting while he spoiled me with tons of morning kisses.

I sat up and wiped his slobber from my face, then put him on the floor beside my feet. I took a deep breath and looked around the living room as I rallied enough strength to not cry, at least not until after I brushed my teeth this morning. Goals. Weekends were the hardest. No work, nowhere to go, and absolutely zero distractions to keep my mind from racing. I kept telling myself we would adjust to this new normal of being on our own, just me and Stormy.

For the past eight months, we've gotten into a pretty good routine. Monday through Friday, we go for a morning walk around the block a few times before I make our breakfast and I get ready for work.

Stormy is old enough now that I can leave him home alone during the day without having to worry about him going potty in the apartment. Just to be safe though, I bought one of those fake grass squares for the balcony, so he could go in and out as he needed to during the day.

Our apartment isn't very big. In fact, the whole place is about as big as your average hotel room. Because that is exactly what my apartment used to be. The building is a hotel that was converted into apartments.

I pushed myself off the couch and walked to my small kitchenette, which consisted of what I referred to as a 'half stove,' with two burners, but no oven. At least they provided each unit with a microwave, small toaster oven and a small fridge. I grabbed a glass of water and headed to the balcony, letting Stormy out to do his business on his square. As soon as I opened the sliding glass door, I was immediately struck by a burst of crisp fall air. I should have put on slippers, but somehow the cold concrete against my bare feet made me feel a little more alive this morning. *I'll take it.* I thought to myself.

When you live in the city on a budget, you pay for location and convenience, not space. When the property management remodeled these rooms, they created a short hallway to the front door to give the illusion this wasn't once a hotel room. I didn't care so much about that. What made us fall in love with this place was this very balcony, with the peekaboo view of Elliott Bay and the breathtaking views of the city lights at night.

I let Stormy sniff around while I took a minute to embrace the calmness of the air and the noises of the city. Like most mornings in my neighborhood, the bakery up the street filled the air with the smell of warm pastries. I guessed Stormy smelled it too, by the little strings of drool that formed at the sides of his mouth. I supposed we should probably get ready for our walk and breakfast before he thinks I am going to starve him to death.

We walked back into the apartment, where the silence hit me like a brick wall. The apartment seemed so empty, even though it was filled to the rim with furniture, books, and other odds and ends. You would think I'd be used to how quiet it was, after living here alone for the last eight months, but I'm not. Sometimes I just don't expect it. It took me so off guard, the silence.

It was so random when the silence would hit me—it could be when I turned off the shower or the tv, or the simple transition from room to room. I just feel this overwhelming emptiness consuming me. All my fears taunt me over and over. The fear of never feeling another woman in my arms—the weight of her head on my shoulder, feeling the softness of her breath flow across my chest as she fell into a deep sleep after hours of making love. The fear of waking up every day in this apartment alone, not knowing if I will ever be able to love someone else again. I feel so betrayed, abandoned...lost. I want to move on. I think.

Sometimes I would lie awake at night and think about all the stories buried deep inside the walls of this old hotel. The families on vacation, kids jumping from bed to bed, the couples who fought and made up, the travelers who were just passing through, the lady pacing back and forth across the floor, practicing her speech before her big presentation at the convention center, and all heartbroken souls who dragged themselves up to the ninth floor from the hotel bar and cried themselves to sleep in this very room. Am I going to be just another story sucked into these walls someday, too? Probably. Thank god for Stormy, he will most likely be the best part of my story.

In fact, all those "who rescued who" bumper stickers you see on vehicles are true. I didn't rescue Stormy, Stormy rescued me. From the moment I laid eyes on him at the shelter, we immediately bonded. I played with him for all of twenty seconds before I told the guy I was taking him home with me. I named him Stormy because his body is all white except for one grey spot in the shape of a cloud on his rump. Stormy just turned a year old, but it seems like we have been together for way longer. He's been through everything with me.

My office building is only six blocks from my apartment, so I walk to work every day. I go to work, a bunch of work-type stuff happens, and randomly throughout the week I indulge in happy hour drinks with my coworker, Bev. Mostly, though, I just come home and fix dinner, go for another walk, and repeat the charade of life until another torturous weekend rolls around.

When the weekend does finally come around, we go for a longer walk in the mornings. Stormy gets a pup cake, I get coffee, and we frequent a local park not too far from our neighborhood. I sit on the same bench under our favorite tree and I desperately try to figure out what the next move is going to be for our lives. I just don't know what direction to move in, because every turn I take brings me back to this same exact place. The place that has me alone with Stormy, doing our same old routine that we just can't seem to break out of. After I contemplate our lives at the park, we go back home. Eventually, Monday shows her face, and the cycle repeats itself.

But just so I don't sound completely pathetic, I will ease your mind by telling you that last weekend I went to my nephew's football game and then we went for pizza afterwards. And on Sunday I had coffee with my coworker, Amy, who is planning her wedding shower she asked me to attend. I wouldn't say I enjoyed myself. It's always awkward discussing someone else's happiness when your own relationship has ended, so to be honest, it was an unpleasant experience, to say the least. I only said yes because she invited me along with three other coworkers. But yay me, I left my apartment twice last weekend!

I decided a shower today was pointless, as it was another drizzly Saturday morning. I'll shower when I get home. Maybe. I do really love this time of year though, always have. Fall is my favorite season. It is October, school is long back in session, football season is in full swing, and the weather is turning slightly undesirable for most people to be out and about, which all together means Stormy and I typically have fewer people and dogs to deal with at the park.

The park was just a big circle around a lake. We got a lot of exercise by just walking laps around the water. There was plenty of grass to sprawl out on in the summer, benches to sit on when the grass was too wet, and paved pathways for walkers and people who like to bike or rollerblade. We found stuck to just the walking part though, it was much safer that way.

I called Stormy over as I finished lacing my sneakers. I grabbed my keys and shoved my wallet into the pocket of my oversized hoodie before we shuffled towards the door to head out.

I kept Stormy's raincoat and walking gear all on a hook by the front door. He has a drawer for his clothes in my dresser. It's just an empty sock drawer. It's not like anyone else is using it anymore, anyway. I put on Stormy's raincoat, then grabbed his harness and clicked it around his tiny body. "Ready to go, bud?" I asked him as I opened the door.

Just as I stepped outside my apartment, I practically knocked over my big sister standing in front of me with two venti cups of coffee.

"Whoa, hey sis," Sawyer greeted me, almost spilling the coffees on herself.

For a good ten seconds we just stood there and stared at each other like we were gazing from opposite sides of a mirror. We could practically be twins if it wasn't for the fact that I chose to cut off all my hair into an edgy pixie cut. We mimicked our nervous tics as we both ran our fingers through our dark auburn hair. Her fingers took a bit longer as her length flowed over her shoulder and slightly down her chest. We shared the lightest of brown eyes that both narrowed while we determined who would speak next. I broke the silence first.

"Hey..." I replied, furrowing my eyebrows.

"You're probably wondering why I am here, unannounced, on a Saturday morning, with no makeup on, and in sweatpants," she said as she extended one of the two cups of coffee at me, which I assumed was a peace offering.

"Mostly the no makeup part. You're scaring my dog." I took one of the coffees.

It's true. My sister would rarely show up in any public setting looking anything but completely perfect. I, on the other hand, tend to be more on the causal side. I like to wear jeans, a cozy sweater, and my baggy sweatshirts on the weekends.

"Ha, well, you haven't answered any of my text messages or phone calls all week. The only reason I know you're still alive is because I can see your movements on the app," she said, holding up her phone so I could see my location pinned at my apartment on what I like to call her "sister stalker," app.

"Note to self, turn off my location on my phone," I mumbled under my breath, while taking a sip of coffee. One of these days I needed to get off my sister's family plan and get my own phone plan.

"Anyways, I was hoping we could talk, you know, hoping you might have given our conversation from last week a little more thought?" Sawyer treaded lightly.

"Stormy and I are just heading out for a walk, if you want to come?" I asked, secretly hoping she would decline as I handed her Stormy's leash.

"Um, sure, why not." Sawyer accepted both the offer and Stormy's leash.

*Ugh! She is never going to drop this!* I thought to myself.

Sawyer is my big sister. Born five years my elder. My parents' favorite child. I know, I know, a lot of people say that about their siblings. *Mom and Dad like my brother or sister more than me.* Well, our parents don't deny the fact that Sawyer was their favorite. They literally say it all the time. Still don't believe me? Then, I will present you, the jury of my peers, with three critical pieces of evidence, and then I will let you decide for yourselves.

Exhibit number one: our middle names. Our parents had children late in life and therefore only wanted one child. When they had Sawyer, they gave her the middle name Evelyn, which means "wished for child." Then along came me. I was a surprise, and an unwanted pregnancy. Not only was I unwanted, but I also came along at the worst possible time. My dad had just lost his job, my mom was sick the whole time she was pregnant with me, her labor lasted thirty-two hours, I weighed ten pounds three ounces, and I was breech. She swears I was a demon inside of her. My mother named me Ember Rue. Rue means "regret."

Exhibit number two: our lifestyles. My sister is a doctor, married to my brother-in-law, Todd, who is also a doctor. He is a dentist, and she is a baby doctor. They have two kids. One is in high school and the other just started the fifth grade. One boy and one girl. They are the perfect all-American family. Almost "perfect", they don't have a dog, which I think is a huge flaw in the whole "all-American" part...just saying. Then there is me. I work as an Executive Assistant for the VP of Marketing at a medium size advertisement agency in downtown Seattle. I have been with the company for eight years and it barely pays the bills. My parents still call me a secretary. Not only did I not follow in my sister's footsteps and become a doctor, but I never even went to college. I am obviously not married. My parents wonder everyday why I didn't turn out "normal" like my sister, but for the most part they have always accepted my partners and been pleasant to them. Except for Tiffany, a woman I dated very briefly—like one date.

Tiffany's demise was when she got a little tipsy at a dinner party that my parents hosted for their retirement community. My parents are always trying to raise money for something to make their retirement center a better place to live. On that fateful night, after a half a bottle of wine, Tiffany told my mother her crab cakes were the best burgers she ever tasted. It was a disaster that ended with my mother crying and my dad laughing. My mother's cooking is not often very well received, but we at least try to pretend we like it. Sawyer tried to make me feel better by saying that no one else noticed how bad mom's cooking was that night because all the guests were old and their taste buds were all pretty much dead. Hey, she's the doctor, who was I to argue with that logic?

I am thirty-seven and, in my parents' eyes, I have no future and will die alone with no family, no retirement, rotting in my little hotel apartment. I am sure there are a hundred other things they consider embarrassing about me, but we will just keep it at a high level for now.

Now I present you with my third and final exhibit. Sawyer has always been the poster child of stability and mental health. If she had a business card, it would say:

*Sawyer Evelyn*
*Family Manager*
*Mental Health Extraordinaire*

My parents perceive her as the strong one, the stable one, while everyone thinks I can't handle my shit, that I am going to step off the ledge. Ridiculous.

This was the reason Sawyer showed up today. She wants me to go to therapy. She thinks I have anxiety. She also thinks I am depressed, she thinks, she thinks, she thinks. When really, I am just over here living my life. It is my life and if I say I'm fine, I'm fine. I can't fix all the fucked up things in the world. This has been the absolute worst year of my life, so you would think instead of my family pressuring me to be perfect Sawyer, instead they might find it in themselves to accept me as I am and let me deal with my life the way I see fit, after all it is my life.

Maybe I just see the world differently, maybe I am just more sensitive, maybe I just want to be left alone, maybe I'm just quick to cry, maybe I just don't have the right words all the time, maybe I am a little quiet, maybe I just miss my girlfriend, maybe they're right to be full of regret... maybe I'm just Ember Rue.

"Ember, you okay? You ready to go?" Sawyer asked as she tugged lightly on my jacket.

I eased back to attention, inhaled deeply, and responded. "Yep, fine, I'm ready, let's go," I said as I turned and locked my apartment door.

# Chapter Two

"What the hell was that!" I called out to darkness as I was suddenly jolted awake. I was now sitting upright on my bed while I clenched my t-shirt with my fist. I threw my head back and gasped loudly as I struggled to suck the air back into my lungs. After a minute, I started to get nips of air again, so I slowly leaned back and rested my shoulders against the headboard of my bed.

I tried to shake the feeling away, but I just couldn't. I crept my hand lower where I found my heart pulsating in my stomach to see if I could regulate myself somehow, but the beats just kept getting stronger and faster. I looked down to see my t-shirt was so soaked with sweat that I could see my bare skin through the thin cotton fabric that outlined the crevice of my bellybutton.

I turned to reach for Stormy and noticed my hands were shaking. I went to pet him, but between the sweat and vibration of my palms, tons of his fur pulled away from between my fingers. I tried to take a deep breath, yet with each attempt, a large lump of air kept getting caught in my throat. I started to cough to clear my airway.

*My god I just want this to stop, please, please, PLEASE stop. I just want to feel normal again. Why can't I just be normal? Breathe. Breathe. Breathe.* I exhaled a few long breaths of air from my lungs.

"FUCKKKKKKK," I screamed out loud. *Please god, take this fucking pain away and just let me be normal.*

I wrestled with this thought as I looked over at the clock. It was 2:00 a.m. I jumped a little when I felt Stormy's small licks across the back of my arm, which I know was his way of trying to calm me down. *We've been through this before.* I shut my eyes and brought my pillow to my lips, then clenched my fingers around the edges of the seams. As I buried my face into the cool linen fabric, I rocked back and forth and screamed until I had nothing left inside of me. This felt like it went on for hours, but most likely only a few minutes had passed before I finally dropped backwards on my bed from exhaustion.

I reached over and pulled Stormy into me so I could cradle his little body. I needed a drink of water, but I couldn't go into the kitchen alone. I couldn't even go to the frickin kitchen to get water. I just laid there, curled up in a tight ball, and begged no one, someone, everyone, anyone, for the morning light to come. I just wanted to hear people walking below my window again, then I wouldn't be alone anymore.

\*\*\*

I stood outside my office building wondering if I even had the energy to tackle today. Last night was rough. I don't normally call in sick, yet something was telling me I should have just called my boss and told her I had the flu, or a headache, or something. Instead, I woke up and managed to take a short shower. I couldn't hold down any breakfast this morning, so I grabbed an apple on the way out the door just in case I felt better a little later.

I really don't understand how people can function without sleep. There is this guy in my office that works in the IT department, Jack, who says that he would regularly stay up all night playing video games and come to work on zero sleep. He would code all day like it's no big deal. He was productive in meetings, very articulate, and everyone trusted him with their computers. I brushed my teeth today. Yep, that's what everyone gets, minty fresh breath.

Jack and I used to have super deep conversations about all sorts of things. Technology, science, life, well, mostly about alien life, but deep alien life stuff. I used to be the person in the office who everyone would jump out of their chair to walk with when I passed by to share all the office gossip with. I would stop by everyone's cubicle to say good morning, and take coffee orders, but nowadays I try to make it to my desk as fast as possible and avoid all eye contact along the way. I could count on the one hand the number of people in the office I actively engage with these days.

I put on my best smile and headed the rest of the way to the front door.

We do have a beautiful office building. As soon as you rotated through the revolving doors, you fell into an open space of marbled floors and forty-foot ceilings. There was an amazing color palette of blues and gold that streamed through the entire entrance to make our lobby look like a museum.

There is a gallery of beautiful artwork, some I am told are centuries old. Mixed in are statues of women made of stainless-steel. The lighting that shines in from the windows hits each woman in such a perfect way that it makes the metal shine with a radiant, magnificent glow. My favorite statue is of a woman dressed in a long flowing dress. Her eyes are mysterious and no matter where you stand, they appear to be following you. It's like she is looking deep inside your soul while her hand is outstretched towards you, inviting you to take it. The tilt of her smile, along with the softness of her gaze, is like someone who wants to hold you, love you—not quite like a lover or a friend but more like a protector. I am deeply captivated by her beauty.

On the opposite end of the entrance is a water feature where children throw their pennies into the waterfall to make a wish. Live plants and flowers surround the waterfall to give the place a more serene feel.

When I have time, I like to take my lunch downstairs and sit with the metal woman and just listen to the water. Some days, it's the only peace I find in my world. It's possible some of those pennies aren't just from the kids. I might have dropped one (or a hundred) penny wishes in there too.

"Good morning, Ember," Mr. Lee called out from behind the security desk that was strategically placed in the middle of the lobby. He looks so small surrounded by the half dozen monitors that provide him and another guard, who I don't know because they seem to change by the week these days, a view of each entrance and the elevator bay.

Mr. Lee had a good twenty-five-year tenure on me at SBTK Advertising. He kept saying this is the year he is going to retire, like last year, and the year before that. Maybe he will, but I kind of doubt it. I remember when I first started with the company, Mr. Lee refused to let me pass the security desk unless I could prove I worked for the company. I told him it was my first day, and I didn't have my badge yet. He called another security officer and told him I was being hostile and to take me in back to "vet" me as a possible "problem". Then they both started laughing and welcomed me to the company. Mr. Lee eventually scanned his badge on my behalf to let the elevator take me to my floor. He still thinks my tears were real.

"Good morning, Mr. Lee." I waved my hand over my shoulder as I passed by his desk to walk towards that same elevator bay while smiling at the memory.

Being a Monday morning, the lobby was as busy as ever. People were racing around and bumping into each other, trying to make their first meetings of the day. The lobby will look nothing like this on Friday. Most likely, I will be one of a handful of people who will show up to the office by the end of the week.

After I waited for three elevators to fill and take off without me, I finally crammed into one with eight other people. I pushed the button for the eighteenth floor on the panel and squeezed my way backwards towards the furthest right-hand corner of the elevator. I always go directly to the back right corner if I can. It's like it's "my" corner. I almost get irritated if someone is standing in "my" elevator corner. I hate being in such tight quarters with people. Even if I know them. Even if I like them. There must be a respectable distance that we must always adhere to. Elevators were not built with this consideration in mind.

I felt my stomach dip slightly as the elevator shot up. Off we went, stopping at seven other floors on the way up.

I enjoyed a couple seconds of silence before the ding of the doors told me to put on my cheery face and go make people believe that all was right in the world of Ember Rue.

"Happy Monday Bev," I greeted my friend and coworker as I passed the receptionist's desk. Beverly and I connected on day one. She is two times my age, but has such a fun, young spirit about her, which made it hard to see her as the motherly or grandma type. She is short, round, and never stops smiling.

Bev had this longing to live through all the younger people in the office. If gossiping was an Olympic sport, "The Bev," as she sometimes referred to herself, would be a gold medalist. She is sixty-six, married to a "mole in a hole," as she calls him, named Ed. She has never, I mean never, missed one day of work in her career. Beverly is an amazing human and my happy hour buddy. Everyone loves them some "Bev-Bev," again, as she sometimes refers to herself. As you can see, she comes up with many terms of endearments...for herself.

Bev stood up from behind her desk. "Good morning, Ember. How was your weekend?"

Digging in my workbag for her package, I replied, "Riveting, in fact, I brought you a thank you gift for staying a little later at happy hour with me on Friday."

"Shut up dog, you didn't." Bev clapped her hands and came scooting around her desk over to me.

"Don't get too excited. I just made some microwave brownies and brought you some." I held them up so she could take them from me.

"Oh, are they the 'bud' brownies? Made with a little, ya know, magical butter?" Bev snickered as she took them from my hands.

"No. I don't cook like that, and I tell you that every time I bake you something," I reminded her with a stern look.

"Oh, I know, I am just poking at ya. Totally okay by me if you do bake with the ganja green though. No worries here, probably good for Ed's arthritis." Now trying to backtrack as she tried a bite of her brownies. "Yummy, Em. These are amazing. Your coffee is by your computer, hon." Bev turned and trotted back to her desk.

"Thank you, Bev-Bev, you're the best," I yelled as I watched her disappear to just a head of hair behind her computer.

I sat down at my desk and started to scroll through emails, only to find myself thinking about my conversation with Sawyer over the weekend. It's not like I don't feel like I need therapy. I probably do. I just wonder if therapy is right for me. When I think about therapy,

I think about the people who have serious shit going on. Can't get out of bed type shit. "Look at me, I am here at work, even though I had a horrible night," I whispered to myself while I ran my hands over my desk, looking around the office at the sea of cubicles that lined the office floor.

I am lucky enough to have a corner desk on the floor with an amazing view of Elliott Bay. My cubicle is about the size of my apartment, okay maybe not quite, but close. I have an L shaped desk, two monitors and a round table that seats four chairs. The wall that sits behind that table also serves as a whiteboard, which often comes in handy when my boss, who sits on the other side of the wall, has "the best idea EVER" for us to work through.

I feel like therapy is for people who can't function. I function. I leave the house, granted it's mostly with Stormy, but we do technically leave the house in a functional manner. Therapy is for people who can't stand the light of day. *I love the sun, totally love it, drink it, I bathe in it,* I think to myself as I look out the window at the sun glistening across the water on the bay. Sure, I get a little down, but who doesn't? I have some anxiety, but again, don't we all get a little worked up over things now and then? *Don't people go to therapy when they can't take it anymore? Have that 'at the end of their rope' feeling?* This last thought felt like a knife sliced through my stomach. *Ugh! I really hate the idea of all of this.*

"Ember," Jack blurted, abruptly interrupting my thoughts.

"Jesus, Jack." I jumped out of my chair. "You startled me."

"I wanted to say goodbye." He stood there stiffly. "I am leaving the company and didn't want there to be any erroneous impressions that you and I would stay in touch. I believe that it is important to be upfront and honest with people and not give any false hope, whatsoever, that we will stay friends. Because we are not friends, we are in fact, just work acquaintances. I have always found you pleasant to work with though, you have great integrity."

Now standing in front of Jack with my arms crossed and my head slightly tilted, I find myself completely dumbfounded by the announcement of his departure. "Oh wow, um, okay, thank you, Jack. Well, we all wish you the best of luck, and I do hope we can stay connected on LinkedIn or something." I put out my fist for the customary bump now that Covid has put us all on edge about shaking hands.

"I doubt that will happen either. Take care," Jack said, bumping my fist and somberly walking away.

I sat back down in my chair, shook my head, and sighed. I went back to considering my conversation with Sawyer. Therapy, what would I even talk about? It's not like my problems are interesting or serious. *Are they?* I mean, I have the same shit as everyone else out there. Parent issues, relationship issues, feelings, emotions. *Right?* I may have a couple of things that separate me from others, *but really don't we all?* Should I really be taking someone else's appointment slot that might really need it for my issues? *God damnit, Sawyer, why do you make me feel like I am always so damn broken?*

I reached over and picked up my cell phone that was lying on my desk in front of me and started to scroll through my contacts. I chose my primary care doctor's number and tapped her name to make the call.

As the phone rang and rang, I started to get this pit in my stomach. *What the hell am I doing? I am not broken. Am I broken? I am not broken.* Then I heard a woman's voice disrupt the silent banter in head.

"Dr. Collard's office. How may I help you?"

"Yes, my name is Ember and I need to set up an appointment with Dr. Collard." I started to bounce my leg under my desk nervously.

"And what will Dr. Collard be seeing you for?"

"I would like to talk to her about me not sleeping well," I sort of lied as I put my head in my hand.

*Baby steps. I made the appointment, didn't I?*

# Chapter Three

Stormy and I got home a little later than normal, but the weather was too nice not to take advantage of it, so we walked around the block two more times. When we walked into the apartment, I shut the front door behind me. I kicked off my shoes at the same time I tapped Sawyer's phone number with my finger on my cell phone, which in turn made me start to wobble. I began to lose my balance as my shoulder fell into the wall while I was trying to keep the phone to my ear and remove Stormy's harness all at the same time. I twirled, and turned like a ballerina, then BAM! I went headfirst into the door. Shit, I could feel a goose egg form immediately right in the center of my forehead.

"Hey Sis, this is Em," I said, rubbing the swollen lump on my head.

"I'm just calling to let you know I made an appointment with Dr. Collard to talk about how you think my mental health is in need of some fine tuning. You owe me dinner for making the call. Tell Todd I said hi and let Bella know I will be over next weekend for her birthday party. By the way, what do you get a fifth grader for her birthday these days? Tell Alex he better be there. I haven't seen him in forever. I don't care if he is almost eighteen. His aunt is his world, and he needs to remember that. Anyway, call me back when you get this. Love you." I tapped 'end' on the call.

I made a pit stop in the kitchen to grab a frozen bag of mixed veggies for my goose egg, then moved into the living room, staring at my phone and plopped down on the couch. I hated to reach out to people after work hours, but I figured it was best to let Bev know I needed my calendar blocked for my doctor's appointment the next day.

I picked up my phone to text Bev. It was no surprise she responded within seconds, even though it was 7:00 at night.

> "Hey Bev, can you do me a favor and block my calendar to show me out of the office starting at 3:00 p.m. tomorrow?"

> "Hellloooo there Ember, you got it. #hotdate."

> "No, Bev, doctors' appointment."

> "Oh Ember, are you sick with the Covid?"

> "No, just a checkup. I swear I am fine."

> "Ok, don't make me worry about you. #heartfailure"

> "How's Ed?"

> "Who's Ed?

"Lol, your husband??"

"Oh yeah, that old guy. He is snoring in his recliner already. Louder than a monster truck, but at least I know he's alive."

"Sounds like you're having yet another thrilling evening over there, just like me."

"Love my mole!"

"Good night, Bev."

"Good night, Ember."

\*\*\*

I sat in the waiting room, wondering how the hell I got to this point in my life. I didn't have much time to debate the issue before I heard the nurse call my name. "Ember?"

"Yep, that's me." I shot my hand straight up in the air like I was reporting my attendance in math class.

"Follow me, hon." She smiled.

I got up from my chair and followed the nurse behind the front desk, which lead us past multiple closed doors with little colored flags that signify patients were occupying those rooms.

"You'll be in this room right here." She motioned to the small room with two chairs and an exam table that looked very cold and sterile. I watched her flip the little orange flag before entering the room behind me, indicating that I was now the proud occupant of this room.

The first thing I noticed when entering the room was a picture of a mountain landscape on the wall. The sun was blazing over fields of lavender, bees were buzzing all around searching for nectar, a mama bear was watching over her cubs as they played in the high grasses while she simultaneously hunted for their food at the edge of a stream and there was what appeared to be a storm brewing in the distance. At first glance, this picture looked so calm and peaceful, but then as I studied the picture more, I saw the reality of this beautiful scene and how much danger was really lurking. The bees, bears, heat, and storm were all so dangerous to an unexpecting, inexperienced hiker. People get lost and die all the time for this kind of beauty.

I sat down in one of the two chairs which were across from a tiny table on wheels along with a small stool on rollers, which the nurse took a seat at. I started to become extremely overwhelmed by the thought of even talking to the nurse, more or less the doctor now.

"So, Ember, what are we seeing you for today?" the nurse asked as she started typing on her laptop.

"I am having some trouble sleeping," I said, trying not to make eye contact because I knew if I did, I might very well start to cry.

"Do you know what's keeping you up at night?" She probed deeper, while still typing. *What is she typing?* I started to panic.

I tossed my arms in the air. "I'm not sure. That's why I am here." I snapped.

"Okay, that's okay." She stopped typing and rolled her chair a little closer to me, so it was clear I had her full attention. "Just so you know, sometimes when you do the opposite thing of what keeps you awake at night, it might just help you go to sleep. Just a little free advice from an old nurse. The doctor will be in soon, sweetheart." She winked as she stood up, walked out of the room, and shut the door behind her.

*That is actually not bad advice*, I thought to myself.

I didn't even have a full minute to try to calm myself down before I heard a soft knock on the door and Dr. Collard walked in. "Hi Ember, how are you doing today?" The doctor inquired.

I looked down and started to rub my thumb in a circle on the center of my palm, "Good, pretty good, I guess, can't sleep worth crap, but good, that's why I am here ya know, because I can't sleep, most nights, not all nights, just some of them, most of them honestly. My sister thinks I need therapy," I blurted out, then stopped rubbing my palm and looked the doctor straight in the eyes with sheer terror.

"Ok, so are you here because you can't sleep or because your sister thinks you need therapy?" she asked as she slowly took her seat, so not to startle me with any quick movements.

"Well, I guess the therapy part. Maybe that will in the end help me sleep better too," I shamefully admitted, returning to look down at my hand and started to rub my thumb on the center of my palm again.

"Why do you think you need therapy?" She probed, now typing into her laptop.

"My sister thinks I am depressed and have anxiety," I said while I tried to look over her shoulder to see what she was typing.

"Do you think you are depressed and have anxiety?" She continued to type my responses into her computer.

"I think everyone does a bit. Maybe at this time in my life, I do a little bit more than normal," I confessed, giving up on seeing what she was documenting.

"Okay then, I will write you a script for an anti-anxiety med to help you with your sleep and give you a list of psychotherapists that you can start to look through to see if you find one that you might want to reach out to. Which I really encourage you to think about doing," Dr. Collard offered, shutting her laptop as she stood up in front of me.

Before she walked out the of the room, she turned and asked, "do you want me to take a look at that bump on your head?"

"It's not why I am here." I replied.

"Ember, do you feel safe at home?" She looked very serious.

*Good question,* I thought to myself. "My hallway is very narrow, and this is certainly not the first time I've gotten a goose egg or a bruise falling into that door. I will assess my options with my landlord and report back. Thank you for asking."

"Please do. How about we see you in six months and see how the medication is working for you?" Dr. Collard held the door open for me to exit.

"Okay, this went well, very, very well, thank you Doctor." I jumped out of my seat and put my fist out for a bump.

Dr. Collard made a nervous laugh and awkwardly bumped my fist. "Take care, Ember."

*Good day.* I thought to myself.

I got on the number seventy bus that would take me back downtown to my apartment. I found a single seater near the front so no one could sit next to me. I wanted complete privacy on this bus full of commuters to look at the list Dr. Collard gave me without someone looking over my shoulder. The list only had the name, phone number and a website for each of the therapists, so it wasn't like I had a lot to go on about each person. Just looking at the names though, I narrowed the records down to five people, all women doctors. I felt like to understand a woman, you need to be a woman, just my opinion. Same with my primary care doctor. When I told her I had bad cramps,

I wanted her to totally understand what bad cramps felt like. I needed to know that she gets me.

I stared at the names of all therapists the entire way home. Wondering if I could really do this. People are successful and fail in therapy all the time. I wonder which category I'll end up in? Let's be real, it's me. I will probably get myself fired from therapy within the first month.

I have seen a lot of therapy sessions in the movies. The client lies on a couch or sits in a chair, and some stuffy therapist with zero personality peppers the client with questions and writes all their answers on a pad of paper while the client wonders what the heck they are writing down. Maybe it's different nowadays, and it's super fun now. Like you go on field trips to nature centers, museums, or amusement parks. Can you image flying down the track of a thirty-story roller coaster screaming "I fucking hate my life," with your therapist right by your side screaming "How does that make you feel?" How epic would that be? Or maybe it would be something a little less theatrical and you just talk over a pizza and beer. Maybe not beer. I am sure there is probably something unethical about beer. Soda, yeah, for sure soda would be okay. I guess when I get home, I will check out all their websites and pick the one I want to call.

I looked out the window at all the different people on the street and imagined in my head that I was sitting across from each one of these therapists while they asked me questions about myself. There was a weird part of me that started to get excited about the idea of having someone to talk to, but at the same time, I was also nervous to open up to a complete stranger.

When I walked through the front door, I was greeted by Stormy. He jumped on my leg to pick him up, which I immediately obliged. I was soaked in his sloppy wet kisses, knowing this was one of his many ploys to get me to take him for a walk and make him dinner.

I put him down on the floor. "It's been a long day buddy. Mind if we just eat dinner and watch a movie? Mommy has a little research to do," I asked my dog, as if he had a real say in the matter.

I fed Stormy his normal dry kibble and made myself a grilled cheese sandwich, then turned on the TV to old reruns of *Murder She Wrote*. I grabbed a blanket and a pillow off my bed and took out my laptop to settle in when I heard a knock at the door. *Odd, no one should be coming over at this hour. It's way past dinner time.* "My god, I am talking like I am a ninety-year-old biddy." I rolled my eyes at myself as I got up to go open the door. Not even caring that I was in my t-shirt and sweatpants already, I opened the door to find a woman who seemed to be around my age standing before me.

I immediately felt a sensual charge of energy flow straight through me as I watched her pull a hair tie from her wrist to pull her dark curly hair back into a ponytail while she lifted her deep brown marbled gaze up to meet mine. We both kind of tilted our heads with the same silent curiosity of "are you?", "because I am…" that two lesbians sometimes share.

"Oh…ahh…hi neighbor, I'm Isla and I just moved in two doors down." She pointed to the same side of the hallway as mine. "This is really embarrassing, but I locked myself out of my apartment already, and my cell phone is also inside," she said as she gave me a pathetic look.

I opened my door wider to invite her in. "Oh no, I am so sorry that happened to you. What can I do to help?"

Isla walked into my apartment, looking around, taking it all in before noticing Stormy, who was jumping on her leg. She squatted down with a huge smile on her face and started to give him some love and ear scratches. "Awe hello little one, what is your name?"

"I'm Ember...oh, you mean my dog." I tried to recover quickly "Um, that little charmer is Stormy." Blushing, I closed the door behind her.

Now rubbing his belly. "Yes, he is, he sure is," she said in a cutesy voice.

"So, would you like to use my cell phone to call Larry, Larry the landlord?" I said in a goofy voice, suddenly realizing how dorky that sounded, and I was again immediately embarrassed.

Isla stood up from the floor. "Yeah, that would be really great, thank you."

Still blushing, I handed her my phone, which she took to make her call.

After she finished the call to our landlord, Isla handed my phone back to me. "Larry is just downstairs, so he is going to meet me at my apartment. Number nine hundred fifteen, in case you were wondering. Thank you again for letting me use your phone. That was super sweet."

I walked her back to the door and opened it for her. "Maybe I'll see you around in the hallways. It was really nice to meet you Isla."

We both shyly smiled at each other as I watched her walk down the hall. I closed the door and stood there for a good minute, wondering what the hell had just happened? Were we flirting or just being neighborly? Just being neighborly, I'm sure.

I returned to the couch and covered back up with my blanket and started to peruse the websites of the five women therapists.

First up is Dr. Natalie. Looks friendly enough, a little older in years, but that's probably okay. Looks like she does all the normal stuff; anxiety, depression, trauma, and OCD. I wonder if she focuses more on families than individuals? Her website has a lot of pictures of families. I'll put her in the maybe pile.

Next up is Dr. Pam. Oh wow, she looks angry. Like really pissed off. I would think if you wanted people to be your clients and confide all their deep, dark secrets, you would start with a warm, welcoming picture of yourself on your website. Dr. Pam is a no. I can't sit across from someone and wonder if they are pissed off at me the whole time.

Okay, who's next? Dr. Tonya. Nope. No. Not going to happen. I'm not going to someone who starts by saying, "God will put you on the right path." Right therapist for someone, I'm sure, just not for me.

Moving on. Dr. Kayla. Looks to be around my age. Also, does all the normal stuff. LGBTQIA+, that's a positive. Good to know I won't be judged there. She looks happier than Dr. Pam, that's for sure. On the list.

Last one. Dr. Sandra. Also looks to be my age and does all the normal stuff as well. LGBTQIA+ too. Again, a big plus.

Now I must decide between Dr. Kayla and Dr. Sandra. What differentiates them?

Pictures on their websites? Both seem warm and welcoming people. I like that. Stormy will like that, too. Oh, I better ask about Stormy. I wonder if they are dog friendly? I hope I get to bring him. That will be one of my questions. I should make a list of questions. What other questions do I have?

1. Can I bring my dog?

2. Can I bring food and snacks?

3. Do I have to come on the same day every week?

4. Will I have homework?

5. Will you tell my sister everything I say?

Oh, here might be a deal breaker. Dr. Sandra only works in her Seattle office on Thursdays. I can't always do the same day every week. I need flexibility in my life. I am a mover and a shaker, or maybe it's a shaker and a mover? Regardless, I am always on the go. Here. There. One never knows where I am going to be, day to day, hour to hour. I will call Dr. Kayla's office.

# Chapter Four

"Happy Birthday to you, happy birthday to you, happy birthday dear Bella, Happy birthday to yooooouuuuuu," we all sang in our worst possible singing voices.

Sawyer and I excused ourselves from the dining room to go into the kitchen so we could cut Bella's birthday cake. I was still half listening to the kids' adorable squeaky voices as we left behind my niece Bella and her four pre-teen friends, who all sat on their knees, bodies stretched out towards the middle of the table to form a tight circle. They giggled under their breaths about how their teacher, Mr. Kramer, fell asleep in class, *again*. Rumor had it this extremely old man, who was somewhere in his late twenties, was moonlighting AT A BAR and would go into the coat closet to take naps while the class took their tests. But enough of that gossip. They switched to drooling over their favorite boy band members.

I smiled and thought about how all these things were so not important in life, but it would be years before they realized that. Their worlds were so small in the here and now. Then a deep wave of sadness rolled over me as I kind of wished my world was a bit smaller right now, too.

Swayer sliced the cake and licked the knife. "So, did you talk to mom yet?"

"I feel like this is a trick question." I took a bit of the frosting from the cake and licked it off my finger. "Yummy sis."

"Now, why would you feel like that was a trick question?" she said with a devious smile.

"That! That right there!" I pointed to her face. "When you smile like that, you make me feel like there is something I should already know that I don't know, or there is something that is going to be happening that I am not going to be happy about, or...NO, nooooo, Sawyer, I am not going to some lame ass dinner party at mom and dad's. I told you I wouldn't do that anymore after what happened with Tiffany." I stomped my foot like a fifth grader.

"Tiffany was your one and only date that you brought to a party, well, since Rayna. Plus, it's been a couple months since they have had one of these. Besides, it's just a few hours, and Todd and I will be there. This one might be kind of fun. It's a fundraiser to, get this, put slot machines in the lobby of their retirement center." She laughed while she put a slice of cake on a plate for each of the kids.

I gave Sawyer a nasty glare for bringing up my ex, Rayna. She knows I don't like to talk about her. Rayna and I were together for twelve years. I had a couple of partners before her, but Rayna, she was the love of my life.

I still remember the morning Rayna stormed into my coffee shop where I worked at the time. She was such a hot mess, budging her way to the front of the coffee line demanding a long list of drinks for a staff meeting that had already started. I had seen her come into my coffee shop before and I thought she was so pretty. Her layered blond hair fell just around the shoulders of her suit jacket. She always dressed so professionally. I didn't know what she did for a living, but I was sure it was a pretty fancy job by the way she held herself. Rayna always seemed so confident. Well, except for that morning.

# THE NEXT 167 HOURS

Long story short, I took over her order, calmed her down, wrote my phone number on her coffee cup, and won her heart. We fell madly in love. We talked about getting married, moving out of the city and buying a little house. But she left me, so fuck her. Yes, I am still bitter, angry, and sad.

I shook off the memories of Rayna and responded, "I hate to admit it, but that does sound kind of fun. But why do they want us there?" I grabbed each plate and put them on the tray to be taken to the dining room.

"To run the card tables, of course," Sawyer said as she picked up the tray of sliced birthday cake.

Dinner parties at our parents' house had a long history of trauma for both Sawyer and me. Especially one night in particular. We both like to pretend like it doesn't bother us, or we often use humor to cover up our real feelings and the impact it had on us, but the truth is, damage had been done. We dubbed it "Shepard Pie" night. Because that is the meal we served that night. I was maybe seven years old, and Sawyer was twelve. Our parents were hosting a fundraiser for our church to support a local family who had lost their belongings in a house fire.

The night was going as you would expect. We were doing our jobs serving drinks and appetizers, then after dinner we would serve dessert. After working us to exhaustion, they told us to go to bed and not step foot out of our room, otherwise we would be grounded for a month.

I didn't need to be threatened because I was so tired that I didn't even bother to put my pajamas on. I fell asleep as soon as my head hit the pillow. No sooner did I drift off to a gentle slumber than I was abruptly awoken by Sawyer jamming her knee into my side and crying that she just saw dad kissing Mrs. Lindal with his tongue. She looked so distraught, so I bolted out of bed and we ran out of our room to the top of the stairs. I remember we wrapped our little fingers around the banister and looked through the wooden railings down to the entryway where we stashed our shoes and hung our apparel. Sure enough, Sawyer was right. There was dad and Mrs. Lindal, kissing and fondling each other while buried among all the winter coats.

We didn't know what to do. I almost screamed out for them to stop, but Sawyer slapped her hand across my mouth and whispered for me to keep quiet. Then we saw mom walk up and say, "George, knock that off. You're drunk and embarrassing Teresa. I am sure she can find her own coat." Dad didn't even defend himself or look embarrassed, he just stumbled off with mom ignoring Mrs. Lindal and walking off behind dad. Mrs. Lindal fixed her dress and, by chance, she happened to look up and see Sawyer and I, a look of devastation on her face. She hurried off, and we just went back to bed. Sawyer slept with me that night. She wrapped us both in the same blanket and covered my ear with her hand, so I couldn't hear what was happening downstairs. The rest of the night she held me so tightly and if I moved in the slightest, she would wake up and squeeze me a little tighter, just so I knew she was still there. She never let me stay scared for very long.

We never forgot about that night, and neither of us had ever asked mom or dad about it. We had so many questions. Was dad a big cheater? Was that the one and only time that happened? Did mom even know what he was really doing, or did she truly think he was helping Mrs. Lindal find her coat? They seemed fine for the most part now, and it is hard to imagine that this was ever a thing between them. I can't imagine mom was that naïve to believe that our father was just helping a woman from our church find her coat.

We headed back to the dining room to serve our little guests their cake. Another amazing talent of my sister. You could add cake decoration to the list. As if she didn't already have enough talents. This year's prize-winning design looked like a two-tier ocean scene straight out of a baking challenge. Bella loved whales, so the cake was a deep mixture of blues, pinks and purples swirled together to create these ocean wave patterns. A whale breached from the first tier up to the second tier of the cake. Along the base of the cake were seashells, crabs, pearls, and so many other little detailed pieces. Mom of the year, for sure. We grabbed two pieces for us, then went to the living room and settled down on the couch to indulge in the chocolatey goodness.

"How's work going?" I asked, taking my first bite of cake.

Digging into her cake, Sawyer responded, "Fine, nothing new, really. I was supposed to be on call this weekend, but another doctor switched with me so I could be home for Bella's party. How about you? How's work?"

"Fine, work is work, you know us secretaries, type, type, type." I winked.

"Stop, mom just wants the best for you." Sticking up for mom like always.

"I found a therapist," I blurted out, putting my plate down on the coffee table.

"Oh, that's so great. Do you want to talk about it?" Sawyer also set her plate down and leaned forward.

"No. I would honestly like to not talk about it anymore. Just let me do this thing. I am checking everyone's boxes. Now just give me some breathing room, okay?" I started to rub my thumb in the center of my palm.

"That's fair, I guess. You know we just worry about you, Em. But if it's space and time you need to work on you, then we support you. I am just glad you are finally seeing this as something you need to do to get better. You know what is best for you." She scooted over closer to me on the couch.

"Whoa, no, I didn't say either of those things, Sawyer. I didn't say this is what is best for me, or this is what I need to, as you say, 'get better.' There is nothing wrong with me. I am just fine. I am healthy, I am happy, and I am as normal as you are. Just because I live my life different than you, doesn't mean I am crazy or messed up in the head. Jesus Christ," I snapped, as I could feel my face start to blaze with anger.

Sawyer tried to keep me calm by placing her hand on my leg. "I didn't say you were messed up in the head or crazy, I just think you have been through a lot and could use someone to talk to. Why is that so wrong of me to want my sister to be okay?"

I threw her hand off my leg. "What makes you think I'm not okay?" I raised my voice.

"By the fact that we can't have a simple conversation about this without you freaking out, for one," she pointed out, putting her hands back on her own lap.

"Maybe that's because you are always trying to manipulate me into thinking there is more to everything than there is. Maybe I am fine, maybe I am just okay with my life exactly the way it is. Did you ever think of that?" I raised my voice an octave louder as I found myself suddenly standing in front of her.

We both turn our heads to a gaggle of fifth graders staring at us. "Mom, are you two going to start wrestling again?" Bella asked in a nervous voice.

"No, of course not honey, we were just having a little disagreement about if we should open presents before we play birthday games or after. How about you girls decide, and we will be right in to join you," Sawyer said, unconvincingly, as she stood up to follow the girls back into the dining room.

I jumped at the chance to end this conversation by grabbing my gift bag and headed back into the dining room as well.

After Bella had finished opening her presents, the girls started passing around her gifts like Sawyer and I were no longer part of their 'in' crowd.

I looked at my phone and saw my Uber had arrived, so I grabbed Stormy off the couch and put on his jean jacket. I waved a small goodbye to Bella, who sent me off with a one of her bright smiles and went back to sharing her gifts with her friends. I asked Sawyer to walk me to the door.

"My Uber is here, so we are going to head home. Looks like the girls are probably getting ready for Bella's slumber party soon anyway. We would just be in the way if I stayed. I really don't want to fight with you, Sawyer. I just need some space. I'm doing this, okay, so please just give me space to settle into all this my way. Don't ask me about it every time you see me, just trust that I'm going to my sessions and doing whatever the good doctor tells me to do. Can that just be enough for now?" I pleaded softly as I stopped and turned back towards her before opening the front door.

Taking a deep breath. "Sure, Em. That can be enough for now," Sawyer replied as she pulled me in close to give me a hug.

I waved at Sawyer from the window of the car that she kindly paid for as we drove off.

As the Uber driver pulled away from the house, he asked, "so heading downtown?"

"Yes, please." I petted Stormy, who was snuggled up on my lap.

The driver turned onto the interstate. "You like living in the city?" he asked.

Here we go. Small talk. My most hated activity in the whole world. I often wonder how best to get out of it. I am not a rude person, so ignoring someone didn't seem like an acceptable means of escape. Being honest and telling them the truth, that I don't feel like talking, also seemed rude, like it could hurt someone's feelings. I wouldn't say I am a complete introvert, but I am definitely not an extrovert either. If you gave me one of those personality tests, I would come in at exactly fifty percent. Dead center. If this driver caught me last week, I would have explained all the ups and downs of living in the city in such great detail that whether or not I liked living in the city would have been the last question he asked me on the ride home because we would have run out of time for any other questions.

Not tonight though. I am tired and cranky and I just knew this man is going to make me suffer through conversation the entire way home.

"It has its ups and downs like anywhere else, I suppose." I sat there and looked out the car window at the people in the vehicles next to ours.

"What's the best part?" He continued his inquiry while taking the second exit downtown.

"Shopping, restaurants, easy access to work, stuff like that, I guess." I wished he would have taken the third exit because it was a more direct route to my apartment.

"What's the worst part?" he asked, getting a little more enthusiastic.

"All the Uber drivers," I said bitchily.

Silence. Oh my god. I can't believe I just said that out loud. We drove in silence for about ten minutes before I felt the weight of guilt suffocating me.

"So, what's the best part of being an Uber driver?" I asked as I saw my apartment come into view.

# Chapter Five

"What a night last night, huh, buddy?" I said to Stormy as we strolled through the park. It was a chilly Sunday morning with a bit of sun that was trying desperately to break through the clouds, but with no luck so far. Inhaling the cool, fresh morning air gave me a sense of the calm that I felt like I really needed after such a draining birthday party last night. "I think if we don't see family for a year or two, it would do us some good. Don't you think, buddy?"

I tugged on Stormy's leash, which got him excited enough to start jumping on my leg. However, he soon lost his excitement for me as the sounds of rustling leaves drew his attention away. I felt the jerk of my wrist and off we went, as he bolted after the colorful storm of fall foliage that whipped through the air as he dragged me along to chase his little leaf tornado.

We walked a couple of laps around the lake before we settled into our spot on the park bench. We fell in love with this very spot the first time we visited this park. The bench sits right next to the lake with a bountiful tree that shelters us from the sun in the summer months, but fully exposes the bench to the elements in the winter when the leaves fall to the ground.

I took out Stormy's pup cake and gave him small bites at a time. Today's flavor was sweet potato, which is one of his favorites. I sipped my coffee and gazed across the lake. With the weather cooling, but the water slightly warmer, there was a mist leaving behind a bit of a mystery as to whether people were out on the water or not this morning.

Winter would probably decide to show herself early this year. The fog was swirling along the walking path and then rolling off into the fields, settling into the empty spaces between each blade of grass. Coupled with the cool breeze and the dark skies, the park was entertaining fewer visitors today, which made my people watching a bit of a bore. A few random people passed by over the next hour. I wondered where they were going, what their lives were like, if they were happy, sad, or if they were like me and had to pretend like they were always fine, someone happier than they really are, just to keep the resemblance of some kind of peace in their lives.

A lady and her Pitbull walked by, which triggered Stormy to bark at them. The Pitbull looked at Stormy like *'are you for real?'* Stormy looked at the Pitbull, like *'hell yeah, I'm for real.'* I apologized to the lady for my brutish dog's behavior and decided that was enough bad ass Frenchie drama for one day and it was probably time for us to mosey on.

We headed towards the entrance of the park to leave when I was stopped dead in my tracks. There she was, sitting on a blanket, my ex-girlfriend, Rayna. I started to freak out and Stormy began to whimper like he always did when he could feel the panic brewing inside me.

My heart started to race as I put one hand to my chest and bent over with my other hand on my knee. I immediately could feel the sweat of my palm soak through my yoga pants. *You seriously cannot have a panic attack in the middle of this park.* I tried to encourage myself. I totally feel like I want to puke right now. I started to get lightheaded, so I decided it was best to turn back around and go back the way I came.

"Hey lady, are you okay?" A young man approached me, looking concerned.

"Oh, yeah, totally fine. I just stood up too fast from picking up dog poop and must have gotten a little dizzy. Thank you for checking on me." I kept walking.

"Do you need a ride home or something?" The man offered. He followed me.

"No, we are seriously fine. Thank you again for the offer." I tried to walk a bit faster.

"Happy to. My car is just across the street." He sounded a little pushy now.

I stopped dead in my tracks and looked him dead in the eyes. "I am fine," I said, a lot stronger than before.

"Okay, okay." He backed off and walked away.

I ran as fast as we could to get away from as many people as possible. I stopped at the other end of the park where I leaned up against a brick wall, desperately trying to catch my breath. My hands were shaking so badly, and my vision started to get blurry. People and cars looked like huge blobs of Jell-O in motion. I kept trying to take deep breaths until my vision started to clear and my heart started to slow, but the shaking just would not stop. *Please, please stop. Deep breaths, deep breaths.*

I walked up and down the sidewalk and beg the universe to help this go away. Stormy jumped up my leg enough times to get me to sit down. As soon as I hit the ground, he curled up into my lap and licked my arm. I closed my eyes and just gently rocked back and forth until I started to feel somewhat human again. It took some time, but I was eventually able to stand, then it took a little longer, but I was eventually able to walk out of the park.

What the hell is going on with me? My god, I need to just go home and lay down. Yes, just breathe. I just needed to go home and go to sleep. It's been a long weekend, an emotional weekend. It's going to happen. *Everyone runs into their ex. It happens. Oh my god, what the hell is wrong with me, can you hear yourself, Ember? I think I am literally going fucking insane.*

I knew that after we got home, I would not want to leave my apartment for the rest of the weekend, so instead of going straight there, we took a detour to stop by the store to pick up a few groceries.

I put Stormy in the cart and headed straight for the wine aisle. I figured this was exactly what I needed to get through the rest of this horrible weekend.

Just as I was turning the corner, I heard a someone say "Hey, Ember, remember me?"

I turned around and smiled as I did, in fact, remember this very cute person.

"Hi Isla, yes, of course I remember you. It's been what, less than a week?" I nervously responded, fiddling with my cart. *Oh my god, why am I all nervous?* I smiled.

"Yeah, I am officially not homeless. I got back into my apartment," she said, semi proud of herself.

"Yay!" I pumped my fist straight up into the air. *I can't believe I just did that. I am such an idiot.*

Giggling at me, she said, "I guess I will see you around the hallways." She gave Stormy a scratch on the head and walked away.

"See you there." I waved, although she was already halfway down the aisle.

"See you there? See you there? Really, Ember? See you there?" I scolded myself out loud for sounding like a complete ass.

# THE NEXT 167 HOURS

\*\*\*

I woke up to complete darkness. *Oh my god what time is it?* I looked over at the clock and realized it was already 7:30 at night. *I can't believe I slept into the night like this. I am never going back to sleep tonight.* My body ached and my head felt tight, like I had a rubber band around it. *Note to self, day drinking is a bad idea.*

I rolled out of bed and brushed my hair enough to look somewhat presentable to go to the small diner that sits on the corner of my street. Not that anyone there really cared what I looked like, but I should probably present a semi alive version of myself.

I grabbed my coat and headed down to the elevator, ignoring everyone I passed by, keeping my head hung low. If I didn't make eye contact, then there was no need for pleasantries. And tonight, I was in no mood for pleasantries.

The rusty old bells that had been attached to these doors for probably fifty years rang as I passed through the entrance to announce my arrival at the diner. Jean, the waitress, waved me to a booth in the corner along the window where I could people watch the happenings on the street. She walked over with a glass of water, a menu and sat it all down in front of me with a thin napkin that was wrapped around some old silverware.

"Hey Ember, it's been a while since you been down here. How you been doing, hon?" She crossed her arms like she was hugging herself, or maybe metaphorically me.

I ran my finger over the menu and replied, "Oh, I'm doing just great. Can I have a glass of red wine and some tater tots?" Jean took the menu from me.

"That's sounds super not healthy," she said, in her best caring tone.

I looked at her with my "I don't give a shit" smile and looked down at my phone as she walked away. "Okay, I will just eat my tots and have a glass of wine or two, no more than two, then maybe a little Instagram surfing to kill a couple of hours. Then maybe I will be tired enough to go back to bed and get enough sleep to make it to work on time tomorrow morning," I mumbled to myself as I logged into my Instagram account.

"You know they have wine that comes out of actual bottles across the street at the hotel bar, right?" she suggested as she leaned into my booth across the table from me, balanced on one knee.

"But all the lovely company is over here with the boxed wine," I retorted, turning my phone over so she couldn't see what I was looking at.

"Seriously, are you doing okay, Ember?" Realizing I was hiding something.

I put my hand straight out towards her face. "No, stop right there. I came here for happy time. I came here for the beautiful, stained coffee marks on the tables." I pointed to a coffee stain on the table. "The dust that covers the lights shades above me." I pointed to the dusty light shades. "The grease that assaults my nostrils as soon as I walk through the door. I came here for everything that feels familiar and happy, so just let me be happy for two god damn hours while I eat my fucking tots and drink my god damn wine, okay, Jean?"

Jean knelt over the table, and rested her hand on my arm, "Okay, sweetie. We also have some chocolate cake, if that makes you fucking happy too." She winked with a slight smile, slid out of the booth, and walked away.

I shook my head, then went back to my phone and started looking at all my old pictures of Rayna and I on Instagram and started thinking about how everything used to be so good, or at least I thought it was good. I never go online anymore. I don't even know why I am doing this to myself tonight.

If a digital picture could fade, it would look like these pictures. They literally looked like they were starting to distort. Like in this picture right here, we were sitting next to each other on a Ferris wheel. The sun was just starting to set behind us. I was smiling at you, and you were looking forward like you didn't even see me looking at you, so full of love. Or this one here, where we were dancing at your sister's wedding, and you were just staring off into the night over my shoulder. What were you thinking about? Were you thinking about me? Us? I don't even look the same as we did in these pictures. I know I look older, worn, defeated, and broken. "No, I am not broken," I whispered.

I closed my Instagram app and went to my contacts to find Rayna's number. I debated, should I call her? She will probably see my name and be like "go to hell" *I had to at least try*. I think to myself. I miss her so damn much.

I hit send. It rings and rings and rings...voicemail. "Hey this is Rayna, can't talk now. Leave me a message, love ya!" She always lets it go to voicemail. *Oh my god, what the hell am I doing?*

My head fell into my hands, then I slightly lifted it and yelled across the diner. "Jean, another red please."

\*\*\*

"Come on, Ember, get into bed now. Take off your shoes. This is the last time you get drunk in my diner; I swear to god," Jean scolded me as she threw one of my shoes across the room.

"I'm not drunk. I just needed to ride home." I fell backwards on my bed.

"We walked, Em, or, basically, I carried you back here." She sounded frustrated, throwing my other shoe across the room.

"Jean, you're cute, with those little badges and buttons all over your uniform," I started to flirt. *Why not? It's been a while.* I poked one of the buttons on her smock.

"Ember, you're drunk, and I'm married. Besides, I am twice your age," she reminded me as she covered me with a blanket.

"Fine, but if you're ever not twice my age, you look me up, waitress Jean, I will be right here waiting for you," I promised, as I tapped the tip of her nose.

"God damnit, Ember, you just stabbed me in the eye!"

# Chapter Six

I moaned as my head throbbed. I sat in front of the toilet and my mouth was watering while a knot formed in my throat. "Oh my god, my head, my head, owwww, my head." I thrust over the toilet and started violently throwing up.

I called in late for work and go back to bed for a couple of hours. *No more drinking on work nights. I am too old for this crap.*

***

I warily walked into the office with my hair a mess and sunglasses on to find Bev standing at the double doors waiting for me. "You look like crap, Ember," she said with a surprised look on her face. Bev grabbed me by the arm and dragged me toward the office kitchen so no one else would see how awful I looked. "Let's get you some coffee. Bev-Bev will take care of you."

If I didn't feel exactly how I probably looked right now, I might have been offended by Bev's comment.

"What did you do last night? It better have been spicy to make how you feel today worth it." She set a cup of coffee in front of me.

"I wish," I said, rubbing both my temples simultaneously.

"Your boss is back from New York and has been asking what time you're going to be in this morning. She seems very high energy today, so watch out. I think her work trip just became more work for you," she said as she wiped some breadcrumbs off the lunchroom table.

"Great, just the kind of Monday I was hoping for. When does she get done with her first meeting? Do I have time to finish this cup of coffee before being—"

"Ember, there you are," Bethany, my boss, announced so loudly that I got a sharp pain behind my right eye.

"Good morning, Bethany. So sorry I am late this morning. I woke up with a bug or something." I looked up at her with only my left eye open.

"No problem. Finish your break and come to my office as soon as possible. Great things are happening." She snapped her fingers high in the air in celebration as she turned and walked away.

I entered Bethany's office to find it in its normal state. Floor to ceiling windows, one wall filled with awards for multiple achievements in the advertisement industry, the other wall lined with pictures of herself and no-name celebrities, and on her desk, a single photo of her family that included herself, her husband, and her daughter. In Bethany's world, everything had its place, down to each pen and paper clip.

Today, the addition to her office was an easel with an advertisement that said, "You are..." That's it. In red cursive font, on a black background. "You are..."

Bethany was the stereotypical VP type you would find heading the marketing department of an advertisement agency. She was tall and slender with flawless dark skin and long locs that flowed down the length of her back. Bethany wore the latest fashion and was extremely smart, articulate, and always professional. Some say she is beautiful in her own right. Others might say it is her powerful position that makes her attractive. I say it is the way she walks into a room, grabs your attention, and captivates you within two seconds and then how she just holds you there for hours. Now that is what made her beautiful or attractive or whatever you want to call it. You couldn't escape her intensity when she locked eyes with you. She made you feel like you were the only person in the room. Bethany had a gift that was truly addicting.

Bethany stood next to the easel. "We have until the end of January to turn this pitch into the world's next earth-shattering message," Bethany said, pacing around her office. "It's for one of the largest fashion icons in New York City. We will need it to be ready for fashion week, and they chose six of us to come back to them with one word that will complete this message and why it's meaningful, and they will print it for their spring line. This could be our chance to really get our name out there, Ember."

"But we don't do fashion," I reminded her as I typed notes on my laptop.

"No, but this is different. They are reinventing themselves as a company and need a campaign slogan," she said as she stepped in front of her desk and leaned on the edge, right in front of me.

I tried not to be intimated by this power move, so I adjusted my position to face the office door and changed my tune. "Wow, this really is amazing, Bethany. I will set up the meetings and get the creative team working on this right now." I stood up and squeezed myself around her to leave the office.

I walked back to my desk with my head still throbbing, thrilled for our new opportunity, but also a bit too tired to really jump right into making everything happen just yet. I decided I had better eat something first, so I sent Bev a text message to see if she was ready for lunch.

> "Hey, Bev! I'm starving. wanna grab a bite to eat?"

> "Sure, sushi? #fishyfishy"

> "Puke, no"

> "Greasy burgers? #gutbomb"

> "Are you trying to make me throw up"

> "Yes. #youdeserveit"

> "Why would you do that?"

> "Slow morning. #iamfun"

> "How about just a salad across the street?"

> "Meet you at the elevators?"

We sat down for lunch in the courtyard at a cute little outdoor hotdog stand across from our building. I debated whether to tell Bev about therapy. I probably should, since I will be leaving the office to go to my sessions. I could lie and say I was going to the chiropractor or physical therapy, but she would know I was up to something. Bev always knows when I am lying, mainly because I suck at it.

Stabbing my salad repeatedly, I finally worked up the courage to just tell her. "I want to tell you something, but I don't want you to make a big deal about it, okay?" I made her promise.

Bev stopped licking her bowl and looked up at me. "Of course," Bev curiously responded, as if I was going to share horrible news.

"I have decided to start seeing a therapist, like a shrink. If that's what they're still called?" I questioned innocently.

"I don't think they call them that anymore," Bev confirmed, setting down her bowl.

"Oh, okay, good to know." I went back to my salad.

Bev reached her hand across the table and placed hers over the top of mine. "Are you okay. Do you want to talk about it?"

"That's just it. I feel completely fine, well most days. I mean, I know everything isn't perfect and maybe I could use someone to talk to, but it's mainly Sawyer and my parents that think I need to go, not me. I am doing this mostly for them. But I am trying to be open-minded to see if...anyway, I am only telling you and you only, Bev, okay? So don't tell anyone around the office that I am going to therapy. I will be going during working hours. I just thought you should know, so you can help me with my schedule."

"I promise I won't say a word to anyone. It's not my business to share. Just let me know what days and times you need me to block on your calendar and I will make sure it all looks discreet," Bev said, and squeezed my hand.

I squeezed her hand back. "Thanks Bev, I love you."

She let go of my hand. "I love you too, dog."

After we got back from lunch, I decided it was time to swallow my pride and call Dr. Kayla to make an appointment, but I got her voicemail on my first attempt.

Dr. Kayla called me back, but I was in a meeting, so she left a message offering a couple of times that she was available for what she called an 'intake session' over the phone. She said it would be twenty minutes to see if we were a good fit for each other.

I called back, again getting her voicemail, and chose Wednesday at ten in the morning. I didn't have any meetings and I could book a little conference room where no one would bother me. Besides, it was only a twenty-minute conversation. Even I couldn't screw up a twenty-minute conversation.

The next couple of days went by quickly. I slept most of the time when I wasn't at work. I hadn't been feeling very good. Maybe I do have a flu bug or something. I'm tired all the time. My body is aching, and I just don't have any energy to go anywhere or do anything. I mostly feel bad for Stormy, since that meant he hasn't gotten to go on many walks. I have been slacking at work, doing the bare minimum just to get my work done so I can go home, eat, and go to bed. I can't wait for the weekend to catch up on some sleep.

Wednesday rolled around, and I went into the conference room at work and settled in to take the call from Dr. Kayla. It surprised me at how nervous I was. What was she going to ask me? What if she thought I was too much to take on? Well, I guess she must already assume I was a bit much, otherwise I wouldn't have called her. What if she laughed at me? What if she doesn't like me? Or worse, what if she judged me?

Maybe I shouldn't do this. I stood up to leave the room when my cell phone started to ring, and I saw Dr. Kayla's name on the screen. I noticed my breathing started to increase and I could feel my heart racing as I hit the answer button.

I sat back down. My voice started to tremble. "This is Ember."

"Hi Ember, this is Kayla." Her voice sounded so friendly. I bet they learned how to do that in college. The friendly voice.

"Hello." I wanted to throw up.

"How are you doing today?" She asked like she genuinely wanted to know. The genuine voice, master's program, for sure.

"Good, I'm good. How are you?" I lied. I really, really wanted to throw up.

"Great, this call, as I stated in my voicemail, will be about twenty minutes and will give us the opportunity to see if we are a good fit for each other. I want to make sure my services and experience will meet your needs, so I just have a few questions for you, and I will also give you some time towards the end of our call to ask me a few questions as well. How does that sound?"

"Sounds good." I started to rub the center of my palm with my thumb.

"Have you been in therapy before?" she inquired.

"No." I rubbed my palm faster.

"What are you looking to get out of therapy?"

"My sister thinks I have anxiety and I am depressed." I pressed my thumb hard in the center of my palm.

"Do you feel the same?"

"I suppose I do sometimes." I started to rub my palm again.

"What is your number one goal at this time, although we may find other goals over the course of therapy, and we can address those as we work together?"

"To prove I am not broken, I guess." Pressing my thumb repeatedly in my palm again.

"Okay, anything else you want to add?" she asked.

"I also don't sleep well at night. I can share my sleep app data with you if that would be helpful. I wear a watch at night, and it tracks my sleeping patterns. My sister got it for me for Christmas a couple of years ago. Sawyer is her name. She is my older sister. She is a doctor too.

Like you, but for babies. I mean, she doesn't see depressed babies, well maybe she does. You know, I will have to ask her if any of the babies she sees are depressed. That would be super sad to just be born and two weeks later, already hate your life." I started to rub the center of my palm again.

After an awkward pause, Dr. Kayla filled the silence. "Okay, yes, please share anything you think will be helpful to get us started. I think we can move forward if you are interested in working together. Do you have any questions for me?"

Opening my notebook, I realized I forgot my list of questions at home. I only remembered one of the five questions I wrote down, so I decided to just ask that one.

"Do I have to come in on the same day every week?" I clicked my mechanical pencil to dispense more lead so I could record her answer in my notebook.

"No, we can see what availability I have on a weekly basis," Dr. Kayla offered.

"Good, because I move and shake." I slapped my hand on my forehead. I cannot believe I just said that.

"Like tremors?" Dr. Kayla asked inquisitively.

Embarrassed that I couldn't get out what I meant to say, I just responded. "Yeah, something like that."

"We can talk about that at our first session. Are you available tomorrow, say eleven?"

Oh my god, tomorrow. Let's just jump right in, Doc. Go for the gold. Take no prisoners. Like this is no big deal. Like she does this every day, multiple times a day, in fact. Tomorrow. Holy hell. Tomorrow?

"Tomorrow, eleven, sure, that would work." I confirmed the appointment while dying a little bit inside.

\*\*\*

When I got home, I couldn't stop thinking about what my first session would be like. I was literally freaking out. I was so nervous that even Stormy approached me slower than normal. I had no idea what I was going to talk about. Would I just dive in? Would she ask me questions and I would just have to answer them, like I did when I went in for my job interview? Maybe we would just sit and stare at each other until one of us talked? Oh lord, what if we have a stare down? I would totally lose. Sawyer used to always beat me at stare downs. She still does.

I was pacing back and forth across my bedroom while holding my phone so tight against my ear I could feel my hand sweating, "Sawyer, I know I told you to stay out of this, but I have my first appointment tomorrow with my new therapist and I am freaking out a little, call me." I tapped 'end' on the call.

I turned on the TV to try to distract myself but that was pointless. I just couldn't focus, so I decided to instead google, "how to talk to your therapist." Surely this would set me up for success, make me look like a pro going in, like I knew what I was doing. "Let's see here. Oh, here's a website with pictures even, perfect." Scrolling through the pictures, I am definitely noticing a pattern. It's like every website I went to suggest it was totally up to me how this all went down.

Well, this is not helpful at all. Be open, they say, be honest, they say, I can tell them anything, they say, therapists have heard it all before, they say. Well, have they considered that maybe I haven't ever told someone all my life stories before? Did they ever think of that? The therapist gets to sit there and think, "not new information to me, I've heard this all before." They're probably bored out of their mind. While I am sitting there saying things out loud that have never left my lips. Hardly seems fair. Dr. Kayla is probably eating her dinner right now, watching a movie, not even thinking about the fact that tomorrow a person is coming into her office for the first time, scared out of her mind. I not only have to sit with my life anxiety, but I had to sit with the anxiety that this whole new person is about to turn my world upside down. Therapists go to school for years for this stuff, but no one gave me any training on how to be a client.

"Why the hell am I even doing this?" I scooped up Stormy and took him to bed and snuggled him. I laid there and watched my phone light up with Sawyer's name on my screen. I changed my mind. I don't want to talk to her anymore. I don't want to talk to anyone. I just want to go to sleep. I quickly texted her back and told her I was already in bed and was feeling better about my appointment after I had some dinner and relaxed for a bit. I lied, but I strongly believed it was for the best, for both of us.

# Chapter Seven

Standing in the rain, I watched the cars drive past my apartment building. I debated whether I should call an Uber to drive me from my work to Dr. Kayla's office or if I should take the bus. Of course, the bus is cheaper, but it's not a direct route and will keep me away from work longer than I probably should be. However, an Uber once a week would drain my bank account quickly on top of paying for my therapy appointments. My health insurance doesn't cover these visits, so I pay for them all out of pocket. I could split the difference by taking an Uber today, so I won't be late for my first appointment, and figuring out the bus schedule over the weekend.

I threw my hands in the air and said to the random woman walking past me, "It's a plan." Then I fell in line behind her to start walking to work. I think I made her nervous because she hurried into the nearest coffee shop and waited for me to pass by.

The six-block walk to work today, although chilly, seemed to ease my anxiety about going to my first session. As I streamed through the crowds of people, I felt like I was invisible. No one acknowledged me with a greeting as they passed by me, no one smiled or made eye contact. If it wasn't for the homeless man sitting against the wall of the bank asking me for money, I might have thought I was invisible. I handed him a dollar as I passed by, along with a muffin that I decided I was too nervous to eat for breakfast.

As soon as I stepped through the double doors of the office, Bev was standing there with my coffee and a devilish grin on her face.

Without being able to take another step, Bev took my workbag out of my hand and replaced it with a cup of coffee. "Take your coffee and go straight to your desk and talk to no one. NO ONE," she demanded.

I did as I was told, accepted my coffee, and started walking towards my desk. It wasn't a hard feat to ignore people along the journey to my desk, as there was not a soul in sight.

I sat down and saw an envelope with my name on it. "EMBER" printed in black ink. I started to get nervous because I couldn't tell by the way Bev was acting if this was good news or bad news, so I decided either way I would have to open the letter to find out. Just as I was about to tear it open, Bev popped her head in. "Did you open it?"

I grabbed my letter opener and started to cut open the envelope. "I was just about to. What is it?"

"It's a million-dollar check, baby." Bev dropped in my visitor's chair.

I cut it open and, although it wasn't a million-dollar check, it *was* airline tickets for a work conference in Las Vegas.

Bev jumped up and started dancing and singing in my cubicle. "We're going to Las Vegas, we're going to Las Vegas, are you excited, Em?" she asked, when she stopped dancing to grab both my hands.

"Well, yeah, I think so. I mean, I haven't left the city in a couple of years. You know what, Bev? Yes. We are going to have a blast. It's going to be amazing, and maybe we will win a million dollars." I stood up and joined her in her dancing charade.

We were dancing all around my cube together, only to be interrupted by Bethany. "Ember, my office. Now please." She gave us a confused look as she started to back up before she turned around and walked away.

Bev and I looked at each other, saluted one another before I marched into my boss's office.

"Ember, I am assuming you saw your plane ticket?" She sat down behind her desk and clasped her hands together.

"Yes, what's up with the work trip? We haven't traveled since before the pandemic." I sat down in her visitor's chair.

"Things are loosening up. They will implement Covid precautions during round tables and different working sessions, but, overall, it seems like they are doing everything they can to keep us all safe. Are you okay with traveling?" She sat back in her chair like a principal.

"Oh yes. I am excited. It's been a long time since we've had a chance to socialize our brand," I said, drinking the company Kool Aide, metaphorically of course. I honestly just wanted to go to the after hours parties.

"Good, I just wanted to make sure. I know it's been a tough year for you." *For the love of Christ will people just leave it be.* I thought to myself. I smiled to reassured her.

"I'm fine, thank you."

Bethany stood up to excuse me. "Great, we will leave next week. I know this is short notice, but we were made aware of this opportunity at the last minute, and I think it's in our best interest if we take advantage of the discounted tickets. Your hotel and food, of course, will all be covered as always, and any entertainment and alcohol you choose to consume outside of event dinners will be on your own dime. I hope this is something that lifts your spirits after such a hard year, Ember." Walking around her desk, she pulled me in for a hug.

"Thank you, Bethany. I appreciate your kindness," I said as I squirmed out of her embrace.

I jumped into my Uber, that had been waiting outside for me now for ten minutes because Bev had decided I couldn't go to my first therapy session on an empty stomach. I hated running late to appointments, but there I was, running late because I had to share Bev's leftover meatloaf sandwich so my stomach wouldn't start growling in front of my new therapist. Little did Bev know that my stomach growling was the least of my worries about the things that could possibly go wrong in front of my therapist. Try puking or passing out. I am worried about those things more.

***

I arrived with about five minutes to spare. I walked into the building and immediately wanted to turn right back around, climb back into the Uber and go back to work. My hands were shaking and sweating. My heart was pounding in my chest. I was a freaking mess. I wasn't a huge people type person, but I also was not normally this nervous to meet new people.

I gave the receptionist my name and told her I was there to see Dr. Kayla. Pretty sure she looked at me with pity. As if she knew I had all the mental health issues. I looked at her name tag. it said her name was Lisa.

"I'm good, Lisa," I said, giving her a wink. "All good." Lisa looked up at me a little sideway, then turned her eyes back to whatever she was doing before I walked up to her desk.

I walked backwards before completely swinging around to go find a seat in the waiting room.

I chose a seat in the corner of the waiting room. I like corners. Typically, there is at least one wall on one side of your shoulder, which means statistically there is a reduced chance of someone sitting down next to you on the other side because they won't want to block you in. At least, that is what I think.

When I was younger and got in trouble, my mom would always put me in the same corner in the kitchen. I had to sit on this small metal stool with these rubber ridges on the seat. It seemed like I would sit there for hours when, in reality, it was probably only the minutes that equaled my age.

I learned to enjoy that corner and found it to be more of a safe place than a punishment over time. On each side of the corner, I was surrounded by these off-white tiles. On one side of the wall there was one tile missing. I used to pretend I had an imaginary friend that lived inside that empty tile, named Ember. I would talk to her, we would laugh, I would cry and tell her how much I hated my mom for putting me in time out for doing nothing wrong, and we would make up stories together. Then one day I overheard my mom tell my dad she was worried I was talking to myself too much and thought I should take my punishments in the form of housework. I missed Ember for the longest time, until I realized my mom was right, I was just talking to myself, and I could still talk to "Ember," but I should probably just do it quietly in my head.

"Ember." I looked up from my seat when I heard my name called.

"That's me." I shot my arm straight in the air.

Dr. Kayla stood at her door. She was taller than I expected, with long brown hair, and her smile was very warm and welcoming. She wore glasses that told me she was probably very smart and ready to deconstruct everything about me.

I stopped in front of her as she motioned for me to continue to make my way into her office, then she shut the door behind us. I just stood there. Not knowing what to do next.

"Please, Ember, come sit down."

I sat down on a small couch and started to rub my sweaty palms against the ribbing of my corduroy pants while I looked around her office. When my eyes returned forward, Dr. Kayla was sitting across from me, staring at me. I knew this was going to happen.

"How are you doing today, Ember?" She clicked her pen and wrote something on her legal pad.

*Oh shit, a legal pad. I knew it.*

"I'm good. How are you?" I returned the greeting, struggling to keep eye contact with her for some reason. I could not quite place where my nervousness was coming from.

"Good. Are you ready to get started? I am happy to kick us off with just some basic background questions to get to know you a bit better, if that is okay with you?"

"Sure, that seems like the appropriate first line of interrogation." I nodded my head, then looked up at the ceiling. This building looked to be older. *Asbestos, I bet there is asbestos in these ceilings,* I thought to myself before Dr. Kayla's voice brought me back to the moment.

"I certainly hope you never feel like I am interrogating you, Ember. My questions will always be thought provoking to help us work towards your goals." She wrote something on her pad of paper.

"Oh yeah, of course." I nodded towards the lamp that stood by my seat, yet hung ever so slightly over my head.

"It's just a floor lamp, Ember." She wrote something down.

"Hmm, okay," I said with skepticism.

"I can move it, if you'd like," she offered.

"Nah," I shook my head.

"Are you sure?" Dr. Kayla offered again.

"Totally, fine. Not interrogating me. Got it." I glanced up at the light, poked it with my finger to rock it back and forth, then drew my attention back to her, and smiled.

Dr. Kayla stared at me for about five seconds, then continued. "Okay, so, I looked over the sleep app data you provided me from your sleep watch numbers, and it appears that you are resting pretty well throughout the night." She flipped through the legal pad's pages.

"Yeah, I don't think that it's actually that I'm sleeping really well, I think it's that I just lay still really well." I shrugged my shoulders.

"Alright, we can talk more about your sleeping patterns later, but why don't you tell me the other reasons you are here? I know you said because your sister thinks you should be here, but you are the one who showed up today. Why?"

She looked at me so curiously, but with so much tenderness and care. I think she knew right then and there exactly what was about to occur. Like the earth was starting to rumble under our feet, only it wasn't the earth, it was my emotions that came reverberating across the floor.

Then it happened. I totally lost my shit. I don't know why, but it felt like a lifetime's worth of pain came pouring out of me, not so much in words but in tears and rage. At first, Dr. Kayla sat there and said nothing. Like it was totally fine. She could have done her nails or read a book while I just sat there and sobbed. She was that comfortable with what was happening right in front of her.

After a few minutes, she leaned in and said, "Ember, you are not in this alone. Whatever it is that has brought you here, we will navigate it together. You don't have to name it today or next week or even the week after that. We have time, so don't feel pressured or rushed. I will continue to hold this space for you, okay?"

I nodded my head as I wiped my nose with the tissues that she had strategically placed by the interrogation lamp. "Okay," I agreed.

We spent the rest of the hour with Dr. Kayla, asking me about my childhood. My parents, my sister, what I like, what I don't like, and my hobbies. I gave her the basics about my life. I didn't know if I could trust her yet or if I even had the energy to try. We ended the session agreeing to meet the next Monday, since that was my only available day before I headed out to Vegas for work. I left Dr. Kayla's office feeling different from when I arrived. I just couldn't put my finger on what was making me feel so different.

I looked at Lisa on the way out and shamefully lowered my head as I walked past her desk. She knew I wasn't okay, but looked away instead of rubbing it in like I probably deserved for being so cocky when I signed in.

***

I called Bev and told her I was talking the rest of the day off. I told her I had a massive headache and didn't think I could show my puffy face in the office again that day. Instead of going home, I decided to go to the corner diner by my apartment and get a glass of wine and an early dinner before heading home. I needed to clear my head.

I walked in and Jean was standing by the counter. She looked at me and immediately turned around like she was upset. I went over to my normal booth by the window and sat down. Jean brought over a glass of water, silverware, and a menu.

"Holy shit, Jean. Do you have pink eye? Your eye is super red and swollen." I stood up so I could get a closer look at her face. I was very concerned.

"Seriously, you're kidding me, right? No Ember, it's not pink eye," she snapped. "What do you want to order, and like I said, you are not getting drunk in here anymore?"

"Whoa, wow, what's up with you?" I slowly sat back down in my booth.

"Ember, let's not do this right now, just what do you want to order hon?" she asked again sounding very agitated, rocking back and forth on her feet.

"Okay, well I guess if I am to a one drink limit for some reason, I will have just one glass of wine and a chicken salad sandwich, and a bag of chips."

"One, and only one, glass of wine, chicken salad on wheat I assume, and chips, got it." She grabbed the menu swiftly from my hands and stomped off.

I sat there and stared at the empty table, not knowing what the hell to think or do next. I felt like I was more lost and alone than I had ever been in my entire life. What the hell was I supposed to do now? I didn't expect there to be this person who would sit across from me and be able to help me make sense of my insides. Help me take my broken pieces and put them back together. "I am not broken goddamnit," I whispered hard through my pursed lips as I wiped my hands up and down the ribbing of my corduroy pants. *Holy shit, maybe I am broken.* I had no idea that therapy might be something I really needed, and now I am just sitting here in this crappy diner, by myself, with no one to talk to.

I quickly wiped away the tears that formed in the corner of my eyes when the panic arose in my chest. I grabbed a pen and piece of paper out of my work bag. "How long will it be until I see Dr. Kayla again?" I frantically asked no one in particular.

I started to do the math on my piece of paper. One week, that is seven days, times twenty-four hours, minus one hour for being in session, oh my god, oh my god. I had to wait 167 hours until I see Dr. Kayla again.

"How the hell am I supposed to get through the next 167 hours?" I said, with fear in my voice, when Jean walked towards me with my food.

"Well, I don't know what you are talking about, but if I you want my opinion, sleep as much as possible, time goes by way faster that way. Or no, don't do that, you're way too young, go out more, quit sitting at home, meet new people, go to parties, travel, see the world, my gosh, Ember just get out of your damn apartment and live a little," she advised as she laid out my food in front me.

I suddenly didn't feel very hungry anymore as I contemplated my new life in therapy. I was so scared thinking about what I was supposed to do over the course of this next week. I had so many feelings that I just didn't have the strength to feel. I wanted to be numb. I didn't want to feel anything anymore, and that scared me the most.

How could therapy be so damaging after one session? How could Dr. Kayla just let me walk out of there and not even tell me what I should do next? She just let me leave. She said that she would see me in a week. Just like that, how can someone just let someone else walk away, knowing they are in so much pain, and do nothing?

I was so confused. Is this what it's supposed to be like? You have this person who supposedly cares for and supports you, then the next 167 hours you spend in absolute silence, just you, living inside your own head, waiting for the next time you can see your therapist. I was lost in my thoughts when I said out loud, "I don't think I can do this."

"Do what, sweetie?" Jean chimed in. "You haven't touched your food, or your wine. What is up with you tonight, Ember?" She stood at the end of my booth, stealing a chip from my plate.

"Nothing, I guess I am just not as hungry as I thought," I replied. "I think you might be right about getting more sleep, though. Maybe I just need to head home and go to bed early tonight. Nothing else is going on, anyway." I gathered my belongings and put them back into my work bag.

"Alright then, do you want me to box this up for you?" she asked.

I put my bag over my shoulder. "No, you can have it."

Jean grabbed another chip. "Okay, I'm not going to charge you for the food and drink. The bus boy can have the sandwich on his break. Hell, I might even have the wine on my break." Jean teased as she started to clear the table.

I scooted the rest of the way out of the booth. "Thanks Jean, and you really should get your eye looked at. Pink eye isn't something to mess with, you could go blind."

Jean gave me a dirty look and sharply turned away and walked through the kitchen doors with my uneaten food.

# Chapter Eight

The front door swung open with such force you would have thought a sumo wrestler was on the other side instead of my seventy-nine-year-old mother.

Holding out her arms for a hug, she simultaneously looked me up and down, silently judging my choice of attire for tonight's festivities. "Hello darling, how are you?"

"I'm good Mom, how are you?" I said, accepting her cold embrace. We hugged quickly, but only from the shoulders up.

"Well, your sister and Todd aren't here yet, your dad is still in the bathroom getting ready, and the food is still in the oven, but the card tables are set up," she said sounding stressed heading back into the kitchen.

"What can I do to help? You have me all night, and by all night I mean until 10:00 p.m., because I left Stormy at home," I reminded her, following her into the kitchen.

"Really Ember, you are a young woman, you need to be out living it up, not sitting at home with your dog on a Saturday night. You know what happens to young women who wallow in their misery, don't you?"

"Enlighten me, mother," I said, sarcastically dipping my tortilla chip into my mom's handmade salsa, then spitting directly into my napkin as taste buds reminded me that my mother is a terrible cook.

"They end up marrying men like your father," she claimed firmly, then walked out of the kitchen.

"What the hell is that supposed to mean?" I demanded to know, as I followed her out of the kitchen to the buffet table in the living room.

"Grab those wontons and cheese crackers on your way out here honey. I need them for my charcuterie board. See, all the different crackers are supposed to look like poker chips, aren't I clever?" she giggled, obviously avoiding her last comment. Then the doorbell rang, and she raced off to greet more guests, as they were now arriving in droves.

Where the hell were Sawyer and Todd? I was never the first daughter to arrive. Ever. And now I remembered why.

I texted Sawyer, but no response. I texted Todd. No response. Finally, I lowered myself to text my nephew, Alex, who might know where his parents were. His response was typical of a teenage boy. "How should I know?"

Finally, they came rushing in with their contributions to the casino night, which consisted of two bottles of rum and four bottles of cola. Of course, Sawyer and Todd were both dressed like casino dealers. She was always so much better at playing the part for my parents' shindigs than me. Maybe I would just take on my old job and serve drinks and hors d'oeuvres.

"Sawyer, we have got to talk," I said sternly. "Now." I pulled her towards the kitchen.

She grabbed my arm and whipped me around to stop me from pulling her and with a look of fear in her eyes she said, "Oh my god, are you okay? Did something happen at therapy?"

"No, it's something mom said. I think mom and dad might be having marital problems," I said, surprisingly getting a little choked up.

"What, no, really?" Sawyer seemed confused and shocked at the same time. She let go of my arms and looked over my shoulder, "Look, let's talk about this later. Mrs. Lindal just arrived. I can't believe she is still coming to their parties. Remember 'Shepherd Pie Night?' God, it still makes me sick to my stomach."

Turning around to see Mrs. Lindal as well, I replied, "Yes, I remember. tI makes me sick as well. Okay, let's talk later. But Sawyer, I really think something is very wrong here." I stressed my concern again before I headed back to the kitchen to get more food for the buffet.

"Okay, Okay. Calm down, I believe you." I heard Sawyer trying to reassure me as she watched me walk away.

Sawyer and Todd, dressed as the casino dealers, covered the card tables, and I decided that my role as the server would be a perfect cover to follow my dad around the party to see if I could figure out what he had been up to. For the most part, he would just stand at the food table and eat, and my lord, could that man eat. Every now and then I would see someone come up and talk to him for a bit while they filled their plate, then walk away. *Was he waiting for someone, or was he just that hungry?* I thought to myself.

"Ember, we are running out of meatballs. Please go to the kitchen and put more on the stove?" Mom said as she shooed me back into the kitchen. I wasn't happy about having to leave my spy station to make more food, but I had no other choice. It was a direct order from my mother. I gave the two fingers from my eyes to my dad's eyes motion at him, but he just returned a very confused look to me.

I was pouring the meatballs into the saucepan when Mrs. Lindal walked in. "Can I help you honey?" she offered as she stood beside me, looking down into the saucepan.

"Oh no, Mrs. Lindal, that is super sweet of you to offer, but you are our guest. You should be having fun, winning some money," I replied, stirring the meatballs.

"I feel better being in here," she said as she sat down at the kitchen table. I was about to ask her what made her feel unsafe when no sooner did my dad walked in. Mrs. Lindal got right up and bolted straight out of the kitchen.

Dad followed her out with his eyes, but turned around and took her chair and asked, "so how's work going Em?"

After I finished making more food, I enlisted dad into helping me keep the food table full. I had this odd feeling that he was the problem that Mrs. Lindal was fretting over tonight. In order to keep mom from killing dad and Mrs. Lindal from feeling unsafe, I needed to make it my mission to keep this man by my side at all times, or at least until I could figure out what the hell was going on with everyone.

It was 10:00 p.m. and the party was finally starting to wind down. There were only a few guests left and I was helping them gather their coats, purses and keys. Dad was passed out in his recliner and mom was already in the kitchen scrubbing the counter. I waved goodbye to the Klines and shut the door, only to turn around and find Sawyer and Todd both with their coats on, also ready to leave.

I instantly stopped her from leaving. "Sawyer, where are you going? You said we would talk."

Pulling on her coat. "Ember, I am tired. Do you know how many old people I had to help by either reading their cards to them or repeating myself fifty times because they couldn't hear me?"

"At least you didn't have to help Mr. Kline in the bathroom by helping him sit down." Todd complained, pulling on his coat as well.

"I get it guys, but there is some weird shit going on with mom and dad that I think we seriously need to discuss. I think they are going to get a divorce," I blurted out as I positioned myself in front of the front door so they couldn't leave.

Mom came into the room, wiping her hands on a dish towel. "Who's getting a divorce?"

Scrabbling now, both Sawyer and I said at the same time. "Neighbors, coworkers."

"Well, which is it, Sawyer, your neighbors, or Ember your coworkers?" mom said suspiciously. "Okay, you two, what is going on? You both have been acting funny all night and I've about had it."

"Well, you made an odd comment about me being alone and if I didn't start getting out more, I would end up marrying someone like dad. You made it sound like a bad thing." I tried to be honest.

"It's true. Do you want that, Ember?" She threw her dish towel over her shoulder.

Both Sawyer and my mouth dropped. We couldn't believe that mom just admitted it would be a bad thing to end up with someone like our father.

"Why would that be a bad thing to end up with someone like dad, besides the fact that I am gay?" I asked.

"Ember, why do you always talk like that? You need to talk more elegantly, like your sister. Look, girls, it's late. Can we discuss this another time? Your dad is your dad and I just want to go to bed. Please lock the door on your way out. Thank you for helping with the party tonight. And don't forget about the Halloween party coming up. We are raising money for an ice cream machine. Good night, girls." Mom turned around and walked down the hall towards their bedroom, leaving dad in the living room, snoring in his chair.

"Holy shit," Sawyer said. "You are right, there is something going on with mom and dad." She walked over to the couch and sat down.

"I told you. What are we going to do?" I sat down next to her.

Sawyer sat there thinking about it for a few minutes, but it was Todd who offered the first solution. "I could talk to your dad, man to man. See what he thinks is going on?" He found himself a seat on the other side of Sawyer.

Sawyer and I looked at each other and shrugged our shoulders. "Sure, why not? I mean, it's not like we have any better ideas," I said.

\*\*\*

Sawyer and Todd dropped me off at my apartment and as I was walking through the front door of the complex, I saw Isla walking up the street, so I thought I would hold back a few seconds to hold the door for her.

"Hey neighbor, how's it going?" I asked as she walked through the open door.

"I'm good. Evening was a bust, but that's okay." She stopped like she wanted to talk for a minute. *Oh wow, I was feeling some butterflies take flight in my stomach.*

"Oh no, I'm sorry to hear you didn't have a good night. Hopefully, nothing too tragic." I tried to sound as empathic as possible.

"Oh god no, just went to a game night at a friend's house where I was supposed to have a blind date, but she didn't show, so the rest of the night was slightly awkward. Now I think I am ready for a drink and probably bed," she said, sounding bummed, but still standing there, as if she still wanted to engage.

I took the bait. "Happy to join you, if you want?" I offered, then instantly realizing how that sounded, "I mean the drink part, not the bed part. Oh my god, I am so sorry. I swear I didn't mean to come off all...let's jump into bed, I'm not like that, I mean I have done that, but–"

Isla cut off my rambling by laughing and said, "I'd love to have a drink. Do you want to go over to the hotel bar across the street?"

I sighed an enormous sigh of relief, knowing she didn't think I was a complete idiot, and smiled as we both headed across the street. We found a spot at the bar, and both ordered a glass of wine. It seemed so weird to be at a bar with someone besides Bev. Bev is the only woman I have been at a bar with in the last several months. I got a little nervous, so I slammed the wine and ordered something a little harder to calm my nerves.

"So, Isla, what do you do for a living?" Putting a few dollars on the bar to signal to the bartender that I desperately wanted another drink.

"I am an artist. I paint," she replied, "you may have seen my work in a few places around the city. I've rotated through high-end restaurants, department stores, art galleries, but those are all my managers' favorite places to sell my work. I personally love to throw a piece or two in a bar and sell it super cheap. I love the idea of some of my work being out there and the owner not knowing what they have hanging on their wall. Sometimes I feel like people put too much emphasis on an artist's name instead of the print or the work itself. That's why I do it, because I want the person who buys it out of a dive bar or little barber shop to buy it because it resonates with them, because it fills their soul, not because my name is on it. Although my name is on it, you just have to really search for it," Isla said as she took a long swallow of her wine.

I sat there on my chair, absolutely stunned. I had no idea who I was hanging out with. Isla was a well-known Latina artist in the Seattle area. She painted pieces with such vibrant colors that you didn't just see, you literally felt, like you were pulled through a portal from another dimension.

Some pieces you found yourself staring at in utter calm, while other pieces brought you to tears. I had never had a piece of art evoke so many different emotions from within me, as I did at her opening night two years ago at the Seattle Art Museum.

I, of course, could never afford an Isla piece, too expensive, but I cherished every minute I got to be in the presence of her work. This woman was going places, It was just a matter of time.

I snapped back to reality when I realized she said earlier that she was supposed to have a date with a woman? I was completely freaking out at this point. I needed to check myself. This woman was totally out of my league.

Trying to play it cool, I said. "I'm not going to lie. I know who you are, and I am very familiar with your work. I just didn't recognize you, I guess in the real world. You are an amazing artist, Isla." I sipped my drink.

"Thank you," she said graciously. Placing her hand on top of mine.

"I promise not to get all fan girl on you. After all, we are neighbors and I hate when people get all... 'Ember, you're such an amazing executive assistant.' It's just weird, and quite frankly overwhelming at times," I said sarcastically.

Isla laughed at this, "Is that what you do for work? You're an executive assistant?"

"Yes, I work for an advertising agency, not like a big, fancy one. Although my boss acts like we are, we have been around a long time, but have never been able to compete with the big guys." I nervously pulled my hand away from hers.

"Are you happy?" For some reason, she seemed all serious now.

"Why do you ask me that?" I answered her question with a question.

"I see you around. I don't know. You don't always seem happy, I guess." She shrugged her shoulders.

I was immediately both embarrassed and irritated at the same time. Famous painter or not, it's kind of rude to deconstruct someone on the first date. Was this a date? Surely not. Either way, it was super rude. "I am fine, totally fine, but I should really get back home and let Stormy out. He's probably crossing his little puppy legs. Thanks for hanging out with me for a bit, Isla. Hope we can do it again soon." I started to stand and put my coat on.

By now Isla was staring at a woman at the other end of the bar, who was just as intensely staring back at her. "I am going to hang here a bit longer if you are okay heading across the street on your own?" she asked without even looking at me.

"Yeah, of course." Noticing how these two women were staring at each other suddenly made me feel like a third wheel.

"Okay, see you later than." Still not looking at me.

I hurried out of the bar, ran across the street, into my apartment, slammed the door shut and slid down the wall, crying the entire way to the floor.

# Chapter Nine

I walked into Dr. Kayla's office on Monday and nodded to Lisa that I was present. She waved and said I was checked in. I would have preferred if Lisa didn't use actual words and just gave me a thumbs up or a wink. A wink might be weird, but a thumbs up would be fine.

Sitting in Dr. Kayla's waiting room was like waiting for any other doctor except I am pretty sure everyone in here was judging me. I know Lisa was. When I sat in other doctor's offices, I didn't really care why other people were there. I didn't sit there and think they were here because they had a cold or a backache or something else entirely. We all just sat there and pretended like the other person wasn't there. But here, we are all messed up and we all know this about each other. I can't remember if these people were in the waiting room last week when I hurried out the door crying. I was pretty sure at least some of them were, because they kept looking at me. I hate my life.

I heard the squeak of a door open, so I looked up and saw Dr. Kayla look at me and smile. I guess it was her way to cue me that it was my turn. I stood up and swiftly walked into her office, keeping my head down to not make eye contact with Lisa or anyone else along the way.

I sat down with a sense of urgency, deciding to skip the formal greetings. "Okay, I am thinking a week between sessions is a bit excessive."

I could see the winkles start to form on Dr. Kayla's forehead and her eyes dart from side to side while she contemplated how to respond, but then she asked, "What would a better schedule look like if you were to choose one?"

"I should probably be here at least three times a week in the beginning, I think, then we can evaluate my condition over the course of the next few months. How does that sound?" I believe we were starting to get somewhere.

With a slight nod of her head, Dr. Kayla adjusted herself in her chair. "Okay Ember, I am going to recommend a couple of things for you to try between our sessions. Now these are only recommendations. You can say no. Totally up to you. These suggestions would just be to see if they help you get through harder moments. If they don't end up helping, we can try something different. How does that sound?"

I shrugged my shoulders, willing to listen. "I guess I can try your way of therapy."

She seemed to appreciate my willingness to let her do her job.

"I would like you to buy a journal, write everything and anything you are feeling, your thoughts, your fears, your dreams, anything at all. Then in our sessions we can discuss them if you would like. I would also like you to try to go for walks, get outside more if you are not doing this already. Find a small pleasure that maybe you used to do that you haven't done in a while that used to bring you joy. Try those three things first, then we can talk about increasing sessions if we need to. What do you think?" she asked.

"You moved your lamp." I realized.

"I did. I didn't want it to be a distraction, or make you feel uncomfortable," Dr. Kayla confirmed.

"Hmmm..." I narrowed my eyes suspiciously.

"In our last session, we started discussing your past relationships with your family. Your parents, and your sister. I know you have told me multiple times that your sister thinks you are broken, however, you have yet to tell me why she thinks that. I want to continue to give you the space to talk about what this means to you and how we might change the narrative of that word, 'broken' into something that describes what you are physically or emotionally experiencing. How does that sound?" Dr. Kayla asked.

"I don't know. I don't know what to feel now or before or in the future, today or tomorrow or next year or last year. Does that make sense?"

"Completely." Dr. Kayla leaned in closer to me. "It makes complete sense, Ember. And we will take the time to explore each of these feelings, whatever they are, wherever they came from. They don't need to define you as a person, although they may have made up your yesterday, your today, they don't need to define your tomorrow. We can start to define those things through our work together. We will organize them into what feels right for you and help them make sense over time."

"Okay." That was all I could think to say.

Dr. Kayla gave me an encouraging smile as she went on to talk about what therapy would look like for the near future. We landed on me starting to journal, that I would get outside more, try to find the small pleasures that I used to connect with. Whatever that might be. We decided that if those things weren't enough between sessions, she would allow another session. That decision made me cry. I felt like such a baby. I just couldn't keep my shit together. Dr. Kayla was so nice, she kept lots of tissues nearby.

I walked out of my therapy session and immediately felt like I wanted to go back in there.

"See you next week," I mumbled to myself, mocking Dr. Kayla's typical closing statement as I walked out the door.

"See you next week," Lisa responded and waved.

Ugh. *Not you,* I wanted to say to Lisa, but I didn't and just walked out the door.

I tried to be open by telling Dr. Kayla how hard this last week was for me, and that was her answer, to buy a journal and write down all my feelings during the week, so we can talk about it the next week's session. Seriously. I wanted her to know I was dying a little more every day while I was waiting to talk to her again. I wanted her to know I wanted to sleep more than I did before, because that meant I would get to see her sooner. Why does she stare at me so damn much? I decided that was going to be the first thing I could journal about. The fact that she stares at me all the time. This journal was going to be in for a lot of abuse, that's for sure.

Maybe getting outside more and trying to fill my days would help between sessions. I am going to try to trust her therapy methods, although it is obvious grown-up therapy is turning out to be a lot harder than I thought it was going to be.

Since I was leaving for Vegas in the morning and needed to pick up some travel supplies, I figured I would also buy the stupid journal when I swung by the store on my way home from work.

I stopped at the corner pharmacy to see what they had. I found the section with the notebooks, calendars, and journals. I wasn't sure if I wanted something with a picture on it, like puppies, that would start me off in a good mood when I wrote about my feelings, or something like a hard back in case I dropped it, then it wouldn't get ruined. But then I found it, or maybe it found me. It was the only one left. It was embossed vintage leather with some sort of tree on it, a tree I have never seen before. The paper was also vintage, aged, and antique looking. There were no other journals like this one on the shelf and there was not a price tag on it either. I gathered the rest of my supplies and headed to the cash register.

"I didn't see a price on this journal." I told the cashier as I was putting all my stuff on the conveyor belt.

He turned it over, looking at the back, inside cover and then asked, "what was the price of the other journals?"

"Around ten dollars." I guessed because I honestly didn't look.

"Ten dollars it is," he said as he punched in the price and continued ringing up my remaining items.

After dinner, I curled up on the couch with Stormy and my new journal. At first, I just sat there and stared at it. I then glanced down at Stormy. "I feel like a fucking idiot. I'm not a twelve-year-old writing in my diary." The little stump of his tail started wagging at the sound of my voice, then he jumped at my face and started giving me a bunch of kisses. "Then you write in the damn thing," I said as I put the journal in front of him and picked up my phone to text Bev.

> "Hey Bevie! All packed?"

> "Please go to the Magic Mike show with me? #hotmen"

> "Not going to happen."

> "The last trip I went to the drag show with you. #hotladies"

> "You had a blast. I had to drag you back to the hotel."

"It was fun."

> "I was just checking what time you were picking me up?"

> "6:00 a.m. still works for you? Who is watching Stormy?"

> "Sawyer is coming to get him after work. She will drop him off on Friday."

"It will be nice for you to have him come home too."

> "Yeah, my first trip away from home."

"Em, you ok?"

> "Yep, see you bright and early, my friend."

"#magicmike #mynewmole."

> "Gag!"

I looked over at Stormy and watched his little chest rise and fall as he slept so peacefully beside my leg. I reached over and started to slowly pet the spot between his eyes, which made him start to snore. He snuggled closer to me, and I started to get teary because I realized how much I was going to miss him. I was glad he was going to be with my sister, but it would be the first time we were ever going to be apart, and I didn't know how I was going to cope without him at night.

~~Dear Diary,~~
~~Dear Journal,~~
~~Dear Dr. Kayla,~~

This was not going to work. Who the hell did a thirty-seven-year-old adult woman address their journal to? Well, I guess this is meant to get me to my next session, right?

*161 hours until my next session*

*What to write, what to write, journaling is kind of dumb. I don't know why I am doing this when I should have therapy sessions multiple times a week instead. 167 hours is a super long time, waiting, hurting, scared, lonely, anxiety, no one to talk to, no one to just be with me.*

*I just can't handle this. How can Dr. Kayla act like she cares so much during that hour, then just let me walk out completely torn to shreds and so casually see the next person? Like, do I even matter? It's probably just a job, like any other job. I guess when someone storms out of one of my meetings all mad, I just go to my next meeting and barely think twice about it. That's probably what it's like for Dr. Kayla too. I cry, I leave, she moves on to the next client and doesn't think twice about it.*

*Maybe Jean is right. I will have to fill these hours between sessions with different things to distract me. Jean said to travel, well I am leaving for Vegas tomorrow. Meeting new people will be hard. Go to parties, well my parents are having a Halloween party. Does that count? Okay, Ember Rue, if you are going to get through these hours, you might just have to step out of your comfort zone, try some new things...like leaving your apartment.*

*Why does Dr. Kayla keep staring at me?*

*~~Love,~~*
*~~Sincerely,~~*
*~~Your friend,~~*
*Ember*

# Chapter Ten

"Vegas, here we come!" Bev called out to everyone standing in the security line at the airport. "Em, are you excited? I'm excited. Even my mole gave me a hundred dollars for the blackjack tables. He said if I win, I can quit work and we will move to a tropical island."

I shook my head and giggled. "Yes, I'm excited. That is if Bethany doesn't keep an eye on my every move like she did in Chicago. Sometimes it feels like she thinks I am more of a personal assistant than her executive assistant." I pulled my carry on up to the TSA agent, so he could check my ticket.

"Ember." I heard a familiar voice yell out. As I turned around, I saw it was Bethany jogging up to join us. "What, no coffee for the group this morning?" Bev and I turned back around and rolled our eyes at each other.

Security was a breeze for me, but Bev packed some herbal teas, so she was stopped by security. Then because Bev is Bev, she started to argue with the TSA agent about how it was for her bad back and not to sell it on the Vegas strip, so I just told the rest of the team to go ahead, and I would wait for her?

I didn't mind. I preferred it to just be me and Bev most of the time anyway. You would think I would want to hang out with women my own age from work, but I didn't have as much in common with them these days. Not that I had a lot in common with Bev either, but she was so damn sweet and lovely. Who wouldn't want to be around her.

The flight to Vegas was quick and boring. But as soon as I stepped off that plane and the warmth of the sun hit my face along with the hot air that immediately made me start to sweat. I felt like a completely different person. I had such a charge of energy flowing through my body that I felt like if I didn't tap into it, I was going to explode. I wanted to party, drink, and just totally let loose. This was ridiculous. This was not me at all, but I was kind of digging this new vibe.

We arrived at the hotel, and everyone checked in. It was nice that we didn't have to share rooms anymore. Back in the day, when I first started with the company, we had to bunk together because there wasn't the budget to support everyone to have their own room. Then people started to complain they felt like their privacy was being invaded and, regardless of the budget, it was inappropriate to make people share rooms. Human Resources agreed and now we all have our own rooms, which I love. I always hated sharing a room, even if it was with Bev.

Sitting down on the edge of one of the two queen size beds in my room, I pulled out my agenda, which was for tonight and the next two days. We will head back to Seattle early Friday morning.

Tonight, there was a cocktail party with a light dinner and drinks. Wednesday, there will be the normal vendor booths at the convention hall, a keynote speaker to kick off the event at 8:00 a.m., and then some breakout sessions throughout the day. Thursday will be a lot of the same, plus an evening dinner to wrap up the event.

I heard my phone buzz, which alerted me I had a text message. I grabbed my phone from my bag to see that Bethany was texting me.

> "Hello, Ember. We will all meet at the restaurant bar at 6:00 p.m. to talk about the agenda for the week."

> "Sounds good, Bethany!"

> "Can you bring me a couple of aspirins? I have a splitting headache already."

> "Sure."

I threw my phone on the bed along with myself. It was kind of weird to think this hotel room kind of felt like home. Besides not having Stormy with me, the room doesn't look that different from my apartment. I rolled over and set my alarm for 5:00 p.m. Out of nowhere, I felt completely exhausted and overwhelmed by the thought of even leaving this room. I kind of didn't even want to be here anymore.

We all met at the restaurant bar at 6:00 p.m., as instructed by Bethany. And, of course, I came with her aspirin, as she requested.

Bev seemed like she had been downstairs for a while by the glow on her face and the smell of alcohol on her breath. "Getting an early start, Bev-Bev?" I asked, finding a seat next to her at the bar.

She leaned over, a little clumsily. "I may have played a few slots. Did you know they give you free drinks in the casino?" She slurred her words a little as she set a five-dollar bill down on the bar and snapped her fingers at the bartender, so she could buy yet another drink.

"Listen up team, we have a busy next two days," Bethany announced. "We have a lot to cover during our time here, so I decided to take a divide and conquer approach. I have created a list for all of you to follow to make sure we capture everything this event has to offer. We will meet for breakfast in the morning to discuss our individual agendas for the day. Together, we will attend the keynote speaker both mornings, then go to our respective events during the day. Everyone is expected to meet for lunch and report on your morning activities to the rest of the team. Dinner will be the same concept. Your evening activities are for you to enjoy. I just request that you remember you are representing our brand and this company, so make sure you always act responsibly." Bethany looked over at Bev.

Bev shrugged her shoulders like she didn't understand why Bethany directed that comment at her.

Bev and I were assigned to wander the convention hall and talk to different vendors, get their business cards, and determine if they were someone Bethany might want to take on as a client. We used to work with almost everyone and anyone who would do business with us, but as our company grew, Bethany became very particular as to who she let have our brand name on or in their advertisements. She believes that holding out for "bigger" money by not accepting "smaller" money was the strategy that would grow us to a billion-dollar company someday. It will be Bev and my job to determine who makes the cut and who does not over the next two days.

Cocktails and dinner were super boring, so I went back to my room as soon as I could. Tomorrow will be a new day. I just wanted this week to be over so I could go back home. I have no energy to even write in my stupid journal. I just wanted to go to sleep and pretend like this life was not happening to me.

\*\*\*

> "Where are you, Em? We are all down here. #Reportforduty"

> "I overslept. Give me 10 minutes Bevie."

> "Bethany is PO'd #bosszilla"

> "Bethany can kiss my ass."

No sooner did I drop my phone back on my bed, then did it buzz again, only for it to be Bethany wondering where I was at as well. *For fuck's sake. I am up!*

> "Ember, where are you? We are all waiting for you!"

> "On my way right now, Boss, can I bring you anything?"

> "Oh god, yes, more aspirin would be great. Thank you for asking. What would I do without you?"

> "You got it, boss. On my way."

Breakfast was quick and the keynote speaker was your typical man in a suit with no tie, wearing sneakers, jumping all over the stage trying to motivate the crowd by telling everyone their personal success story of how they started their business in their basement with just a notepad, pen, and rotary phone.

After the presentation, Bev and I headed to the convention hall to start our search for our new future clients. No sooner did we step into the hall was I beauty struck by a woman behind a booth who I knew I would never forgive myself if I didn't at least say hello to.

I tried pumping myself up to make my move by reminding myself it was Vegas and the worst that could happen was, one, she'd not be interested in me, or two, she'd end up being straight, which would most likely lead me back to number one.

Finally, I confidently walked right up to the booth and introduced both myself and Bev to the woman. "Hi, my name is Ember, and this is my coworker, Bev. What do you all have going on over here?" I held out my hand to shake.

The woman looked up at me, and I was immediately mesmerized by her frosty blue eyes. She smiled and then extended her fist instead. Oh, I liked her already.

"Hi, my name is Cara, I'm the buyer, and we sell different types of cookware," she said. *Shoot, no way Bethany will go for cookware*, I thought to myself.

Bev, being oblivious to my attraction to this woman, immediately tried to size up whether this vendor was even worth our time, while all I wanted to do was get her number. "Who do you typically market your cookware to?" Bev asked.

"We market to high-end restaurants, classic chefs, and some culinary schools," Cara responded.

Trying to insert myself professionally, I said "Cool."

Bev looked over at me like, *"What the hell are you doing? I am a receptionist! You are the executive assistant! Bag this deal, woman!"*

I stammered a bit. "Um, are you currently represented by an advertising company or is that why you are attending this conference?" Picking up the different pans trying to act interested in the product.

She gave me a sweet, crooked smile like she was picking up on the fact that I was interested in more than her pots and pans. "That is why we are here. We will interview multiple advertising companies to help us with our campaign. Do you have a card or a number that I can give my boss?" She took the pan from my hand, which drew my eyes up to connect with hers.

I stood there, taking in her smile for a moment, when I was jarred back to attention by Bev hitting my arm as I saw our business card in front of my face. "Oh yes, here is our card. I will write my cell phone number on the back in case you have any questions. Hopefully, we will see you around one of these evenings. It was very nice to meet you, Cara." I offered my fist with a smile. Cara bumped my fist slowly, connecting our knuckles together for a couple of seconds longer than I expected, which sent a flutter of excitement through my body. She then turned and held out her fist to bump Bev's as well.

Later that evening, after dinner, I decided to go down to the hotel bar instead of gambling with the rest of the team. I have never been a big gambler. Maybe it's because I never had any money to gamble with. I sat at the bar on my third beer and my second shot of a drink called the 'Mind Eraser'. I must say, the shots were definitely living up to their reputation when the sweetest voice said my name. "Ember, right?" I turned around to see the woman from the cookware booth.

"Hi, yes, that's right. My name is Ember. How are you? Would you like to sit down?" I stood up and pulled out a barstool.

"I am not sure if you remember me. I'm Cara. We met this morning. I was selling cookware." She seemed a little more nervous now.

"Of course I remember you. How could I forget that smile?" I said, backed by my newfound alcohol confidence. Cara blushed, obviously sober, but taking the seat I offered.

As the night wore on, we both drank and flirted. Both of us seemed to become bolder with each drop of alcohol that we consumed. I leaned in closer while talking to her, just to feel her warm breath against my cheek when she replied to my questions. I softly brush the tips of my finger across the top of her hand that laid flat on the bar, and when I stopped, she would trace the side of my hand with the edge of her pinky. At one point I even took a chance by lightly laying my hand on her thigh, but just long enough to tease her when I excused myself to go to the restroom. The sexual energy between us was growing by the second. I didn't think I could last much longer.

The evening was coming to an end, and I hoped she was thinking the same thing I was thinking. I knew if I didn't just take my shot, I would regret it. "Can I kiss you?" I asked her gently while taking in every bit of those iced blue eyes of hers.

Cara looked a little surprised, maybe because we were sitting at a bar in the middle of a hotel, or maybe because it was a work event, I'm not sure, but then she whispered, "Not here. Let's go to my room." I said nothing, I just took her hand and led her to the elevators.

Cara slammed her hotel room door shut and pushed me against the back of the door with such eagerness that my breath loudly escaped my body. She didn't even bother with words but instead immediately drove her hand down the front of my pants while kissing me with such passion that I wasn't sure I would be able to last an even minute by the way she touched me.

I couldn't believe how she went from sweet and shy Cara at the bar to this sex crazed ninja in the click of a door latch. For a second, I thought I was going to lose complete control and scream, feeling her move her fingers against me, but then she stopped and stepped back and started to undress.

"I am married, I hope that doesn't bother you. I just want you to know that it's just tonight. I love my wife and I don't know why I am doing this, but anyway, it's just tonight, okay? You can't try to find me or anything after this, okay?" She kept undressing and was now standing completely naked in front of me, walking back towards me.

"I don't know what to say." Suddenly, I wasn't feeling the vibe as much anymore. "Maybe we shouldn't do this if you're married. I'm not here to mess with anyone's relationship."

Cara took my hand and placed it between her legs. "Please," she begged. Just feeling how much she wanted me suddenly made me not care about anything else she had going on outside of this room. I started to slowly move my fingers. "Please, oh god please," she begged.

I pushed my fingers deep inside her and pulled her body against mine. "Just tonight," I whispered.

\*\*\*

The next morning, I made it to breakfast just in time to give Bethany our debrief. "Bev and I were able to connect with four different vendors, of which three of them seemed to be very promising future clients." I reported proudly. "Today our plan is to hit the east side of the convention hall and then possibly do one round on the west side if we have time."

Bethany was staring at me with confusion. "Only four?" she said, sounding disappointed. "Well, a lot of these vendors took our cards, but didn't really seem like the type of new client that we are looking for. You know, with our new "big money" strategy."

Bethany sighed, then moved on to the next person for their update.

Bev leaned over to me and whispered. "Where the hell did you end up last night? I texted you a hundred times. I was worried sick Ember."

I turned ten shades of red and whispered back. "I met up with that Cara woman from the cookware booth for drinks and ended up hanging out with her until about two in the morning. I was so tired and a little drunk that I must have just passed out cold when I got back to my room and missed your text messages. I am so sorry, Bev'er." My sheepish smile was begging for forgiveness.

"Do you like her?" Bev asked, seemly hopeful.

"It's not like that. We are just going to be friends, I think. Probably we'll never see each other again." I didn't feel like explaining how complicated all this was to an elderly straight woman.

After breakfast, Bev and I hit the convention center. We walked in and I thought I would at least go say good morning to Cara. I went over to her booth, and she looked up and at me, then back down at her paperwork. *Odd*, I thought to myself. I picked up one of the frying pans and I teasingly said, "Hey do any of these pans get hotter than you did last night?"

Cara responded so coldly, like I was a stranger. "Can I help you with something?"

I was so taken off guard by her rudeness that I didn't know whether I should walk away or stay. "Um, no, I just wanted to stop by and say good morning is all."

Cara looked around to make sure no one was watching us and said in a low voice. "Just last night, okay? Take care, Ember." Cara then picked up her paperwork and turned her back to me, leaving me stranded in utter disbelief.

Bev saw this exchange from a few feet away and straight woman or not, elderly or not, complicated or not, Bev knew my feelings were destroyed. She walked over and took me by the arm and pushed me straight out the exit door and held me so tight while I cried in her arms for an hour, begging her to take me home.

# Chapter Eleven

I decided that Jean's idea of meeting new people sucked, so I might want to find something else to do to kill time between sessions. Sawyer dropped off Stormy after I got home from Vegas on Friday morning and asked if I wanted to be a chaperone for Bella's "Weekend in the Woods," dance camp outing at the last minute, since she had to work, and I jumped at the opportunity. The leader of the Dance Club said I could even bring Stormy, which made both Bella and I super excited. From nightmare Vegas on Friday morning to forest bathing in the woods Friday night. I so needed this.

I tossed my feet on the arm of the couch and pulled up the email on my phone that Sawyer had forwarded to me. I started to make a list of everything Bella and I would need for the weekend. Each family was required to bring their own tent and sleeping bags, but other than that, they would supply everything else.

According to the pamphlet, there would be games, a hike on Saturday, a bonfire on Saturday night, some sort of yoga event on Sunday morning, followed by lunch before we head back to the city. My niece was obviously giddy about her weekend in the woods because a text message popped up from Bella as I was reading through the agenda for the weekend.

# THE NEXT 167 HOURS

> "I'm so excited for this weekend. Thank you for taking me, Aunt Em."

> "We are excited too. Stormy loves being in the woods. Do you mind cuddling with him if he gets cold?"

> "Yes! Yes! Yes! I wish mom would let us get a dog."

> "I know, right? What is wrong with your parents?"

> "idk"

> "I will meet you in the Dance Studio parking lot tonight at 6:00 p.m. sharp. I promise I won't be late. Love you, Bell."

> "Bye"

I could just feel her energy coming through my phone, which makes me feel even more excited to get out there and let go of all my stress.

I decided I had better get packed. There were only a few hours to spare before I had to meet her at the dance studio to get on the bus. I slapped my hands on my legs and stood up from the couch and strolled towards the closet where I kept some of Stormy's camping gear. Opening the closet door, I pulled down his little puppy backpack I could strap around his waist. I unzipped the bag and first threw in his winter vest, then his rubber boots and a knit scarf for the hike. For the Bonfire, I thought a cute argyle sweater that would match my own would be super cute. Last, for the yoga class in the morning, he would wear his one-piece swimsuit. I had no idea what I would wear for yoga, since I had never been to a yoga class before. Probably sweatpants and a t-shirt.

I found his sleeping bag on the top shelf of the closet. I figured he could sleep between Bella and I so he would stay extra warm. Stormy typically liked to carry a toy with him, so I would have to bring one of his camping toys so that if it got lost in the woods, at least it would be biodegradable and wouldn't hurt any other animal or nature.

My backpack was similar. Stuff for the hike and clothes for the events. The only items that were different were yummy unhealthy snacks of chocolates, potato chips, candy, and soda. I packed a flashlight in case we had to find a bathroom in the middle of the night. I brought some cards so we could play games in our tent if we got bored and I also threw in my therapy journal.

***

We boarded the bus at 6:30 p.m., which was on schedule according to the agenda. I was a bit disappointed because I was hoping Bella and I would be sitting by each other, but instead she and her friends gathered at the back of the bus and all we could hear were their little giggles about who knows what. Not getting to sit with my niece meant I had to sit with the other moms, who I didn't know. Frustrated, I found a seat at the very front of the bus, thinking to myself that I did not sign up to hang up with a bunch of dance moms.

# THE NEXT 167 HOURS

No sooner did the bus pull out onto the highway for our two-and-a-half-hour journey southeast than the moms pounced on me like a cat on a ball of yarn.

"So, Ember, it is Ember, right?" One of the moms said to me.

"Yes, my name is Ember," I replied with growing discomfort, as I smiled and shifted in my seat towards the mom who was speaking to me.

The mom leaned closer to me. "How is it that you, of all the people Sawyer could have chosen to come on this trip, you ended up being the person she picked? I mean, I am not trying to be rude, but I would have thought Bella's grandmother, or someone more, how do I put this, more in line with our values, would have decided to join us this weekend."

My stomach dropped to the deepest pit of my stomach, but before I could respond, another mom jumped in and said, "Julie, shut the fuck up. You are such a snob. My lord, and yes, I said 'the lord's' name completely in vain. Bella is lucky to have an aunt who would come on this trip with her. Go back to reading your bible and pray for yourself."

The mom who stuck up for me smiled and winked at me, and I returned the smile. "Thank you. I didn't realize there were religious requirements for this trip."

"There's not. Julie just likes to spread the word wherever she goes. Such a bitch. This is a dance trip for girls. We do this yoga and meditation camping trip once a year because dance as a sport is very high stress and competitive. We want the girls to learn skills to stay grounded. It's important for their mental health." She turned around and went back to reading her book.

I also turned my head, but I didn't have anything to read, so I just watched the trees race past the window and wished I could escape this nightmare as quickly as those trees were passing me by.

We arrived at the campsite in complete darkness. I didn't get the feeling the kids were going to be roughing it all that much because the second bus that followed us was full of spotlights, generators, large cooking stoves, and other accommodations that made me think we were staying at a five-star campsite. What kind of dance club did my niece belong to?

While the adults set up everything for a late dinner, they told us we should go set up our tents. Bella and I took all our gear off the bus and found a nice flat spot to pitch the tent. Once the tent was up, I climbed inside, spread out the blankets across the bottom of the tent.

Rayna and I bought all this camping gear years ago. We used to love to go camping. Our favorite camping spot was up in the mountains on a ledge that overlooked a beautiful lake that spread out for miles below us. I remembered unzipping our tent in the early morning hours when I could tell the sun was starting to rise, she would roll over and nuzzle her head into the dip of my shoulder and I would just hold her until the sun would form a full fiery circle in the sky. When the warmth of the sun would begin to fill the tent, it was my cue that it was time to get up and make us coffee and breakfast.

I started to let myself drift off into dangerous memories when I felt a pillow hit me on the side of the head, along with the silly little giggles of my niece. I grabbed a pillow and gently hit her back and yelled, "Pillow fight!"

***

Bella was the first to wake up on Saturday morning. "Aunt Em. Aunt Em." She shook me awake.

"What Bella?" I muttered while I turned over and rubbed the junk out of my eyes to see her sitting up, already dressed and ready to go to breakfast. "Ugh, give me two minutes. Can you put Stormy's vest and boots on?" I tossed her his backpack.

We strolled into breakfast at the same time as everyone else, so at least we weren't late. Bella ran off to sit with her friends and I found a table by myself avoiding the Jesus loving mother, Julie. I was putting Stormy dry kibble under the table so he wouldn't bother me or anyone else for food when the woman who stuck up for me yesterday sat down across from me.

"Hi, my name is Nat. Sorry about Julie yesterday. She can be a total asshole. Sawyer really is the best at dealing with her." Our heads both rotated over to where Julie was sitting.

I played with my food a bit and looked up to where Nat was looking to see Julie staring back at us. "To be honest, even though I have been talked to like that my whole life by people I know and even strangers, it doesn't get any easier and it still hurts."

Looking me directly in the eyes. "We are an all-inclusive club, which means everyone is welcome. We have other gay and lesbian families who come to the studio." She pointed to herself.

I looked around the dining tent curiously. "Oh, which little one is yours?"

Nat pointed to the little girl who sat across the table from Bella. "That is our little Jilly. She is just the sweetest." Nat was beaming from ear to ear with pride.

"She is adorable." I added.

Nat picked up her plate and stood up. "Stick with me. I won't let Julie or anyone else bully you, Ember. We really do want you and Bella to have a nice weekend."

Standing up and putting out my hand for her to shake. "It was very nice to meet you Nat, and thank you for having our backs."

***

*I am so out of shape. Note to self, quit drinking when you get back home and put some inclines into your daily walks.* I was already scolding myself and we weren't even five minutes into the hike. They told us the hike was going to be six miles round trip. Three miles to the top of the summit and three miles back. When we arrived at the top, the girls would gather for some ritual they do every year where they meditate. Sawyer said the dance teachers have been pumping the girls up for this experience on the summit for weeks now. The plan was they would arrive at the summit, form a circle, meditate, then they would be handed a handwritten letter that their mothers or a significant female figure in their life had written to them to read privately for spiritual guidance.

They encourage the rest of us to find our moment to meditate or at least separate ourselves from the girls so they can have the time for themselves. I am sure Stormy and I could find something to do out in the woods.

When we finally reached the summit, the girls went off for their spiritual awakening, so Stormy and I kept hiking further up the trail. We weren't even an eighth of a mile up the trail when we decided to veer off the trail for a while, which is something I was experienced in doing, so I wasn't too worried about it. I knew we had exactly one hour to kill. We were about three hundred yards off the trail when the trees opened to a clearing that had a rocky bank with a small rushing stream.

I walked over to the stream and knelt at the water's edge. I put my fingers in the water to let the icy wetness flow through my fingers. At first the fridge temperatures hurt, but the longer I left them in the water, the less I could feel the pain. Oddly, it was somewhat soothing as I pulled up a few stones from the bottom of the stream and skipped them across the surface of the water. I decided I had better pull my fingers out of the water before I did any permanent damage to my hands.

I sat down on a rock that graciously gave me a seat to rest my tired body and clenched my fingers into a tight fist to try to warm them back up. I slid them into my coat pockets and drew in another long breath of the fresh mountain air. The stillness of the air was so silent, except for the acoustics of the water pitching up and over the rocks as it flowed down the stream.

While I looked at the fog filling the valley below, I felt a warm tear roll down my cheek, then another rolled down, this time filling into the crease of my lip. As I pursed my lips tightly together, I could taste the saltiness of my own sadness. A lump started to form in my throat and a tightness in my chest that made me feel like I was heading for a complete breakdown. I didn't want this to happen while I was on this trip with my niece. I tried so hard to keep my shit together.

Then, an unexpected thing happened. I heard a noise. We weren't alone. Stormy edged closer to my side and buried his head behind my leg, timid about what we were both witnessing.

I lifted my eyes over my coat where I had my face tucked in to keep warm and saw that a deer had strolled up across the stream at some point. She was just standing there, staring at me. I had never seen a more beautiful creature in my life. She was tan, with white spots all over her thin body. Stormy let out a soft whine, but I didn't move or say anything. We just sat there together, me and this doe.

I unclenched my fist and reached towards her, ignorantly thinking she might want me to pet her. She looked at me with a tilted head. Like she knew me or something. Then she just did her thing. She lowered her head and drank from the stream, and I just did mine. I lowered my head back into my coat and cried harder than I have ever cried before.

I was able to pull myself together in time to find Bella and head back down the hill with her. "How was your spiritual awakening, Bella?"

Looking very disappointed, she kicked rocks on our way back down the trail. "Very underwhelming Aunt Em."

"What? Really? Wanna talk about it?" I offered, kicking my own rocks.

Stopping me, she pulled me down to her eye level and whispered, "Mom's letter was super lame. She basically just said to follow my heart, and all will fall in place."

I put my hands on her shoulders as I knelt in front of her. "What's wrong with that? Were you hoping for something different?"

Bella turned and started walking back down the trail again. "Maybe something like, this is your path, God is or isn't real and here is proof, or aliens do exist, or global warming is real, and we all are going to melt, or if I only have one bit of my burger left and one french fry, which do I eat last? You know she still hasn't answered that question either, Aunt Em."

I quickly stood up and jogged to catch up to her. I grabbed her jacket to stop her and turned her around. "Bella, I think these weekends are supposed to be all about you finding your own spiritual awakening and defining your own beliefs, and your mom's letter is supposed to be supportive of your journey."

She looked unconvinced. "Aunt Em, how am I supposed to know if there is a heaven? It's important that I know these things." She turned and ran ahead.

"Fucking Julie," I muttered as I stood there shocked and started to walk back down the hill. I didn't know that I could help her with this one. *I don't know Bella. I wish I did though.*

Bella fell asleep early, so I decided I would take a stab at writing in my journal.

*40 hours until my next session*
*Well, that was deep and unexpected. My niece is contemplating life and is asking me, of all people. Like I fucking know. Does heaven exist? Global warming? How the hell do I know these things? I can barely put two sentences together most days.*

*Aliens? Or course there are aliens and yes, absolutely you must eat the french fry last, everyone knows this. Other than that, I am going to take a pass on her other questions.*

*I am sitting here watching her sleep, thinking back to what life was like when Sawyer and I were her age. I don't know that I was worried so much about global warming and heaven. What torture it must be for this generation of kids to have to wonder if there will be a planet for them to live on when they're older.*

*I want to help her, but I can barely help myself most days. She is sleeping peacefully now. I want to wake her up and promise her it's all going to turn out okay. But will it? Would I be lying to her? If someone told me that everything would turn out okay when I grew up when I was her age, I would scream 'liar' in their face. Because the fact is, it's not okay, nothing turned out okay. My whole life is not okay. I would be lying if I sat here and told her she wasn't going to hurt, that there is a beautiful, happy ending in store for her. I'm sorry Bella, I don't know if there's a heaven, I don't know if the earth is melting under us as we lay here in this tent, but I know your mom and I love you, and we'll do everything we can to keep you safe. Always.*

*Ember*

# Chapter Twelve

I decided to take Monday as a personal day, which I desperately needed. I did my sister a big favor by taking my niece on her camping trip over the weekend, so already getting together with Sawyer so soon to discuss our parents was honestly starting to wear on me. Before heading to the coffee shop, I thought I would see if maybe Isla was around and wanted to go for a morning walk with Stormy and me.

We stepped outside our apartment only to find Isla already in the hallway, saying goodbye to a woman, probably a date from the night before. I waved at them and decided Stormy and I would take this walk on our own. We didn't need new friends anyway.

The elevator door started to shut when a hand came through the door to stop them from closing. Then the same woman who was saying goodbye to Isla jumped in with us.

Out of breath, probably from running down the hall to catch the elevator, she said, "Good morning."

"Good morning," I replied.

"You must live in this building too," she asked.

Small talk with Isla's one night stand. Awesome. "I do, yes indeed live in this building." I nodded and looked at the floor.

"Cool, well here's the lobby." She pointed as the doors opened. "See you around."

I smiled and waved to the girl as she walked away, even though she was already half down to the lobby exit and didn't even see me.

Once we walked out the apartment door, the warm sun embraced us and it seemed to make all the other stuff of the morning a little lighter. *Isla sure had the life,* I thought. We started our journey towards the coffee shop when I realized I had forgotten my phone and needed to go back upstairs to get it.

"Sorry buddy, this will just take a minute," I said to Stormy as we retraced our steps back to our apartment.

Just as I was putting the key in the door, Isla stepped out of her door in nothing but a t-shirt and asked me, "Did you need something earlier? You looked like you might have been coming over to my apartment?"

Trying to keep my eyes from wandering over her body. "Um I was, no not really, just going to say good morning, or hi, mostly good morning though because it's before noon, so saying good morning and not good afternoon seemed to make the most sense, and it's a nice thing to say, to be neighborly. Because I am in fact your neighbor, me Ember." Pointing to myself. "Oh, and Stormy," I tugged at Stormy's leash. "Say good morning to Isla, Stormy." I was hoping his cuteness would save me, as my face turned as red hot as the rest of my body at this point.

Isla, sensing my attraction by the fact I could barely make a cohesive sentence, got a huge grin on her face and said, "Good morning, Ember, and good morning, Stormy." Then she turned and shut the door. Poof. She was gone.

*Wow, Ember, you're a catch,* I thought to myself. I turned the key in the lock and pushed my apartment door open as quickly as possible, then went inside to die a slow death of embarrassment.

\*\*\*

Sitting across from each other at the coffee shop, I watched while Sawyer dunked her croissant into her coffee. She said, "You know mom and dad have always been a little weird about talking about their marriage."

Looking down, I dipped my tea bag in and out of my hot water and replied, "Well, it's not like we ever ask them a lot of questions either."

She brought her croissants about halfway to her mouth to reflect on this for a moment. "Yes, true, but they never say anything at all, like about their anniversary, or their lives together before us, just normal things parents talk about."

"Yeah, but maybe they are just old fashioned and private." I sighed and relaxed back into my chair.

Todd walked in, pulled up a chair next to Sawyer, snagging her croissant from her plate and taking a bite. We knew he had just met with our dad to talk about what had been going on with him and mom, so we both sat up a little straighter in anticipation of what he would tell us about his outing with Dad this morning.

"Well? Tell us everything. Did you ask dad about him and mom?" Sawyer took her croissant back.

"Sort of. I need to order a coffee before I get into all of this. And if was the two of you, I would put a little vodka in your drink before I tell you what I am about to tell you." Todd stood, then moseyed up to the coffee counter.

"That does not sound good," I said to Sawyer.

"No, it does not," she agreed.

Todd returned with a coffee and a cinnamon roll. He pulled his chair up to the table and started to eat without saying a word. Simultaneously we both said, "Todd."

With his mouth full of cinnamon filled gooeyness, he looked up at us like he forgot why he was even meeting us here. "Oh yeah, okay, so dad thinks mom is trying to kill him. He has been suspecting her of trying to plot his murder for months now." Todd said rather seriously, then going back to eating his cinnamon roll.

I slammed my hand on the table. "Todd, focus, that is ridiculous. He was joking, right? Please tell me he was joking?"

Todd looked me dead in the eye. "He wasn't joking, Em. He was dead serious. He thinks your mom is trying to kill him."

Sawyer laughed nervously. "Okay, let's all calm down. What proof did he provide you of our five foot one, ninety-eight-pound mother trying to murder our twice-her-size father?"

Todd sighed. He looked at Sawyer, then at me, wiped his mouth with a napkin and calmly said, "He heard her on the phone with a hitman."

Our mouths hit the floor. "A hitman." I repeated.

"A hitman." Todd confirmed.

Sawyer leaning over the table, slowing moving all our drinks out of the way so to clear a path for a now more serious conversation. "Let's go over this again. Dad heard our mother on the phone with a hitman? And what made him think it was a hitman that she was talking to?" Sawyer asked.

"Well, he admits he can't hear as good as he used to, but he said it's like clockwork. Every Thursday she talks to her hitman on the phone. He hears all these scary things like 'money up front,' 'thousand before, thousand when the job is done,' and 'make it look like an accident,'" he replied.

"That is pretty convincing." I agreed.

Sawyer, always being the reasonable one, said, "Okay, let's think of other people she could have been talking to that fit a conversation such as this, other than a hitman."

We all just sat there, staring at the table. Todd jumped in excitedly with the first explanation. "His birthday is coming up. Maybe it's a surprise party."

Sawyer looked like she was about to agree, then thought better of it. "But for two thousand dollars and to have a party that looks like an accident? That doesn't make any sense."

Todd crossed his arms. "Well, I say we leave it on the table."

I offered my two cents. "Maybe she wants a new car, and she is having someone create an accident with her old car?"

Todd shook his head. "She'd get way more with a trade in from that car."

Sawyer stood up. "I got it," she exclaimed. "She is trying to set him up so she can simply divorce him and make it look like it's all his fault. She doesn't want him dead. She wants him alive, broke, and miserable."

"He's not moving in with me." I put my foot down. "We cannot let them get a divorce. We had to find a way to save their marriage. Sawyer, get mom on the phone and pretend like you are just curious how they are doing. You know, take their temperature. Put her on speakerphone so we can all hear what she has to say."

Sawyer got out her phone and dialed mom's number. Mom answered right away.

"Hello." Mom sounded in a good mood. That was a good sign.

"Mom, this is Sawyer. How are you?"

"I know who this is. It comes up 'Sawyer, My Favorite', right on my screen. Don't tell your sister I said that. I'm just teasing, I'm not...t easing, but if she happens to ever hear me say it, tell her I'm teasing, okay?" said mom.

I sat back in my chair and rolled my eyes. "Whatever." I whispered. Sawyer hushed me.

"I won't, Mom. What are you and Dad up to today?"

"I don't know where he is still at. He left this morning to have coffee with some of the guys. He hasn't been home since. I am sewing our Halloween customs. You and your sister will be here, right? And you promised you will dress up, right?" She sounded excited.

"Yes, we will all be there, and we will all dress up." Sawyer promised.

"Don't tell me what you're coming as. I want to be surprised."

"Okay, I won't. So how are you and Dad doing lately? Are you two okay? Because Dad is a little concerned that you might want him a little dead. He is hearing you say things on the phone." Sawyer asked causally.

"Oh, that is just silly, such a drama guy. We are fine. Your dad had his appointment with Dr. Francis on Thursday. The doctor called with the results and said he must have some good genes in his family because he has the heart of a twenty-year-old. He said he will probably live to be one hundred years old. I laughed and told your dad, 'Not if I had anything to say about it.' Look honey, your dad just got home. I better go. Love you, bye."

The phone went dead and there was silence. We all looked at each other and sat back in our chairs. I was the first to speak. "She did not just say that?"

"She did," Sawyer confirmed.

Todd didn't waste any time chiming in. "I told you guys," He said, licking the frosting off his fingers.

***

I walked into Dr. Kayla's office, not at all ready for the session. My last week had been an absolute nightmare. I guess I could talk about Vegas, the camping trip, or the fact that my father thinks my mother is trying to kill him, but why waste a session on my drama. I really didn't want to take up all her time on my problems.

I sat in the waiting area to see if I could eye lock Lisa instead of checking in with her at the front desk. "Hi there, I have you checked in," Lisa announced from across the room. She smiled and went back to whatever she was doing.

Seriously, will she ever get the fact that I am incognito over here?

I could not understand why I was always so nervous before each session. My hands were sweating, my heart was pounding, and I felt so nauseous. I don't think this is normal. I heard the squealing of the door hinges and looked up to see Dr. Kayla smiling back at me. I stood up and pointed at her with a quick whistle to confirm my readiness for therapy. I immediately regretted the whistle.

I came in with nothing today. I didn't know where to start, how to start, what to say, how to say it, so I just sat there and picked a focal point on the wall behind her head.

"Ember, how was your work trip?" Dr. Kayla asked.

Oh god, I had not planned on a social question. I didn't even know that was legal in therapy.

I squirmed in my chair and looked over her right shoulder. "Um, it was fine, for the most part, work is work, ya know. I talked to nine people. To be honest I didn't count them. That would be weird to count the number people you talk to. Seventeen, it was seventeen people. I logged seventeen people that I talked to. Lots of people there, I like people in some settings, in other settings I don't like people, but sometimes in those same settings if I am drinking, I might like them a little more, sometimes too much. Ever been to Vegas?" I asked. "I'm not a big fan myself." My leg began to rapidly bounce up and down.

Dr. Kayla smiled and said, "My partner and I went to her best friend's wedding in Vegas last year. It was okay. I don't need to go back."

Then I just sat there in a daze, as I replayed what she just said over and over in my head. So simple, but just hearing her say a non-therapy sentence made my heart skip a beat, and I felt these tingles all over my body. I had this same odd sensation the last time I was here. *What the hell has been going on with me lately?*

"Ember, what would you like to talk about today?" Dr. Kayla probed.

My head shot up in exact alignment with hers, but then I immediately turned and looked away. "Um, maybe my sleeping issues." I could feel myself starting to panic, and by the way she looked at me, I knew she could sense there was something amiss.

*I now know what is wrong. Oh my god, it was totally making sense. I think I had feelings for my therapist. I liked her. I like,* liked her, *liked her.* "Fuck." I accidentally said out loud.

Dr. Kayla leaned in closer and looked at me with curiosity. "Is that really what you want to talk about today?" I threw my head back and stared at the ceiling because I couldn't look her in the eyes. Not today, not with what I just discovered about my feelings. "Yeah, that's sounds like a good place to start. I lay awake thinking about a lot of stuff at night. I can't shut my mind off it seems."

She leaned back and wrote something on her legal pad. "What is it you are thinking about?"

I exhaled, wondering what she had just wrote down. "Well, work, family, my dog, things I should start doing, things I should probably stop doing, and why I can't sleep. Normal stuff, I guess."

"What things have you tried to do to fall asleep?" She was still writing stuff down.

Try? Try? I had tried everything; sleeping pills, crying, screaming, drinking, tossing, turning, and begging the universe to take away my nightmares. "I just lay real still." I replied, rapidly bouncing my leg.

"Would you like to try some different relaxation techniques?"

"Yes. I would absolutely like to relax right now. I need to really, really find a way to relax right now. Yes, please. Let's do it." I closed my eyes and pinched my pointer fingers and thumbs together in a meditation position.

Everything was too quiet, so I opened one eye to find Dr. Kayla staring at me.

"This is not exactly what I meant, so let's just start with a few deep breaths."

I learned a lot of relaxation techniques in the session. I just hoped they would work when Dr. Kayla crept into my thoughts as I tried to go to sleep at night.

Dr. Kayla looked at me as if I was holding something back, and she wasn't wrong. I was a sweaty mess. I couldn't even make eye contact with her without blushing.

"As we are nearing the end of our session, Ember, I want to make sure you feel supported going into this next week. Is there anything I can do? Anything else you want to discuss in the time we have left that would help you feel supported? Anything else you would like to talk about with the time we have left?" Dr. Kayla asked, as if she was opening the door for me to let out whatever was bothering me.

"Why? What do you want to know?"

"I just want to make sure that we have covered everything that is important to you in our session today."

"And?"

"And... you feel you have the tools to be successful as you move forward into this next week."

"Okay, well, if that is the only reason you are asking such cryptic questions." I was so nervous that she already had me figured out.

Dr. Kayla stared at me for a second, wrote something on my legal pad, "Okay then Ember, if you don't have anything else, I guess we'll see you next week then."

"Yes, good talk. See you next week, Dr. Kayla."

\*\*\*

I walked out of my session and headed straight home, tormented by the fact that I now had to deal with the weight of something I had no idea how to navigate. Could I go back next week, or do I need to find another therapist?

One shirt flew over my head, another flew over my left shoulder. *Where is my damn journal?* I was frantically throwing my clothes onto the floor that were once folded neatly on my bed. Shoot, it wasn't there. I next moved to the couch and threw the pillows onto the floor as I looked between the cushions. Where the hell did I put it? Now shoveling through the books on my coffee table. The one time I actually felt like writing in the damn thing, and I can't fucking find it. I was about to flip the hell out, and then I saw it sitting by the stove. I grabbed it, went back to the couch, plopped down, and immediately began panic writing all my feelings.

# THE NEXT 167 HOURS

*167 hours until my next session*

*Welp, I have a problem. A ginormous problem. I can't even go to the one place I am supposed to be able to take all my problems to. I just realized, sitting in therapy today, that I have feelings for my doctor. So, I have developed a list of questions for myself to figure out what to do next.*

*1. What the fuck is wrong with me?*

*Answer: Everything*

*2. Who does that, who falls for their therapist?*

*Answer: Well, apparently, me.*

*3. How the hell do I go back and pretend like this isn't happening?*

*Answer: Don't look her in the eyes*

*4. What if you like her eyes?*

*Answer: Don't look her in the eyes*

*5. What if she likes you too?*

*Answer: She doesn't, don't be stupid*

*6. What if she smiles at you?*

*Answer: Why are you asking yourself this question?*

*7. Because you like her smile too.*

*Answer: Don't look at her smile*

*8. Should you tell her?*

*Answer: Yes, ~~you probably should just tell her~~*

*Answer #2: Absolutely not! You should not tell her.*

*9. What if she kicks you out of therapy?*

*Answer: Find a new therapist*

*10. What if she lets you stay?*

*Answer: Good question. What if she lets you stay?*

*Question: You can't answer a question with a question?*

*It would really help if she would stop being nice to me. It's not like I deserve her kindness. Sometimes I show up, sit down, and within ten minutes I am crying. She just sits there and holds me, well, not physically but emotionally. I never show up with anything to really talk about. I don't have the guts to. I want to. I want to tell her everything. I need to tell her everything. Next session, for sure. I will tell her everything. Crushes are hard. Being honest about my life is hard. Why is this all so hard? This is going to be so fucking hard. Ugh. I expect a bad reaction when I tell her I like her, but that's okay. I'm used to bad reactions, so I got this.*

*Ember*

I tossed my journal back on the coffee table and leaned over to kiss Stormy on the forehead. "Be glad you're a dog, because being a human is not for the weak of heart, my friend."

# Chapter Thirteen

Saturday night rolled around quickly, and although I rather enjoyed Halloween parties, I wasn't sure I wanted to attend one at my parent's retirement community. "Come on, we need to get ready to go to Nana and Papa's Halloween party." As soon as Stormy heard two of his favorite names, he zoomed off the couch and straight to the front door. "We need to put on our costume's first silly. If I have to wear one, you have to wear one."

We arrived at my parents' house a half an hour late, but considering I showed up early to the last party, I was okay not being the first daughter there this time. I rang the doorbell, but no one answered. I rang it again and added a knock, but still no answer. *Odd,* I thought. I retrieved the key that my parents gave me for emergencies and slipped it in the keyhole. As soon as I opened the door, everyone yelled. "Surprise!"

Completely stunned, I turned ten shades of red. "Oh my god, what the hell is going on, and why am I the only one dressed up for this Halloween party?" My mother ran over to me, grabbed both my hands in hers. "Surprise! Don't worry honey, we are all going to get dressed here soon. You won't be the only one, but it's your birthday and we wanted to celebrate with you. We knew you'd never let us throw you a party, so we surprised you. Look, all your friends are here too." Mom took a step back and looked at me up and down. "Are you a waffle and Stormy a piece of chicken? Is he a drumstick?"

"Yes, we dressed up as chicken and waffles for the Halloween party," I said as I took in all the people who were already back to mingling with each other. I saw Bev and a couple of other girls from work, Sawyer, Todd and the kids, but most of the people who were there were my parents' friends.

I can't believe I forgot today was my birthday. It literally didn't even occur to me that I just took another trip around the sun and I didn't even notice. I stood there dripping in plastic syrup while Stormy was chewing his stuffed chicken that I let him bring with him. "Aren't we a pair, buddy," I commented, while we moved towards the crowd.

Bev just returned from putting on her costume, which was a potted plant. "I like your costume, Bev-Bev, very creative."

She winked at me, then twirled around to give me a full view. "I am pot. Get it?"

I shook my head and started to walk away smiling. "That's not how it works, Bev."

I was super curious what my mom decided to pull together for our parents this year being my dad was so obsessed with the thought that my mom wanted him dead, but I couldn't find them. "Hey Sawyer, have you seen mom and dad anywhere?" I asked as I scanned the room.

No sooner did we both look towards their bedroom door did we see dad looking at Todd with the fear of god in his eyes. Sawyer nudged my arm, trying not to be obvious. "Ember, are you seeing what I am seeing?"

I raised my drink to my mouth to cover my shock, "If you are seeing that mom made dad a fork costume and her an outlet costume, then yes, I am seeing what you are seeing." We stood very still as all their friends rushed them with compliments on their costumes.

Todd pulled us into a football huddle. "It is becoming more and more obvious that something is seriously wrong with your mother, girls."

I pulled my head out of the huddle and looked at mom and dad, then lowered my head back down, "I don't disagree, Todd, but what do we do?"

"We obviously have got to call her doctor. Something is seriously off with that woman," Todd suggested.

Sawyer lifted her head out of the huddle and looked over at mom and dad, then quickly dropped her back down, "Shit, mom is coming over."

We all quickly broke the huddle at the same time to turn and face our mother. "Hi Mom, are you enjoying your party?" Sawyer asked.

Mom looked at us suspiciously with pursed lips and said, "Well, it's not just my party, it's your sister's party too you know. It's her birthday. Happy birthday, Ember."

I smiled at my mother, "Thank you Mom, this was quite the surprise. I certainly didn't expect such a big deal for a non-decade birth year."

Mom hugged me. "Well, it's been a tough year, and we all thought it would be nice to see you smile a bit more." She leaned back, holding onto my shoulders, giving me one of her pitying looks, then she rubbed both my arms softly before she turned and walked away.

I rolled my eyes and looked disgustedly at Sawyer. "Did you know about this?"

She backed away slowly. "I did, but no matter how much I tried to convince her you would hate a party, she insisted."

Birthdays are low key events in my family. I have never experienced a surprise party, especially from my family. In fact, my birthday had always flown under the radar. As a kid, we ate a family dinner; I opened presents, then we ate cake. As an adult, my mom called me and left me a voicemail with a "Happy Birthday, Ember. Enjoy your day, honey. We love you."

There was one year when I turned thirteen, a very important birthday for a teenager, I had my first sleepover party. I invited all three of my friends, including my first crush, Patti. Of course, Patti didn't know I was absolutely head over heels in love with her, but it didn't matter. I had everything planned out perfectly. I even made sure to put mine and Patti's sleeping bags next to each other's just so I could be close to her when we slept.

Everything was perfect until my mother fed everyone lasagna. But it wasn't any lasagna, it was a vegetarian lasagna. It had peppers, onions, cucumbers, and radishes in it. Besides being a disgusting dinner, unknowingly Patti was allergic to radishes, and we spent half the night in the emergency room waiting for her parents to get there, since they were out of town. My dad took my other friend's home. Patti ended up being okay, but we didn't hang out much after that night and eventually never spoke again. I never cared to celebrate my birthday after that.

As the evening wore on, I had figured out exactly eleven different escape stories of why I must immediately leave my own party, but of course, none of them would have worked. So, Bev and I just did Jell-O shots until we were both brave enough to try a slice of my mom's birthday cake. This year was a banana and apple cake, with chocolate frosting. There were also these little fried discs on top that I thought were just crumpled up cinnamon spices, but nope, they were fried pickles. So gross. This woman should not be allowed to bake.

I could not sit and listen to the Monster Mash song and watch my mother shove my father's fork head into her outlet stomach one more time before I was literally about to go insane. I finally convinced my mother that I should take Stormy home and she released me from my own personal hell. I said my goodbyes and called for an Uber. I just wanted to go home and pretend like this birthday never happened.

\*\*\*

When I got home and stepped off the elevator, I heard music blaring. I looked down the hallway and noticed it was coming from Isla's apartment. She must have decided to have a Halloween party of her own tonight. I wasn't invited, which I guess I couldn't be upset about since we are just neighbors, not friends.

I started towards my apartment when I saw a few people walk out of her apartment. "Oh my god, I love your costume," said one of the two girls, "and your little puppy's outfit is so cute, what a clever idea. You have to come in and show Isla. She will just die." Grabbing my arm, she dragged me into Isla's apartment.

"Isla, look at these two," the girl lightly pushed me in front of her. "I'm sorry sweetie, I didn't catch your name," the girl asked me.

"I'm Ember, I actually just live a couple of doors down." I pointed to the wall that faced my apartment.

"Yes, we know each other. Super cute costume, Ember. Would you guys like to stay for a drink?" Isla offered.

"Sure, if you don't mind, we just came from my parents' Halloween party and my birthday party." I regretted saying that immediately.

"Oh well, happy birthday." Isla embraced me with a hug. Just feeling another woman against my waffle made me get all tingly inside. I knew right then and there I was too drunk to stay, but not drunk enough to go home and pass out like I probably should.

I decided it was best to run Stormy home quickly and come back over. I walked over to the buffet table to grab what looked like a fruit punch, but tasted like pure alcohol. Being that I was already tipsy, the first drink hit me hard and fast. I popped a piece of shrimp into my mouth and watched the party goers move in slow motion across the room. Everyone seemed to move from couch to chair, person to person, some embracing, some laughing hysterically, others were staring at me, judging me. *Maybe I should just leave,* I thought, but as soon as I turned around, a man stopped me.

"Are you a friend of Isla's?" he asked as he dipped his cup into the punch bowl.

I tried to pick one of his faces to respond to, when the room started to spin violently. "Sort of. We are neighbors." I saw dark.

\*\*\*

When I woke up, I was in a strange bed. I slowly sat up, but the room started to spin again, so I laid back down and closed my eyes.

The next time I opened my eyes, the sun was shining through a crack in the curtains of a bedroom that was not mine. I swung my legs over the side of the bed and gingerly stood up to navigate my way towards the door. Doing so, I bumped into every obstacle that stood between me and what I was hoping would be my silent escape out of this embarrassing nightmare.

I slowly opened the bedroom door and looked out into the living room where a few people were either lying on the floor or on the couch, passed out. I started to tiptoe across the floor, being as quiet as possible, when I heard a familiar voice.

"You want some coffee?" Isla asked as she pushed the button on the coffee grinder.

"Oh my, that's a bit loud, but yes, I would love some coffee." I held my hand to my forehead, then sat at the island in the kitchen. "What happened last night?" I tried to sound inquisitive instead of guilty.

Isla slid a ceramic coffee cup to me that said "-feel color-" with a heart made from swirls of different colors of the rainbow in the center. I would expect an artist to have a lot of coffee cups like this.

Raising her eyebrows at me. "Well, let's see, should I start with you bobbing for shrimp that you threw in the fruit punch bowl, or no, how about when you threw up in the fruit punch bowl?"

My head fell solidly in my crossed arms on the counter. "I did not do those things. Please Isla tell me you are joking to get a rise out of me."

Isla walked around the counter and sat next to me, and slowly sipped her hot coffee. "I wish I was."

We both sat in silence and stared at the kitchen wall before I was the first to speak again. "I am so incredibly sorry. I will pay for all damages that can be paid for in monetary value."

Isla looked over at me and smiled. "Honestly, it's okay. Most people got a kick out of your waffle dance." She stood up and walked towards her bathroom. "I am going to jump in the shower. I have a meeting with my agent in a couple of hours. I assume you can you see yourself safely home?" She winked at me and turned away, then back around again and pointed at me curiously. "Oh, there was one other thing. You kept trying to call some girl named Rayna, but she didn't answer. You left her like a thousand voicemails. Is that a friend, girlfriend, ex? Just curious, you don't have to tell me. You seemed very frustrated that she wouldn't take your calls is all."

The look on my face had to say it all. I didn't want to talk about it. "She's my ex, I guess. Sorry to cause that drama." I left it at that.

I took one last drink of coffee, stood up, and pushed my chair under the counter. "I should probably go home and take care of my little drumstick."

Isla smiled and nodded, silently agreeing to leave it alone. "Hey, on second thought, I do need to meet with my agent, but would you like to go to my studio with me today? I mean, it's totally cool if that sounds totally lame."

"Not lame. I would love to. I mean, yeah, that's sounds fun. I should probably grab a shower and feed Stormy first. Meet you in the hallway at 11:00?" I smiled back.

"Alright, guess I will see you around the hallways then," she said.

I think this was our new saying.

Isla disappeared into the bathroom, and I headed to the front door. But before heading out, I admired how stunning her apartment was. I bet this was the Presidential Suite back when this was the hotel. The kitchen alone was the size of my entire apartment. The living area had a fireplace with a beautiful stone mantel. There were two bedrooms and an office. I peeked in the office door that was slightly ajar, which she obviously used as an art studio. We really did live in completely different universes.

I took my leave and headed out the door. As I walked down the hall to my apartment, it hit me: Isla winked at me. She liked my waffle dance. Wait, what the hell was my waffle dance? Then she watched me have a breakdown over Rayna. Fuck! That wink was most likely her way of saying she felt sorry for me, or she knew what drunk I was. Probably both.

# Chapter Fourteen

I was ten minutes early, so I just stood by the elevator and greeted all the neighbors coming on and off the elevator. It's amazing how long it's been since I have seen any of these people. It was kind of nice to socialize a little bit. I used to stop in the lobby and chat with different neighbors all the time. I felt good to get caught up on what was happening in the neighborhood. Having the type of camaraderie among people that live side by side, and that you can reach out to if you need a cup of sugar or, apparently, if you lock your keys in your apartment, still means something. I can't wait to tell Dr. Kayla I did I little something that used to bring me pleasure. I know I haven't been in therapy but a few times, but I am wondering if Dr. Kayla might be right about these little things helping me until I can see her again.

I released a small breath as Dr. Kayla's face came into my mind when I was startled by the feeling of a hand on the back of my arm.

"You ready to go?" Isla asked.

"I am." I let her leave her hand on my arm as we walked onto the elevator.

Isla's personal driver pulled up, got out of the car, and opened the door to the SUV that smelled brand new. The inside of the doors were lined with blue neon lights and there was a black tinted window that was halfway down between us and the driver.

"Wow, I don't think I have ever been in a car this fancy. I typically take an Uber or Sawyer drives me in her Toyota."

"Who's Sawyer?" Isla asked.

"Oh Sawyer, she's my older sister. We are pretty close. It was just the two of us growing up. Our parents were hard to deal with, I guess you could say. She has two kids who I absolutely adore. Anyway, you probably don't want to hear everything about my family. How about you?" I turned towards Isla and put my arm around the top of her seat above her head.

"I come from a large Latino family. We are all very close. They are wonderful, supportive, and I just want to take care of them. They are beautiful people. I am the oldest myself, so I get what it's like being the oldest sister."

For some reason, her comment turned me off. What was she trying to say? That she saw me as a little sister? Was that what this day was about? Taking me under her wing? Helping the poor pathetic drunk neighbor girl out? No, thank you. Isla was going to have a disappointing day, if that is what she had in mind.

"We are here. Are you ready?" Isla said as she jumped out of the SUV and offered me her hand.

"Let's do it." I hesitantly responded as I took her hand looking up at an old, abandoned warehouse.

We walked up to a side door next to a double wide garage door full of graffiti. "Don't worry, that's my work on the doors. Do you like it?" Isla smiled.

I nodded my head in approval while I just stood there and took it all in. I must have driven past here a hundred times this year alone and never thought it might be Isla's work. But standing here and taking in all these small details was breathtaking.

"I had been known to tag a bit back in the day. That's how my agent, Janelle, found me. She saw one of my tags. Hunted me down, then asked to see more of my work. Of course, I don't tag anymore, not as much anyway. Can't afford to get arrested. I mean, you know my art is only good enough for galleries, not for brick walls?" Isla rolled her eyes and pushed the iron door open with her shoulder.

Once inside, it was obvious that her career was massive. There were not just the few pieces that she would end up showing in there, but her entire life was on display in this building. There had to be over a hundred paintings in here, some finished, some half done, some with just a few blotches of paint on the canvas.

"I need to go meet with Janelle quick, feel free to look around. When I get back, I will give you the official tour. Don't run off on me, okay?" Walking backwards, then turning around, she jogged off.

I started to walk around, casually looking at each painting while I waited for Isla to come back from her meeting. I felt like I was intruding a bit. Here I was in this big warehouse packed with easel after easel, canvas after canvas. Some of these paintings looked deeply personal. Not at all like her other work.

There was a painting of a woman in a burgundy dress, running in the rain down the middle of a city street barefoot. Her hair was dripping wet. The woman was holding up her dress like she didn't want to get the bottom of it wet. You could tell by the deep reds and blacks Isla used and the dim streetlights that this woman was in pain, she was hurting. But why? Who was she?

"That piece will never see the light of day." I heard Isla's voice echo from across the warehouse.

I turned around. "Sorry, I didn't get very far looking around. This painting stopped me in my tracks. She looks so sad. Who is she?" I asked.

Isla walked closer to me. "Shonda, my ex. She was sad. That was the last time I saw her. I broke up with her that night. It was at my opening. I saw her with another woman in a back room. A mutual friend of ours. After I saw her...with her, I just couldn't handle it anymore. All her lies of where she was at night, when she wasn't coming home, the phone calls she took in the bathroom. Honestly, I think we were both just pretending, and we had been for months. So, when I had the chance, I pulled her aside and told her I sold a piece for nine hundred thousand dollars. Her eyes lit up. Then I told her we were done, to get out of my show, that I never wanted to see her again. She begged me to reconsider. She cried, and I pleaded with her to just leave. She took off her shoes and threw them at me and took off running down the street, crying. I never saw her again. I call this piece 'The Last Time.'"

"Wow. That sounds horrible. I am so sorry."

"We've all been there, right? Is that what happened with Rayna, cheated on you?" Isla probed.

"You said you'd give me an official tour? I can't wait to see the rest of this place. It's massive."

Isla exhaled a long breath that I took as disappointment for me not wanting to have a big kumbaya over break up stories, but she took the hint and decided to just move us along to show me her studio.

As we walked around the warehouse, I just couldn't believe that Isla was trusting me with her art. I mean, I could be secretly snapping pictures every time I blinked or recording everything through a button on my shirt. It takes a lot to trust someone to bring them into your world. I wonder if I will ever be able to be that strong, that brave again. I really want to be. But I barely know this woman.

At one point, Isla took my hand and smiled at me while we continued to walk through her life of easels and canvases. She took me into so many different worlds and landscapes. Fantasy worlds that must have resembled what it was like to be on an acid trip. I kept thinking about how much Bev would love some of these pieces. She showed me pieces of children begging for food, two elderly women with their arms wrapped around each and their heads softly laid against one another's, their eyes shut with thin smiles across each of their lips. Isla captured a love so deep in the painting. Goals.

I cried and laughed while we walked. At times, I was completely silent as I took it all in. Over the next hour, Isla showed me so many different pieces and told me about all the stories that led her to create them. It felt nice to be close to a woman like this, even if she did just see me as a friend.

As we walked around a group of easels towards the back of the warehouse, I was immediately drawn to a canvas that was half covered with a painter's cloth. I dropped Isla's hand and went over to it while she was still talking about a bird that was nesting in a tree downtown that she painted. I slid the cloth from the canvas and stood there in shock. I heard Isla stop talking, then noticed the cloth suddenly reappear over the painting.

"Isla, that looks like the park Stormy, and I go to. That kind of looks like us on the bench too?"

"It's not done. Pretend like you didn't see it, okay? You weren't supposed to see that one." She sounded nervous and busted all at the same time.

"I don't know what to say. It's beautiful." My heart fluttered.

"Thank you. I appreciate the compliment. I don't typically paint a lot of greenery scenes. I was just trying something new."

"Oh, yeah, of course. Well, like I said. It's great. Great job." My feelings were a little hurt because, for a second, I thought it might have been something special for me.

"I should probably take you home, Ember. It's getting late."

"Yeah, late. Stormy is probably wondering where I am at or something. You know how dogs worry." I turned to walk towards the garage door.

"Ember, wait, I'm sorry. I didn't mean to snap at you about the painting. I just get a little sensitive about people seeing my unfinished work."

"Seriously Isla, this place is full of unfinished work. Why is that one so different?"

"Because I haven't gotten the woman in the painting as beautiful as she is in real life yet." Isla said softly, staring at her shoes.

"Ha! Okay, good save. I promise I'm not mad, but you don't need to tell me all the lies." I smiled at her for being nice, then continued towards the door.

# Chapter Fifteen

I arrived at the therapy office while everyone was out to lunch, which made it eerily quiet. I was the only one in the waiting room for the first ten minutes, so I decided to shake off the spookiness and explore my surroundings a bit. I meandered around by first checking out the magazine rack. They mostly kept health magazines.

Next, I examine the water filtration system. Looked clean.

Onto Lisa's space. I leaned over the counter that was attached to her desk to get a better look at all her pictures. *Awe, she has a picture of a small human.* A little girl who looked to be about two years old. There was a family picture as well. *That must be her significant other standing beside her, holding the little girl.* He looked to be older than Lisa. Maybe it was his beard, or maybe Lisa was just born with good genes and looked younger.

"Hi Ember." Startled, I slid off her counter, knocking all Lisa's appointment cards and a cup of pens onto the floor. "Checking in?" she asked as we both started to pick up the mess I just made.

"Yes, present, I am here," I said anxiously as I tried to help her, but then decided to just stop when we almost knocked heads. I saluted her as a thank you and turned around to go take my normal seat in the corner.

My routine was all jacked up. Not only was I the only person in the office when I got there, but then Dr. Kayla came strolling in the front door which totally threw me off.

She was always in her office when I arrived. I hated that she wasn't in her office and was now walking through the waiting room. I never saw her outside of that room.

It was like a movie in slow motion, her stride was long and full of purpose as she passed by my chair, she gave me a thin, closed lip smile, then her hair naturally flipped over her shoulder while she looked away to unlock her door. She pulled the door closed behind her and then poof she was gone like a shooting star that fizzled out across the night sky.

I wasn't sure how much time had passed, but I heard the familiar squeal of the door, and I looked up to see Dr. Kayla waiting for me with that same inviting smile. *This is torture.* I stood up and walked in with my head down, trying not to make eye contact in fear that she would be able to tell I was feeling the feels.

I sat in my normal spot and Dr. Kayla sat across from me in hers.

"How has your week been? Anything that you would like to begin our session with today?" Placing her legal pad on her lap.

"Not really. I got here early today because the bus came ten minutes early, which made me ten minutes early. I dropped all of Lisa's pens."

Dr. Kayla stared at me smiling, for about five seconds before she continued. "In our last session, you seemed to be distracted. Lost in your thoughts. I didn't want to interrupt your process, but was thinking maybe we could explore some of those thoughts together today? I also would like to check in to see how your relaxation techniques are going?"

I started to tap my fingers on my knee, then make small circles over my knee cap. I knew what she was talking about. I was distracted by the fact that I was attracted to her, that I had feelings for her. Now I had to sit here and try to figure out how to not let her see right through me. For god's sakes, I am not a fifth grader like my niece, who giggled over her crush every time she said his name to her friends. I can act like an adult, have a crush, and still get through a therapy session with this woman.

I looked up and saw Dr. Kayla wasn't going to let me off the hook, so I giggled, "Oh, I was just thinking about how it must be an interesting process to pick magazines for your waiting room."

"No, you weren't. Sorry to be so blunt, but Ember, I believe you were involved in something much deeper, even emotional, perhaps?"

Giving her finger guns. "Okay, you got me. I was, in fact, involved in something much deeper, even emotional perhaps. I was thinking about life."

This seemed to interest her, like finally we were getting somewhere. "Okay, what about life?" She leaned back, putting the tip of her pen to her legal pad.

I also sat back to appear relaxed and looked up to the ceiling before I engaged her with my deep words of wisdom about life, but I was nervous, so I tapped my fingers on my knees again. "Well, life is obviously a four-letter word that starts with L and ends with E." I looked back down to see her put her pen away. I looked back up at the ceiling to continue. "Same as like, live, love, which are nice words I guess for the most part, but then there are other words like lone, lame, lose, that are not so nice of words. So, you could end up on either side of the word life, I guess. The nice side or the shit side."

I looked back down from the ceiling to find Dr. Kayla was sitting back in her chair, staring at me again. This time not smiling. She was probably thinking this was all very profound.

"Alright Ember, maybe we will try something new today. I think you will really like this for a change of pace. I will explain it all to you, then you can tell me what you think. How does that sound?"

*I think it sounded like a horrible idea.* "Sounds good," I replied.

She seemed to get excited by the way she scooted to the edge of her seat. "Okay, great. I want you to think about your happiest memory. It can be yesterday, one year ago, or when you were a child. Can you tell me about that memory?"

I sat there and stared at her when my lip started to quiver. She immediately felt it. I felt it. We both felt it. She brought her hand up as if she was about to say, *oh no, I am so sorry, I just triggered something, didn't I?* Then once again, I lost my shit and started to cry.

"Ember, what is triggering about me asking you about a memory?"

Through my hyperventilating sobs, I mumbled softly, "Because I miss her."

"I'm sorry Ember, I didn't understand what it was you just said, but I feel like it was really important, could you repeat it?"

I took one of those deep relaxation breaths that Dr. Kayla taught me how to do and said, "I am hurting on my insides, which makes happy things sad to talk about."

"Is there a particular sad thing that makes happy things hard to talk about?"

"Yes." I froze. I just couldn't go on. I looked at the clock. We had so much time left, and I just wanted to run out of her office and never come back. How could I want to be here so badly, need to be here and want to run away all at the same time?

"It's okay if you are not ready to talk about this Ember. We don't need to solve everything today. We can talk about something else."

"Really, like what?" I asked.

"Anything you want, this is your time."

"So, if I want to talk about doilies, we can?"

Dr. Kayla titled her head curiosity. "Do you crochet?"

"Would you like me to?"

"I want to support you in the hobbies that bring you joy."

I sighed. "Okay. That seems important to know."

I stopped by Lisa's desk to hand her one of the pens that I found on the floor by the edge of her desk and to say I was sorry again. She could tell I had another rough session, but just waved me off like it was no big deal. "See you next week, Ember. Take care of yourself." She was always so nice to me.

***

By the time I got back to work, Bev was ready for happy hour, and I was too. We decided that after how hard things have been lately, we could both use a little girl time, plus who doesn't like to gossip over a few beers and some nachos.

Ollie's Bar was just two doors down from the entrance of our building. We could pop out our office door and right into the bar's door, so it was super convenient to head there after work.

It's an older establishment built back in the late eighteen hundreds. The inside was wall-to-wall brick with a slight odor of stale cigarettes that hung in the air from when people could still smoke in bars. The lighting at the back of the bar was so bad the owners had to put small lamps on each table just so customers could read their menus.

"You grab us a table, I will get us a pitcher of beer," I yelled from over my shoulder as I headed towards the bar.

"Make it two pitchers. Wayne from accounting made me look at the eczema on his knuckles again today."

I stopped and turned around. "Seriously, isn't that some sort of HR violation?" Bev shrugged her shoulders, then went off to look for a table.

We met up at a table in the back of the bar by the dart boards and the bathrooms. Being a weeknight, it wasn't too busy, so we found a decent table right away. "So how is Ed? You barely spoke of him the last few times we've seen each other."

Bev took a long guzzle from her beer. "He's good, for the most part. Tired a lot. I keep telling him he needs to retire from driving the delivery truck, but he won't listen. He thinks he'll be bored at home."

I took a sip of my beer, then put my glass down. "Is it his arthritis that worries you?"

Bev had a look of worry in her eyes. "No, it's something else. He sleeps all the time, and he never wants to do anything or go anywhere. I guess we are no spring chickens, though."

I giggled a bit at this, because it was so rare to hear Bev admit to being older.

"I am sure he is just tired because of the holidays, and he is working double time with the increase in all the package deliveries. Happens every year, right?" I suggested.

Bev just shrugged her shoulders and patted my hands like she always did when she wanted to change the subject.

"So, how was therapy today?" Bev asked.

"Same as always." I poured us another glass of beer, being careful not to include as much foam this time.

Bev looked at me curiously. "Are you getting anything out of it? I mean is it helping?"

# THE NEXT 167 HOURS

I laughed and smiled at her. "I am getting some feelings out of it" I winked at Bev.

She laughed, then quickly got serious. "You're kidding right, you know you can't get a crush on your therapist. There are all sorts of rules about that. Ember, that will never happen, you do know that right, you cannot date your therapist. It's practically illegal, I think."

I shook my head and looked Bev deep in her eyes. "I totally got this Bev-Bev. I don't worry about your love life. You don't worry about mine."

Bev looked super concerned, but knew I wasn't going to argue with her about it, so we just moved on to another topic. "So, about Wayne's knuckle eczema..."

When I got home, I gave Stormy a bunch of loving because he looked so sad. He didn't even jump on my leg. "What's wrong buddy? Do you want to go for a quick walk or just eat dinner?" As soon as I said the word dinner, he jumped almost to the ceiling with excitement.

After I poured Stormy some dry food, I made myself a bowl of chicken noodle soup. We both curled up on the couch to see if we could find a movie to watch. This would be the first weekend coming up in some time that I didn't have a family obligation or any other plans. I was a little nervous with the thought of being by myself, going back to Stormy's and I's normal weekend routine.

I grabbed my journal from my work bag and moved to the floor in front of the couch to write. If I had to wait another week to see Dr. Kayla, I would take her advice and try to make more use of this thing. These hours between appointments were getting unbearable. How do people manage it? I don't know what to do with myself anymore.

*161 hours until my next session*

*It doesn't really matter whether I am in a room full of strangers, coworkers, friends, or even family. It's all the same, that loneliness I still feel. Sitting here on this couch with not another human around feels the same to me as when I am sitting at a family dinner. The emptiness in my soul makes it impossible to feel any sort of joy being around others.*

*I often wonder if it comes from when I used to watch Sawyer leave with my dad to go on adventures and I would be stuck at home with my mother. I would sit in the window and watch them drive away. Sawyer said they would just go to the store, and it was boring, but she was always so excited, jumping in the front seat of the car. I would cry and cry for them to take me, but they never would. Mom would set me on the couch and turn on cartoons and leave the room to clean or do dishes. Even if she sat in the room with me, she would just knit and not speak a word to me. I guess I just learned early in life how to be alone, even with other people sitting right next to me. Okay, I can't keep sitting in this apartment. What is something I used to enjoy? A little pleasure? I know! Adventure day with Bev!*

*Ember*

I threw my journal on the coffee table and leaned my head against the couch to stare at the ceiling, rallying the courage to just pick up my phone to text her. "Okay, yes, I can do this, okay, adventure day with Bev. Here we go, buddy," I said to Stormy as I grabbed my phone and texted Bev.

> "Bev! Let's go on adventure."

> "I'm…on…one…right…now. #alltheprettylights"

> "You know what I mean, let's go do something crazy, fun, take me out of my misery."

> "I will plan a day you will never forget! #trustthebev"

> "I can't wait. Love you, Bevie."

> "Love you too, Em."

I tossed my phone on the couch beside me when I heard a soft knock on the door. Stormy jumped up first and raced to the door. He brought back an envelope and dropped it in front of me before I could even get to the door. "What is this?" I petted his head.

I opened the front door but saw no one there, so I shut the door and flipped over the envelope to read the mysterious writing. All it said was "Jewelry Heist Apt. 915." I ripped it open to find an invitation to what I assumed was one of those "whodunit mystery parties" that Isla was hosting this coming weekend. Change of plans. I have plans now.

It shocked me that she was inviting me back to her place after the spectacle I made of myself at her party and how I intruded on her artwork of Stormy and I in the park. Time to make a few rules for myself. Maybe just one.

Rule number one. Don't make a spectacle of myself this coming weekend.

# Chapter Sixteen

I had very specific instructions on my invitation of what items to bring to this "whodunit mystery" party at Isla's. Me. I guessed I was just a partygoer, so my contribution would be to bring myself.

I wasn't complaining that my role was small in the grand scheme of the evening. I tend to like to hang in the background and watch things unfold. I gave myself a two drink limit, so I wouldn't ruin mine or anyone else's evening.

I decided to bring Stormy with me, as he loves to be around people. I dressed him in a tuxedo. We got to Isla's place right on time. I went to knock on the door, but before my knuckles even hit the wood, the door flew open to reveal a man introducing himself as Detective Frank Ortega, who invited me in. *I already hated this.*

Detective Frank guided us into the living room where at least seven other people sat on the couch and various chairs, staring at Stormy and I. Detective Frank took my invitation and announced my arrival as Ms. Ember and her pug dog. I corrected him. "Stormy is a French bulldog." *Asshole.*

I sat down on the only seat available by Isla on the couch. Everyone sat in silence, so I did the same. Silence can be very difficult for me, so I finally broke it and leaned over to Isla and asked, "This is a pretty serious game, huh?"

She leaned over and whispered, "This isn't a game. Someone stole my mother's sapphires the night of my Halloween party, and I am going to find out who did it!" I leaned back, very confused. This was a game, right? Isla had to be messing with us. My two drink limit had already expired without me even consuming a drop.

Detective Frank paced around the room with his finger on his chin like he was thinking about how he wanted to start his speech. "Thank you all for coming tonight. Some of you may know why you are here, some of you may not. By the end of tonight, one of you will go to jail, and the rest of you will go home."

Everyone gasped, and I rolled my eyes. I came for the booze and finger food, not a theatrical performance. "On the morning after Ms. Isla's Halloween party, each of you was present. Isla last reported seeing her mother's precious jewels at 5:00 a.m., when she put her own jewelry away in her jewelry box. The only people in this apartment were the seven of you." He slowly rotated as he pointed at all of us.

"This is absurd," said a man in a sweater vest and scarf. *Guilty*, I thought.

Another woman jumped up in agreement. "Ridiculous, none of us would steal from our friend." *They are obviously in cahoots. Round them up and throw them in jail so we can get to the drinking.*

"Does anyone else have anything to add before I move on?" Detective Frank asked. The room fell silent again. I looked around to see if I could get a sense of who might be squirming or showing signs of shifty eyes.

"There was only one person known to be in the bedroom at the time when Isla put her own jewelry away and when she noticed the sapphires were missing, and that was Ms. Ember." He thrusted his pointer finger in my direction as everyone again gasped and started to whisper to each other.

"Ah hell no, I am innocent. I didn't steal anything. I don't even wear jewelry, especially sapphires." I defended myself.

Detective Frank immediately jumped on my statement as some sort of admission. "I never told this group what type of jewelry was stolen. How did you know it was sapphires that were missing?"

I looked at Isla. "Tell them Isla, you told me when I walked in, when I sat down that was what you told me. You were missing your mother's sapphires."

Isla looked away from me. "I don't know what she is talking about."

My mouth dropped open. I felt like all I could do at this point was raise my hand in the air and request a drink. "Double whiskey please."

"I saw Jim walk into Isla's bedroom when she was in the shower," a younger woman in a chair near the kitchen called out.

"Tell us exactly what you saw," the detective requested.

She sounded very nervous, which I thought was amazing acting. She went on. "Well, I was laying on the floor in front of the couch. I heard Isla, and Ember saying goodbye. Ember left and Isla went to take a shower. I was debating whether I should go home or go back to sleep when I saw Jim creep toward her bedroom. I decided to pretend like I was asleep so he wouldn't talk to me. I… I always kind of found him, well, creepy. He was only in there for about two minutes, then ran out of the bedroom. He went straight through the kitchen, out the door and left like he was in a hurry to get out of here. That's it. That's all I saw."

Jim shot up out of his chair. "I went in there to get my coat. I couldn't find it on the bed where I left it, I found it halfway under the bed. It took a couple of minutes, okay? Then I just left. I wasn't in a hurry. I just walked out the door like a normal person. Bitch." Then he gave a dirty look to the young woman, who refused to look his way.

"If you want my opinion, I think Sal is the one who you should be looking at. He was the one I noticed was selling all sorts of jewelry online last week. Gold, silver, and yes, sapphires."

Everyone looked over at Sal. "Whoa, whoa," Sal motioned for everyone to calm down by pushing the air down to the floor with his hands. "I am a jeweler. It's what I do for a living. I don't steal jewelry and sell it. I buy it through vendors from all over the world. I have receipts. I can prove all my purchases and sales."

Detective Frank walked around the room as if he was getting exactly what he wanted, people turning on each other. Not me though. I was not going to fall for this game of cat and mouse. I was going home tonight with my hands clean.

"Maybe it wasn't any of us." I offered to throw a wrench in the evening.

Isla leaned over and whispered, "what are you doing, Ember?"

I ignored her. "Maybe it was you, Detective Frank. Maybe you brought us all here to distract us from the real thief, which is you." I stood up and pointed at him as everyone sighed collectively.

"Um, Ms. Ember, that's not actually how this works. It's going to be one of you, so if you would like to just sit back down and enjoy the rest of the evening. Please." Detective Frank offered my place on the couch with the motion of his hand. I sat back down.

"I have a video from that night. I was just recording everyone in their costumes, and I caught something," a soft-spoken voice came from behind me.

We all turned around to see a young woman who I don't personally recall being at the party that night, but then again, I was a little tipsy.

Detective Frank didn't hesitate to grab the young woman's phone and hook it up to the TV so we could all see the new evidence from the night of the crime. The video started to play, as we drew our attention to the partygoers who were laughing and dancing, when suddenly we all jumped up and collectively gasped, pointing to the TV. "Isla!"

The detective yelled for us all to calm down and take our seats. We did as we were told. Isla stood up and started to fake cry. "It was me. I was the one who stole my own sapphires. I did it to pay for my mentor's eye surgery. I can't fathom the idea of her never painting again. If I could prove they were stolen, I could get the insurance money and pay for Maria's surgery, and we could continue to paint together forever. I am so sorry, everyone." Isla fell to the floor like she was devastated.

To all our surprise, an older woman walked around the corner from the bedroom and said, "Isla, darling you shouldn't have done this to pay for my surgery. If I go blind, I go blind. It's just nature's way of saying I need to retire."

We all spun around to see who this woman was and to our surprise, it was Maria Tomas Winters, a semi-famous artist who has been around for years. I mean, I don't know a lot about art, but even I knew how impressive it was to have her here tonight. We were all so fan-struck with excitement that we immediately jumped up and ran over to ask her for autographs.

Isla was still on the floor fake crying, and I didn't know what to do. Do I comfort her? Should I clap? Then everyone else started clapping, so I started clapping too. Whew.

Isla then stood up and acknowledged our applause. "Thank you, thank you. I hope you all enjoyed tonight's festivities. As you know, I don't throw holiday parties, instead I try to do something a little different before Thanksgiving and Christmas, so thank you for showing up with your openness to just lean into something a little different. Drinks and food are in the kitchen. Oh, and Maria's eyes are just fine. So happy holidays everyone." We all started clapping again.

I took Stormy over to the food and gave him a little nibble of one of the cucumber sandwiches and grabbed a beer. Seemed like a safe drink to start the evening. No one approached me, probably because of the way I acted at the last party. Even though I didn't completely understand what I did, I knew enough not to pretend that I was innocent of making things awkward that night. I decided it was best to just take my beer and a small plate of food and go find a place to sit down.

I sat and people watched for a good twenty minutes, thinking about how different it was when Rayna and I used to attend parties like this together. We would always walk around mingling, discussing world events, things going on in our lives, and our future plans, even if it was just a trip we planned to take that next summer. I got out my phone and sent her a text message.

> "I miss you so much."

I put my phone away. What the hell am I doing? I stood up to grab a harder drink and decided to try to do the mingling thing when I heard some yell, "shots."

After I don't know how many shots and beers, I almost passed out on Isla's couch. I thought Stormy and I should probably head home. *Stormy, oh my god, where was Stormy?* "Stormy," I yelled frantically, looking around Isla's apartment when Isla walked up with him in her arms. I grabbed him and kissed him all over his little face. "You scared mommy, buddy."

Isla was petting his head and looking at me. "Can I walk you back to your apartment, Ember?" I looked up at her and was about to tell her I was fine, but I wasn't fine. I was sad and lonely. "Yeah, that would be nice."

She took my keys from me and unlocked my apartment door. I placed Stormy on the floor, and he ran straight for the patio door to go relieve himself. I threw my shoes off and headed back to the bedroom and Isla followed me. "Are you going to be okay, Ember?"

I sat on the edge of the bed. "Yeah, I'm fine, just a little too much to drink, I think."

She sat down beside me and put her hand on my thigh, which sent a shock of excitement through my body. "Is there anything I can do to make you feel better?"

I leaned in to kiss her, but she lowered her head. "Not like this, not when you're this drunk. I'm sorry. I should get back to my party. I just wanted to make sure you got home safely. Goodnight, Ember." Isla got up and walked out the front door.

"Damnit." I mumbled, as I rolled over, not even bothering to get undressed. I just wanted to go to sleep and not wake up for days.

# Chapter Seventeen

"Ember, I know you are in there." I heard Bev's voice with the continued pounding on my door.

"I'm coming," I yelled as a slithered out of bed and practically crawled towards the door.

I swung the door open to find Bev with two cups of coffee and a box of pastries. "As you requested, my friend, it's Bev and Ember's big adventure day."

Even though I felt slightly shitty from the whodunit party the night before, I couldn't help but smile at Bev's sentiment. "Okay, let me get dressed and brush my teeth and we can head out. What are we doing?" I asked.

Bev laughed in an evil voice. "Now, why would I tell you that? Today is a surprise, but I do have to be home by five to make sure my mole takes his diabetes medication."

"Of course, Bevie." I hugged her and left to go get ready.

The bus stopped at the center of downtown and we got off, but I was none the wiser about what our day was going to bring. "Come on, are you going to tell me what we're going to do or not?" I pleaded.

Bev finally caved. "Okay, first stop we are going to bust some shit up."

"Ohhhh, nice. That sounds super fun. I sooo need that right now. What kind of shit are we going to break?"

"I don't know. We will find out when we get there." She grabbed my hand and pulled me towards the building.

Once we got inside the facility, they handed us all our safety equipment, given a few rules and let loose in a room full of old TVs, vases, glass things, wood things, you name it. If you could swing a mental pipe or a bat at it, you could smash it.

Bev and I never laughed so hard. Bev took her bat and started to pound a computer screen and screamed profanities at her boss for a good five minutes straight. I decided it was no longer a therapeutic experience for her, so I tried to drag her away, only to find her laughing so hard that I just let her go back at it. We spent the next blissful hour taking all our stresses out on inanimate objects, and it was one of the most freeing experiences of my life.

Next, Bev took us to an activity that was supposed to give us the opposite results of the last stress reliever: meditation. Unfortunately, we were kicked out in the first ten minutes because Bev couldn't be still or quiet. She giggled with every deep breath until the teacher kindly excused us from her class, so we decided to stop for lunch at a hotdog truck on our way to our last adventure that Bev said would "knock my socks off."

I stood outside the tattoo shop in awe. "Are you crazy Bev? You want to get a tattoo?"

"Yep, they have these gum ball machines that you put your quarter in and whatever comes out, you get that tattooed on you. You said you wanted an adventure."

"Okay, let's do it." I did ask for this day, after all.

We walked into the tattoo shop, and both put our quarters in the machine. Bev got a cute bumble bee suckling on a bundle of flowers, and I got a fawn lying in a bed of daisies and sunflowers on the inside of my forearm. I laid fine for my tattoo, but Bev threw a fit, kicking and screaming the whole time.

"Maybe putting a tattoo on your rib cage wasn't the smartest place, Bev-Bev." I said to my friend.

"Shut up, Ember. I did fine." I just laughed at her bitchiness.

Bev dropped me off about at home, and I gave her a big hug and thanked her for the best day ever. "I love you, Bevie, I really do."

"Ouch, don't hug me so tight, ugh, I love you too, dog." She inched out of my embrace.

I was glad to have the rest of Sunday afternoon alone. I decided not to leave my apartment for fear of running into Isla. I have officially embarrassed myself not once, but twice now in her presence.

I had no idea how I would spend the rest of the evening, but now that the rain had moved in and I could clearly see it pounding off the pavement below, I found my myself snuggled even tighter under my blanket on the couch listening to the cold winds whistling through the small cracks in my window seals. It didn't look too appealing to be outside anymore.

I picked up my phone to scroll through the news. It wasn't shocking to see all the horror that plagued the world. War, crime, death, with a just sprinkle of enough goodwill in there to keep readers coming back for more. Balance.

My favorite news story today was about a dog who was jogging with her owner and stopped in the middle of the street. Something distracted the dog, who became really stressed out and wouldn't continue running any longer. She just sat in the middle of the street. Every time a car came, the dog ran to the side of the road, let the car pass, then ran back to the middle of the road and sat down again. Finally, the owner realized the dog was drawn to the manhole and figured something must be down there that was upsetting her dog. By this time, a few bystanders came to ask what was going on with her dog and the woman was able to convince them to help her remove the manhole to see if there was, in fact, a reason for her dog's behavior. Sure enough, there was a whole litter of baby kittens in the down there. The dog was a hero. Dogs are the best.

While I was scrolling through other news stories, a text from Sawyer popped up on my screen.

"Hi Sis, whatcha up to?"

"Reading the news, you?"

"Just got off the night shift. Three babies born last night. It was a long night."

"I hear you. I had to help solve a jewelry heist."

"A what?"

"Never mind, long story. Are you going to bed now?"

"Yes, but I was wondering if you want to come over for dinner tomorrow night?"

"During the week? On a work night? Not really. Why?"

> "We are just having a few friends over and thought it would be nice for you to get out."

> "Get out? What are you talking about? I get out all the time? I do have friends, Sawyer."

> "Really, besides Bev, who is two times your age, by the way. name one other real friend?

> "Storm...phia"

> "Exactly. See you at 6:30 p.m. and try to wear something that makes it look like you care about yourself. :) Love you, bye."

With her final demand, I tossed my phone on the couch next to me. I had zero desire to Uber all the way out to her house on a work night, especially when I have therapy the next day. I would go, but only because if I didn't go, she would worry that I was being closed off, or non-social, and I am so tired of everyone always worrying about me.

That was an interesting comment. When she asked me to wear something to make me appear to care about myself, what is that all about? I will wear whatever I wear to work that day.

I grabbed my journal from the coffee table and started to pen a new entry.

*39 hours until my next session*
*Sawyer asking me today to dress like I care about myself for dinner reminded me of when our parents used to get us all dressed up for when they invited the priest to come to our house. It was always a big event if the priest accepted an invitation to come to your house for Sunday dinner.*

*Mom would make pot roast with potatoes and carrots, hot rolls, and corn.*

*Priests came and went in our congregation, so whenever a new one arrived is when my mom would invite them to break bread, and to make the newcomer believe we had a wholesome family. This particular year, the priest was younger and Sawyer had a big ol' crush on him. I, being the bratty little sister that I was, had to make sure he knew it.*

*Father Reily sat at the table, said grace, and as we all began to eat dinner, I asked if I could speak, like a good catholic daughter might. I was given permission. I asked Father Reily if he was married. He said yes, to God. I then turned to Sawyer and said, "Sorry Sawyer, he's gay."*

*Sawyer screamed "Mommmmm!" with embarrassment, and I was sent straight to my room, without dinner, and was grounded for two weeks. I had to write Father Reily an apology letter. Turned out that Father Reily was gay, he left the church and married a man. As far as I know, he is old, gay, and happy, living his best life.*

*I will give her a hug tomorrow and tell her I am sorry. I don't know if I ever told her I was sorry. I need to start telling the people in my life I am sorry more when I make mistakes, so they will stay.*

*Ember*

\*\*\*

I left work forty minutes early to beat rush hour traffic. I was hoping to arrive a little early to see if I could help with dinner. I sat in the back seat of the Uber being thankful that this driver was rather quiet for a change. The rain was a bit heavier tonight, which wasn't that surprising for this time of year. I watched the stream of red taillights blinking on and off as the traffic crawled at a sluggish pace. I used this extra time to plot my escape plan for the evening. Sawyer would never believe anything about Stormy as an excuse. Or work. It would have to be something clever that she couldn't argue with. I decided I would arrive with a headache, so I could use that excuse later to leave early.

As soon as I walked in the front door, my nephew Alex ran up to me and lifted me in the air with one of his big bear hugs. I can't believe he was already a senior in high school. I remember his first day of kindergarten. We dropped him off and he went running in like he owned the place. Sawyer got a call about an hour later asking to come get him because he wasn't feeling well. When she picked him up, she discovered he was faking it and just missed us and wanted to come home and play. Those were the days I would pick him up and snuggle him with big bear hugs. Funny how life comes in full circles.

"How's my little man doing?" I wheezed out the words with the little air I could breathe because he was squeezing me so tight.

Putting me back down on the floor so the air could escape my lungs, he replied, "I'm good. I got all my college applications filled out and in the mail. I should know in a couple of months which ones accepted me and then I will choose where I want to go."

Putting my work bag on the entrance table, we walked towards the kitchen with my arm latched on to his arm. "Do you have a favorite school picked out?"

"I think so. I want to go to med school like mom and dad and staying local seems like it would be cool. I think I want to go to the University." I punched him lightly in the arm. "Well, you can always crash at my place if you need to." He kissed the top of my head and ran off to his room.

I walked into the kitchen to find Sawyer putting garlic season on a pan of veggies before going into the oven. "I can't believe how big Alex is. How did he go from riding on my shoulders to being able to pick me up?"

Sawyer put the veggies in the oven and set the temperature to four hundred degrees. "He is six foot one and still growing, I swear. And get this, I am pretty sure he has a girlfriend. I caught him texting a Melinda on his phone with little heart emojis, cute right?"

I giggled. "Super cute."

I went to sit down at the counter when the doorbell rang. Sawyer yelled for Todd to get the door. "That's probably Steve and Amy, and don't get mad."

With a confused look, I glanced up at Sawyer. "Why would I get mad?"

Putting her hands in the air as if she needed to protect herself. "Because they are bringing a friend with them, a lady friend. A lady lesbian friend."

Immediately pissed. "What the fuck are you thinking? Are you trying to get me back for Father Reily? He was always gay, you know." I said in my loudest whisper.

"What? Who? Father Reily? Are you kidding me, no, Ember–"

"Don't you think you could have asked me first if I was even remotely interested in a blind date? Fuck, Sawyer."

Sawyer started to apologize when the kitchen door swung open and there stood Todd, Steve, Amy, and this woman, who was probably very nice, I am sure.

Sawyer and I whipped around to face our guests, smiled, and everyone started to politely greet each other with handshakes.

I was introduced as Sawyer's little sister to Steve, Steve's wife Amy, and their friend Harper. Why little sister and not just sister, you ask? Well, because this was Sawyer's way of always protecting me.

"Shall we all head to the living room for some cocktails?" Todd suggested.

We all followed one another in a single-file line from the kitchen, passing Todd on the way, each taking a drink from his hand as we found our way to a seat in the living room.

I opted for a comfy chair instead of the couch to not feel obligated to sit too close to Harper. Oddly enough, she sat on the arm of the chair I was sitting in. *This wasn't going to be an awkward night at all.*

Harper leaned over and whispered in my ear. "So, come her often?" Then laughed at her own joke.

I slammed my drink. "I used to, but the crowd is starting to get a little shady." I fake laughed at my own joke.

"Good one." Harper laughed along with me. "Look," she said. "I know this is weird, blind date and all, but why not just make the best of it and have a little fun. It's not like we are going to elope at the end of the night. Unless you want to." She nudged my arm playfully. "If you don't like me at the end of the night, we go our separate ways, no hurt feelings. What do you say?"

After her speech, I felt a bit guilty about my behavior. I guess it wasn't her fault that my sister and her friends set us up like this. "Okay, deal, let's just have fun tonight and go our separate ways at the end of the night." I put my fist out for a bump. Harper bumped my fist against mine, then held it there for a couple of seconds while giving me a soft wink. *Gag.*

Even though Harper and I made a pact to just enjoy the evening, dinner was anything but enjoyable. We had nothing in common, and she was very confrontational and would rudely debate everything. She refused to listen to anyone else's opinions. Whenever someone told a story, she would have a better story. Then the kicker for me was when Harper said she wasn't a fan of animals. How could anyone not like animals? I found all this very unattractive in a woman.

I tend to be more reserved and like to listen more than talk. But I could not handle another minute of this woman's voice. There were many times throughout dinner where I would catch Sawyer mouthing "I am so sorry." from across the table at me. There were also many times throughout dinner when I would raise my middle finger to her in response.

As the evening wore on, Harper continued to drink enough cocktails for all of us. She wasn't a very nice drunk, either. I watched her argue with Steve about to what degree climate change is because of people or fate. It was getting really heated, and I had no plans of intervening.

I decided to pour myself another drink while I waited for my Uber to show up, when Harper suddenly appeared next to me. "So would you like to come over to my place for a few drinks this evening, could be fun?"

I finished pouring my drink and looked at her with what I was hoping was a disgusted look on my face. "No, that does not sound fun, plus I have work in the morning."

I felt her arm slide around my waist. "I promise to get you to work on time in the morning."

I pulled her arm from my waist and looked her directly in the eyes. "Look, Harper, I think you are kind of an asshole. You have been rude to everyone all night, then you have the audacity to think I would want to go home with you for a drink, and oh my grossness, for you to even think for a second, I would consider spending the night with you? You are fucking nuts, lady." I didn't even look at her. I just walked away.

My Uber was waiting outside when I walked out the door. Following me out to the car, Sawyer apologized the entire way. "I am so sorry. I promise never to try to set you up again."

I stopped and gave her a hug. "I love you, but I don't need you like this. I don't need you to help me find love, or get laid, or whatever this was tonight. Okay. Just don't. Ever again. Just don't." I turned away, got into the car, and shut the door.

Sawyer started to walk back towards the house. "Sawyer." I called out. She quickly turned around. "Yeah?" she said with a hopeful look on her face.

"Did you pay the driver?" She sighed and came back to the car. She likes to help.

# Chapter Eighteen

Something in Dr. Kayla's office was different today. She moved stuff around. No, it wasn't that. She added some things. There it was, by the door. It was a new picture. I started to rub my shoulder while I stared at the picture from across the room. It was a long wood frame with a light blue colored matte that had all these little watercolor images of different shapes and sizes. I was curious what Dr. Kayla was trying to discover about her clients with these shapes. I bet they were some sort of ink blot test. Yes, that had to be it. As I looked at them, I figured them out right away. Easy. I was going to ace this part of my mental health test.

"Chicken, pear, blowfish, tooth, cactus, snowflake and vagina. How did I do?" I looked over at Dr. Kayla, who just stared at me with her head slightly tilted.

"I'm sorry. How did you do with what?" She looked thrown off.

"The ink blot test, over there, on the wall, by the door. How did I do? Did I get them all right?" I pointed to the new picture by the door.

Looking over her shoulder at the door, Dr. Kayla laughed a little bit. "Oh, that picture. It's not an ink blot test. Those are hieroglyphs. From Ancient Egypt. I am kind of a history buff."

"Fun." I had nothing else to say about that.

"So, Ember, what would you like to talk about today? I know we tried a of couple new things last session that seem kind of tough to talk about. We could talk about what was hard about those topics or we could talk about something completely different. It's up to you?"

I started to massage my upper arm again and looked down at the floor. "Well, you asked me last week about my favorite memory, and I thought about it, and I have one that I can share. I have a lot of favorite memories, but one that always comes to mind is from when I was a kid."

Dr. Kayla gave me such a warm, inviting smile that came with what felt like such a rush of love. "I really want to hear your story, Ember," she replied softly.

Alright. She wanted to hear my story. I didn't really know why, but she seemed genuinely interested. It was like when Rayna used to ask me questions about my past, what I liked or didn't like. When we first started getting to know each other, we were learning everything there was to know about each other. Everything was so new and exciting. This exchange with Dr. Kayla felt like that, someone who wanted to get to know the real me.

"Okay, well, my mother is from the Seattle area, born and raised, but my dad is from Tennessee. From when I was probably a baby to when I was twelve, we would spend a couple of weeks in the summer vacationing up in the Smokey Mountain." Dr. Kayla seemed like she was enjoying my story so far. It felt nice to share this moment with her, so I continued.

"Of course, I only remember the later years, maybe starting around six or seven years old. We always brought so much stuff on these trips. We packed up the station wagon full of suitcases, camping gear, and coolers. My mom created a small area in the car with blankets and pillows for Sawyer and me to sleep on." I paused, feeling a little overwhelmed by this memory, but in a good way. I took a deep breath and continued, "To sleep on," I repeated.

I felt like I was going into a trance as I told my story. "The trip always seemed so long, but when we would finally arrive, Sawyer and I were thrilled beyond belief. I remember as soon as we jumped out of the car, the thick, sticky heat would suck the air out of my lungs. The humidity was like nothing I ever felt back home."

Dr. Kayla interjected, "How old were you on this trip?"

"Twelve," I replied.

I went on. "Dad would get busy setting up our tent, and mom would start making us a meal depending on when we arrived. By the time night fell, the temperature didn't change much, nor did the thickness of the air. We would sleep on top of our sleeping bags because the heat and humidity were unbearable most nights."

Dr. Kayla sat quietly taking it all in. She wasn't taking any notes. In fact, she wasn't even holding her legal pad anymore. I kept on. "Every morning we would wake up to the smell of mom cooking us breakfast. It was always different. Some mornings it was pancakes, other mornings it was eggs, even oatmeal on the occasion. Sawyer and I would devour our meals and run down to the lake as fast as we could, ignoring the rule about not swimming for two hours after you ate. Not growing up with local swimming pools or easy access to any warm bodies of water, this was a daily occurrence on our vacations. Mom and Dad had to drag us back to the campground for lunch."

I stopped talking for a minute and looked at Dr. Kayla. "Ember, what is happening for you right now?"

I was feeling a little exposed. I didn't normally talk about myself very much with strangers, so this was starting to feel personal and I wasn't sure I wanted to keep talking about this. "I guess I am just feeling a little weird telling you about this. I feel dumb talking about being a kid and playing in the water."

She leaned forward and looked me deep in my eyes. "Ember, I really want to hear the rest of your memory, if you want to share it, but you don't have to. It is always up to you what you share in our sessions."

My stomach started to twirl as her eye locked with mine. I wish I didn't want to be this close to her. I tried to break her gaze, but I just couldn't, then she did it for me. "Would you like to continue or take a break?"

I looked at the floor. "I think I will continue."

I swallowed hard. "Okay, yeah, so my parents never got along, and they were always arguing about one thing or another, so we tried to do our own things most of the time. We were isolated for the most part in the park, but there were other families within walking distance of our tent, so on the weekends, all the different families would get together for a big barbecue. We played tag and kickball with the other kids and that year, someone's parents even put up a volleyball net. We had a blast. When it was over, everyone went back to their respective campsites, and we all went to bed."

I started to rub the inside of my hand because I knew that as much as this was the best part of my memory it was also the most personal part as well. I started to breathe a little heavier as my heart started to pound a little harder.

"Ember, are you okay? Do you want to stop?"

I glanced up at her and stuttered a bit, "n-n-oo, I just needed to take a breath for a second. I'm okay." She wasn't convinced, but let me go on.

"Well, this particular memory was from our last family trip to the Smokey Mountain. Like I said, I was twelve and Sawyer was seventeen. She would be a senior in high school that following year. It was the middle of the night that I woke up to my mom and dad whispering about something my dad did at the barbecue. My mom was crying, and my dad was saying she was seeing things. I remember lying on my side, and feeling my sister cover my one ear with her hand, like she didn't want me to hear what they were saying. I must have fallen back asleep because the next thing I remember was Sawyer waking me up. It was still dark outside. She told me to be quiet, that she wanted to show me something, something special that she made just for me. She slowly unzipped the tent so my parents wouldn't hear us and wake up. We slid out a small opening and took off running as fast as we could."

I stopped long enough to warn Dr. Kayla that I had never shared this story with another soul, not because it was bad, but because it was mine, and from my sister. I don't know why I felt the need to tell her that, but I felt like it was important that she knew.

"We were running and giggling at our great escape, then Sawyer stopped me and said she needed to blindfold me before we could go any further. I didn't hesitate. I completely trusted Sawyer, so I let her. We walked for what felt like forever. I was tripping and bumping into her back, every other step." I heard Dr. Kayla laugh a little, as she was probably imagining this awkward little girl stumbling through the woods.

"Finally, we stopped, and Sawyer took off my blindfold. As soon as the bandana hit the ground, so did my tears. I started crying so hard. It was the most beautiful thing I have ever seen. At first, I slowly turned in circles as I tried to wrap my brain around what was happening. I had never seen anything like this before. It was then one of the hundreds of little fireflies that landed on the tip of my finger and just blinked at me like it was saying 'hi.' I looked up at Sawyer with my eyes full of water and my mouth gaped open. She placed her hand over her heart, also with her eyes full of water, but with the biggest smile on her face just staring back at me. I began spinning and dancing like I was going to be lifted into the air and flown away by these tiny little flashes of light. I didn't know what they were at the time, so I asked my sister if she was doing a magic show for me. She laughed and said no. Then Sawyer grabbed me to slow my motion and tenderly lowered me to the ground, where we sat crossed legged, knee to knee."

I could feel myself getting wet in the eyes, so I stopped talking for a moment. Dr. Kayla and I both sat in silence. After a minute, I was able to continue.

"She held my hands and told me whenever I was scared, sad or lonely to just close my eyes and remember this night. Our moon bugs, she called them. She put her hands on my cheeks and brought our foreheads together, wiping my tears away at the same time. She told me if we were ever lost, the fireflies would always help us find our way back to each other. She told me she loved me so much and I just laid my head on her lap as her fingers ran through my hair. I watched Sawyer's magic show of all the little moon bugs blinking in the night until I fell back asleep.

That next year, Sawyer went off to college, and we never went on another family vacation again."

For the first time, Dr. Kayla wasn't staring at me when I looked up at her. When she did look at me, her eyes were glossy, like she had tears in her eyes. "Oh shit. I am sorry, it really was a happy memory for me. I am super sorry that I upset you."

She smiled and shook her head. "It was a beautiful memory, and thank you for sharing it with me."

\*\*\*

When I arrived home, I was feeling pretty good about my session with Dr. Kayla. It was the first session I didn't leave a complete basket case. I swooped up Stormy and carried him to the kitchen with me. "Are you hungry, buddy? Do you want to share an apple with me?" I grabbed an apple from the fruit bowl and went to the couch to sit down. As soon as I plopped down, I immediately felt this rush of sadness. I am almost three hundred days older than I was the day I was labeled single. *Jesus, I can't do this right now. Maybe I just need some fresh air.*

I patted my leg to get Stormy's attention to follow me out to the balcony. I stood up and opened the door to a gust of cold wind. I could smell the bakery and it was making me hungry, but I didn't feel like eating. I kept very little on my balcony during the winter months because of all the rain, but I did have a plastic bench. I sat down on it, not even caring if I got my pants wet. I tried to call Sawyer, but my call went straight to voice mail. Instead of leaving a message, I just hung up.

I looked across the city streets. It was rainy, dark, and gloomy. I could see the halos around each of the small lights, whether they be the streetlights that dangled over the roads or headlights from the cars making their way to their destination.

As my tears welled up, all the lights became even more burry, so I squinted my eyes and I pretended I was up in the mountains at the water's edge with Sawyer, surrounded by all those fireflies, spinning around and dancing, but instead I just started weeping and screamed "I can't do this anymore."

Then a voice from two balconies down replied, "Yes, you can, and I am coming over."

Within seconds, Isla was sitting beside me, holding me so tight, rocking me, and telling me everything was going to be okay.

# Chapter Nineteen

The fourth elevator just lifted off without me. As the week dragged on, fewer people tended to show up to the office, so by the fact that I was still standing here waiting to catch a ride to my office was a bit of a concern.

"Ember, hi how are you? Did you get the invitation for my wedding shower? I was just curious because you haven't RSVP'd yet," asked my coworker Amy.

The doors to the elevator opened, and I motioned for Amy to enter first. "Yes, I did. I am so sorry, of course, mark me as already there. With a gift in hand, or a bag, or wrapped. Do you prefer it wrapped? Because if you do, I can totally wrap it. My mom used to make these homemade bows out of ribbons. I could probably try one of those. Or I could do both. Yes, I could do a wrapped gift with a homemade bow *in* a bag..."

The elevator door opened, and Amy quickly scooted out. "Um, I'm I just really glad to hear you are coming, don't feel obligated to bring a gift, but if you want to, I put where I am registered on the invite and all those places will wrap it for you." Amy smiled and hurried away.

Bev's head followed Amy rushing past her when she saw me and handed me my coffee. "What did you say to her?"

I stopped in front of Bev and took a sip of my cup while I watched Amy turn the corner and disappear. "Nothing, I just told her I would go to her party and bring a gift."

Bev shrugged her shoulders. "Yeah, I'm going too. We should go in on a gift then head over together." Bev suggested as we headed towards my desk.

Bev leaned on the edge of my desk, looking out at the water, which had an amazing marine layer of hazy air floating on top of it today. I gazed out at the water as well, thinking about Isla's tender embrace last night. I decided not to mention it to Bev because I didn't want her to think it was more than what it was, and I certainly didn't want her to worry about me.

Last night there was just a nice neighbor who noticed another neighbor on her balcony in distress and was caring enough to show up and hold her blubbering mess neighbor with such warmth and support... *Snap out of it, Ember, she is way out of your league.* I scolded myself.

She didn't stay long after I calmed down. She asked me if there was anything she could do or if I wanted to talk. I was so embarrassed, I just wanted her to leave. I thanked her for coming over and told her I just wanted to go to bed. She offered to stay until I fell asleep, but I declined. I mean really, I am sure she could be on a hot date with a model or at some VIP party, not sitting there watching her loser neighbor sleep. She finally gave up and left. That was it. Nothing happened.

"What are you thinking about?" Bev asked.

I looked over at her and said, "Oh, nothing much, just wonder what I have on my calendar for the rest of the day? I would love to hit mid-week happy hour."

Bev flipped open her laptop and started to run through my list of meetings. "You start your day with your normal two-hour weekly review with the executive team, then is an early lunch, there in a new client intake meeting at three, oh bummer a last-minute meeting with you and Bethany at to discuss the New York Fashion Week just popped up on your calendar. I guess happy hour will be a little later tonight. Are you okay with that?"

I made all sorts of grunting noises to show my dissatisfaction, then grabbed my laptop and notebook to head to my first meeting.

Most of the morning was uneventful, but that all changed with my 3:00 new client intake meeting. I sat in the corner of the conference room and not at the table with the rest of the team. It used to bother me I didn't have a seat at the table, but over the years I started to appreciate being in the background and not having to participate. This room was full of C suite executives, CEO of Human Resources, or Finance, or Technology, all the bigwigs that would onboard the new client. Well, let's be real, all the bigwigs that would give orders to their teams to do all the real work. They were just here to hear who Bethany landed.

The table of muckety-mucks was busy in chatter about their weekend plans while I scrolled through social media on my phone until the door finally opened and Bethany walked in, and the room became quiet. "Hello everyone, thank you for joining me today for this very exciting news. As you all know, our goal for the new year is to transition our business model to 'big money.' We have been playing it safe for many years and going forward, we are going to be a lot more selective as to who we do business with, and that time starts now." Everyone looked at each other with excitement and eagerness to hear more.

Bethany lowered the lights and turned on the big screen TV to display the company we had just landed from the conference. Across the screen read 'Simmer and Sauces Pots and Pans.' My eyes tripled in size. "Holy shit." I said out loud.

Bethany looked over at me, "Yes, everyone, please give a round of applauses to Ember as we have her to thank for nailing the buyer on this one." *No pun intended*, I thought to myself. Everyone began clapping for me, but I was anything but happy about this. I really hoped that I wouldn't have to see that woman again. Cara, yes, that was her name.

Bethany spent the remainder of the hour going through each slide before the lights finally came back on. Everyone gathered their things to head to their next meeting, but before they left, she had one last announcement. "Oh, and please make sure you all attend the Christmas party this year. We invited our Simmer and Sauces friends to join us, and I want to make a good impression." *Seriously, could this nightmare get any worse?* I thought to myself.

I left the meeting room and raced over to Bev's desk. "We need to talk."

Bev looked up from her book on indoor gardening and hurried around her desk to follow me to mine. "What is going on? Are you okay?"

Instead of going to my desk, I pulled her into a small conference room and shut the door behind us. "Bev, we just land the pots and pans company."

Bev grabbed my shoulders and pulled me in for a hug. "Oh shit. This is horrible news," she said.

"That's what I said," I replied, taking a seat. "It gets worse. Bethany invited them to our company Christmas party this year."

"Double shit." Bev sat next to me, both of us quiet for a minute as we strategized a plan in our heads. "We just need a plan, a really, really, good plan. I got it. I got it. You just ignore her, like it never happened. Yes, make her feel like she made you feel. Pretend like you don't even know who she is. I mean, after all, that is basically what she wanted, right? Just a one-night stand, never to be contacted again?" Bev suggested.

"You are brilliant, Bev'er, and so right. I just need to play it cool, ignore her, and pretend like I don't even know her. Yes, that is exactly what I will do. If she even comes. She might not come, her role in all of this might be done. Which would be the best-case scenario, honestly."

Bev jumped up and opened the door. "You better hurry up. Your last meeting with Bethany is in five minutes, then we can head to happy hour. So, go. Go. Go." She rushed me off.

I ran to my desk and grabbed my other notebook that I used for my solo meetings with my boss, then rounded the corner to her office. Bethany wasn't in there yet, so I took a chair at the small table and put the date and a reason for meeting at the top of the page in my notebook.

Bethany hurried into the office at twenty minutes past the hour. "I only have about ten minutes to give you because I need to pick up my daughter from day care," she said, gathering her things while attempting to meet with me at the same time.

"Okay, no problem, so what can I help you with?" Bethany handed me a piece of paper that was blank, and then pointed to the easel that she showed me a few weeks ago that said "You are..." I took the paper from her hand. "This paper is blank." I looked at her, confused.

"That's the point, Ember. We still have nothing to submit for New York Fashion Week. Thanksgiving is in the next week, Christmas in a month, New Year's a week later and before you know it, we are supposed to hand over an entire campaign. You have been with me long enough to know how long it takes to pull something like this together, so you are very aware that time is running out. Get my drift?"

I stood up and headed towards the door. I turned around and looked at Bethany. "I have never let you down and I won't this time either. I will get all the right meetings set up to make sure the team gets working on this right away. I am sorry I haven't done that yet. I am on it. First thing in the morning, I promise."

She nodded and sort of smiled. She was disappointed I could tell. "I am going to be off the rest of this week, so have a good weekend, Ember. Get some rest because I need you one hundred percent on Monday, okay?" I gave her two thumbs up and walked out.

Bev and I walked over to the bar next door. Since we arrived an hour and a half later than normal, we couldn't get a table and had to sit at the bar. "Do you want a pitcher or a pint?" Bev asked.

I looked at the bartender. "Give me the largest glass of beer you have behind that bar."

She laughed and drew the tap back as I watched the beer flow into the frosty covered mug. "You must be having a shitty week," she said.

I dropped my head into my arms. "You have no idea."

The bartender placed my beer in front of me. "You ladies want your nachos tonight?"

Rubbing my upper back, Bev looked up at the bartender. "Yes, please."

I sighed and asked Bev. "So, any big plan for thanksgiving this year?"

Bev got super excited about this topic. "Well, me and the mole are going to a friend's house, so I don't have to make a big meal, but I am making a couple of side dishes," she said smiling.

I tipped my head to the side with a smile. "Bev'er, what are you making?" I asked suspiciously.

Bev wiggled proudly in her seat. "Well, I am making Satan's Spinach dip and Sinner's Stuffing."

Now I was concerned. "Bevie, these people do know what you are bringing, right?" I grabbed her hand.

"Of course, yes, it's healthy. The stuffing will also have pears in it." She winked at me.

I was now on my third mug of beer when I saw a small group of women walk through the door and sat at a table near the bar. As soon as I looked over, this woman and I made eye contact, but it wasn't just any woman. It was my therapist. I was about to wave at her, but she turned her head and started talking with her friends. My heart dropped into my stomach, and it took everything inside of me not to cry in front of Bev.

"Ember, are you okay?" Bev asked.

I started to gather my things. "Yeah, I just think I have had enough to drink, and it's been a long week. I should probably go home now. Yeah, I think just want to go home, like right now, okay Bev?"

Bev started to quickly gather her things as well because she knew nothing was okay, but also knew better than to ask, but just to get me out of there. I loved her for just knowing.

We got outside and Bev grabbed my shoulder to stop me. "Em, what is going on?"

I started crying. "I just saw my therapist in there with some women and she totally ignored me, and I just want to go home." Bev pulled me in for a hug. "Oh Em, I am so sorry, honey. Of course, let's get you home. It has been a long day."

Bev gave me one last squeeze before we separated and went in opposite directions. I walked up the hill and Bev across the street to catch her bus.

I walked into the apartment and Stormy did three little spins to show me his excitement to see me. "At least I can always count on you, buddy, to be happy to see me."

I filled his bowl as I started to cry again. I went straight back to my bedroom and sat down on the edge of my bed, and began undressing. After getting out of all my clothes, I slowly crawled up to the top of my bed and slid under the covers. I just laid on my side and stared at the darkness, thinking about how big of an idiot I was. Thinking that this woman might have thought about me too. I leaned over and turned on my lamp, and grabbed my journal. "You want me to write, Dr. Kayla, I will write." I could feel my jaw clenching while my fingers gripped my pen as I began to write.

*111 hours until my next session*

*You saw me, I know you saw me. You just looked at me, then looked away like you didn't even know me. I think I understand now. I only exist in your world between two turns of a doorknob. Once, when I enter your office and then when I leave.*

*I only live in your world for sixty minutes once a week, then I no longer exist. Then you move on to someone else, another client. Thank god for schedules, otherwise you might forget I exist altogether.*

*That is why you have me write in this journal, then never ask me about it. That is why you say we can talk more about a topic next week that we didn't finish, only we never do. It is because you don't think about me again after I walk out your door, do you? It's because you can't see me as a person outside of your room. I only exist in your therapy room.*

*I am more than that. I am so much more than that. Don't you know you are like my human diary? You are the one damn person who has the key to unlock me. Without you, who will ever read my truth, my fears, my joys, my traumas, my new beginnings? I am not broken, but you, you have broken my heart.*

*Ember*

# Chapter Twenty

I rolled over in bed and grabbed my phone to see there were four missed calls from my mom, but no voicemails. I figured since she didn't leave a message, there wasn't an emergency.

I crawled out of bed and headed to the kitchen to get a glass of water. "Do you want to go to the park this morning, buddy?" Stormy hit the hallways with the zoomies, so I took that as a yes from him. We hadn't been to the park since my last panic attack, but I think we both needed to get back out there, plus the sun was out and if we didn't take advantage of these nice days, we would probably regret it.

After doing a couple of laps around the lake, we found ourselves sitting on our favorite bench. Stormy devoured his pumpkin pup cake, then fell asleep at my feet, so I decided I should probably just suck it up and call my mom back.

"Hey Mom, I saw you called a few times this morning. Is everything all right?" I asked, even though I knew everything was just fine.

"Oh Ember, so nice of you to find the time to call me back. I know how busy you are these days," she said sarcastically.

I rolled my eyes. "You called pretty early, then we were on a walk. Sorry it's taken a bit too long to call you back. What's up?" I asked again.

"Well, Ember, what's up is that this week is Thanksgiving and I need you to go shopping for a few things and make something. You can contribute. You are old enough to bring something, you know," Mom snapped.

"Wow mom, are you sure you are okay? You sound super cranky." I tried to be supportive, but call her out on her bitchiness at the same time.

She let out a long sigh. "It's your dad. He wants to let some residents from the retirement community come over for Thanksgiving dinner that don't have other family and I just don't know how I feel about it."

"Oh, that's sweet, don't you think? I mean, if they don't have other family members, then they shouldn't be alone, right? Who are they?"

"Mrs. Fredal, Mrs. Tapers, Mrs. Girders, Mrs. Parses, and Mrs. Lindal. Are you seeing a pattern, honey?" Mom sounded irritated.

"Oh, yeah, maybe we keep it just the family. We will talk to him. What do you want me to bring or make?" Trying to wrap up this conversation.

"Can you just bring a pie?" Mom asked.

Stormy and I hit the store and bought an already made caramel apple pie, then headed home. I called Sawyer to have her take care of the guest list for Thanksgiving. We narrowed it down to just the women from my parent's church, which were Mrs. Lindal and Mrs. Tapers. Mom wasn't happy, but it was important to dad, so we compromised.

\*\*\*

I was dreading therapy this week. I didn't know if I should say something about what happened at the bar or if I was supposed to just pretend like nothing happened. I felt like I wanted to throw up when I heard that same familiar squeal of the door and I saw Dr. Kayla standing there smiling at me.

I walked past her but didn't make eye contact. I am sure she could tell I was uncomfortable today. I was never able to hide my feelings very well.

"How are you today, Ember?" Dr. Kayla's normal opening. Like nothing was different. Like we didn't have this moment at the bar last week.

I just looked at the floor. "Fine, I guess."

There was a change in her voice. "Ember, is there anything you want to address? If not, there is something I think we should."

My stomach flipped. I knew what was coming. "Is this about the bar?" I asked.

Leaning forward, "Yes, this is about the bar. Is it okay to talk about that?"

I looked up at her and sighed. "Yeah, I guess so."

Dr. Kayla continued. "I did see you, and I know you saw me. I didn't approach you or say hello because legally I am obligated to keep your privacy confidential and can't say hi to you first. If you approach me or talk to me first, I can engage, but otherwise I need to pretend like I don't know you. I hope you can understand why that is important."

I felt like a complete ass and realized that I overreacted. "Thank you for explaining that. I didn't know you couldn't make the first move." Dr. Kayla smiled at this comment.

"Right, I can't talk to you first. I am glad we could clear that up. So, what would you like to talk about today? The holidays are coming up. How are you feeling about that?" Dr. Kayla asked.

This immediately reminded me of my last holidays with Rayna and my heart just sank. I missed her so badly. I looked up at Dr. Kayla with tears in my eyes and her head slightly dropped as she leaned back in her chair.

"I love turkey." I said in a shaky voice. "And cranberry sauce and pie, I love *PIE*..." I groaned and started bawling into my hands.

"What makes the holidays so emotional for you?"

I couldn't be honest. I couldn't tell her my heart was broken, that I was alone and single. That I was still attached to the unattachable, still crying over someone who would never again cry over me. "My mom refuses to have the Thanksgiving Day Parade on the TV and it just ruins the whole vibe of the day." I lied.

"While I would love to believe this is what makes Thanksgiving emotional for you, I think there is more to this day than what you are telling me. I want to remind you that this is a safe place to share your feelings. We don't have to talk about what makes the holidays hard. But maybe we can come up with some strategies to get you through the day?"

"I don't know how that will be possible when everything this year will be totally different than last year."

"How so?"

"Mainly the people."

"Okay, is this a good thing or a bad thing?"

"Bad." I responded.

"How does it make you feel?"

"Sad."

"What is something you can do to make the day a better?"

This time, I just stared at Dr. Kayla. *Better? Better? I am alone.*

I shook my head to come out of my thoughts. "Um, I guess spending time with my little niece is always fun. She likes board games. We could spend the day doing that. That might make the day better."

"Ember, is there something else about the holidays that is hard?"

"I am alone." *God, that was hard to say out loud.*

"Do you want that to change?"

My voice was trembling. "I don't know."

"Was there someone special recently in your life that you are no longer with?"

"Yes."

"Is this a relationship you would like to reconcile, or are you glad it's over?"

"I would do anything to have her back." I said, as my tears rolled down my cheek and neck, soaking my shirt.

"There is no need to rush into dating after a breakup. Some people wait years to date again. Some people can stay friends with their exes, some people find it better to completely go their separate ways. No matter what type of relationship you were in, you deserve to take the time you need for yourself and find what it is you want for your next relationship. Sometimes it's okay to be alone while you heal and figure out your next move. It can be a healthier growing experience."

"Yeah, I have a lot to figure out, that's for sure." I wiped the tears from my face.

"We can take our time to understand this one. Breakups are super hard and emotionally taxing. We'll get you through this."

At the end of our session, I got up from my seat and gathered all my tissues and started my journey towards the door. I continued to drop tissues on the floor, picking them up, only to drop another on the floor again. I did this all the way to her office door. Before I left, I turned to Dr. Kayla and smiled through my red, swollen face, "Happy Thanksgiving, Dr. Kayla."

She gave me a little wave and a sad little smile. "Happy Thanksgiving, Ember."

\*\*\*

All the guests, including Sawyer's family and myself, arrived at my parents' apartment building at the exact same time. Mrs. Lindal and Mrs. Tapers walked over together from another building. There were multiple buildings in the complex for different levels of income. The buildings my parents were in were for couples, the buildings the ladies were in were for single people.

We all congregated in the lobby to greet each other and decide who was going to take what out of the older lady's hands. Sawyer handed one casserole dish to Alex and the other to Todd. I offered my arm to Mrs. Tapers and Bella offered her arm to Mrs. Lindal, then we all headed upstairs to my parents' place.

The elevator's doors opened to a hallway full of smoke and my father waving a dish towel out the front door of their apartment. "Your mother burnt the rolls, so we'll be having bread instead," he said as he kept swinging the towel.

I gave him a kiss on the cheek and walked past him into the kitchen to find my mom in a complete panic. "This is not the day I was hoping for, I just wanted a simple meal with my girls, but your dad had to invite the church ladies and put all this pressure on me to make more food than I planned, now everything is just ruined." She turned around, putting her hands on the counter and started to weep.

I put my arm around her to bring her closer to me. "Mom, go into the living room and just socialize. Sawyer and I will finish up in here." I offered.

She pulled away, picked up the plates with the silverware off the counter, and shoved them into my chest. "Just go set the table, and Sawyer, you fill the water glasses. Then I want everyone to sit down and get ready to eat. Now. Go," she said, shooing us out of her kitchen.

We were all sitting around the table when mom came out with a large sliver plater with a covered lid. She sat it in the middle of the table and lifted the lid to reveal our dinner.

Mrs. Tapers was the first to speak. "Oh Joyce, so non-traditional to make a ham instead of a turkey for Thanksgiving."

Mom dropped the lid on the table and stormed out of the dining room, crying. Mrs. Tapers looked around the table at us, all confused. "What did I say? It's a beautiful ham."

I patted her hand. "It's okay, Mrs. Tapers, holidays are always emotional for mom, I'll go talk to her."

Sawyer and I walked into the kitchen to find our mother sitting at the table blowing her nose. "She's a senile old witch. She did that on purpose to impress your dad. She knows it's a turkey."

Sawyer sat down next to mom and started rubbing her lower back. "She is a senile old witch. Do you want me to throat punch her?"

Mom started laughing. "This is why you are my favorite, honey."

I rolled my eyes. "Can we just go back to the dinner table?" We all stood up and went back to the dining room.

I felt like things were going fairly well until dad announced he had a toast. "I want to make a toast. Everyone, please raise your glass." We all raised our glasses as my father went on. "This has been a year, a good year, a bad year, a year of learning, and a year of loss." I shot a look at my dad for him to stop. "Ember, we know this year has been especially hard on you, but we want you to know that your family is here for you and that we are thankful for you and that you are getting help."

I looked around the table at everyone staring at me, then shot the dirtiest look at Sawyer. "Ember, I only told them because they worry about you." Sawyer tried to defend herself.

I put my hand in Sawyer face. "Stop right there, Sawyer. Shut up, all of you. People break up all the time. You all have got to stop this right now. Please stop this right fucking now," I yelled and threw my napkin on the table as I noticed everyone looking at each other, but no one was looking at me.

I stormed off into the bathroom and slammed the door behind me. I took my cellphone out of my jacket pocket and dialed Rayna's number. She didn't answer. I hung up and dialed it again. She still didn't answer. Voicemail. "Hey this is Rayna. Can't talk now. Leave me a message, love ya!"

This time, I left my message. "Rayna, it's me, it's Ember. Why won't you take my calls? I miss you so much. Please come back home. Please Rayna...please...oh god, please...why won't you come back home?" I slid down the wall, crying so hard. I pulled my phone away from my ear and just stared at Rayna's name on my screen, then threw it against the wall so hard it made a hole in the drywall.

Knowing I was not in any condition to go back to the table, I decided I needed to collect myself so no one would see how fucked up I was. If anyone saw my hands trembling like this or my breath catching every time I tried to inhale, then they would probably take me to a hospital. Instead, I just closed my eyes. I had no idea how long I laid on the floor before I heard a soft knock on the door. "Ember, it's me, Sawyer. Can I come in?"

I opened the bathroom door, handed my phone to Sawyer, and went back to my seat at the dining room table.

"Em, our family phone plan doesn't cover cracked screens. You're going to have to wait for our next upgrade this spring." She handed my phone back to me.

Everyone was still sitting in their seats, but all the food was now replaced by a piece of pie in front of them. As I expected, everyone was staring at me, but I didn't care. I was so exhausted and hungry that I just sat down and quietly began eating my pie.

My mom cleared her throat. "Well, I don't think anyone will argue that this has been a complete disaster of a year and even a worse holiday. I think we could all use an end of the year pick me up, so I say we spend Christmas in Hawaii. What does everyone think?" We all looked around at each other and nodded our heads in agreement.

"Yeah, let's do it," Todd said.

"I could use a vacation," I agreed.

Sawyer squeezed my hand. "I will get another doctor to cover for me," she added, smiling.

"It's settled then. We are going to Hawaii for Christmas," Dad declared.

\*\*\*

Day after Thanksgiving, shopping was my second most hated activity right behind small talk with Uber drivers. However, it has been our family tradition for years now, and I could not disappoint the family by not going. Sawyer and Bella picked me up first at 3:00 in the morning, then we picked up mom.

Our first stop was to hit the electronic store for Alex's video game system that he just had to take to college with him. After waiting in line for an hour, we finally got in and luckily there were a few gaming systems left. His big gift was done.

After that, we headed to breakfast to plan the rest of our day. Most of us just wanted clothes for Christmas, so mom and Sawyer decided we should all try on what we wanted, then we would buy each other exactly those items, saving the hassle of returns. It would have been a great idea, except for the fact that I hate shopping and I despise trying on clothes even more.

The rest of the day was just as they planned it. I spent all day following my niece, sister and mother around each store, watching them try on clothes and being forced to participate.

I was standing in the dressing room looking at myself half naked in the mirror, poking my belly, when my mom and Sawyer burst in with an outfit they wanted me to try on. Suddenly my mother gasped. "Ember, do you wear that kind of underwear on dates?"

I blushed like I have never blushed before. "Mom, I can't believe you just asked me that."

Sawyer stared at me with disappointment. "Seriously, sis, you really should upgrade to underwear that might actually get you laid."

My mom looked at me and said, "your sister is right, you will never get any action in those Mrs. Lindal panties. Sawyer, go find your sister some sensible underwear."

Sawyer left the dressing room. "I'm on it, Mom."

But before she could leave, Bella came bouncing in jumping up and down, all excited "Mom, mom there is an Escape Room in the mall, can we go, please, please," she begged, then turned towards me, with a look of total disgust. "Wow Aunt Em, why do you wear your underwear up so high?"

I sat down on the seat beside the mirror. "Everybody, get the hell out of my dressing room. Right! Now!" I angrily whispered.

# Chapter Twenty-One

Bella exploded through the front doors of the Escape Room activity center with such excitement that even the adults were getting excited to try this adventure. She hadn't stopped talking about finding our way out of the Ice Cave Escape room for a solid twenty-four hours now.

Todd thought we should all wear ugly sweaters to commemorate this occasion, and Alex did not disappoint us with his choice of attire. He wore a lime green and pink sweater with large snowballs around the bottom. In the middle was a bulldog wearing sunglasses. Todd's sweater was a little less exciting. It had a Christmas tree with actual lights that lit up on it. Sawyer and Bella had matching mother, daughter, baby blue sweaters with tinsel, sequence, and a snow woman wearing a dress. I went with a sweater that Rayna left behind. It was a rechargeable black light sweater with everything neon. A green Christmas tree, a blue penguin, a white snowman, some yellow presents, and a pink flamingo.

Now that we were inside the activity center and paid for the escape room, we all gathered around for the woman to get us started on our adventure. I was really happy to have this family day. Small pleasures.

Bella was bouncing up and down while tugging on my arm. "Can we go in now?" I looked down at her and smiled at how wonderful it must feel to be without a care in the world.

"Okay, it looks like you are all ready to enter the ice cave. Please remember it is very cold inside, but it looks like you are all dressed for the weather. Thankfully for all of you, it has warmed up the last few days, so it is a toasty fifty degrees inside the cave today," said the Escape Room lady.

Bella giggled. "Will the ice melt?" she asked.

"No little miss, it will not melt. You will be safe as the ice has been there for thousands of years." The woman's voice instantly lowered, as she crouched to half her height and sprawled her arms across the room to animate her story. "Your assignment is simple. You are to give a tour of this ancient ice cave to a group of special Christmas Eve tourists. As your tour begins, you find out the special guests in your tour group are Santa Claus and his elves. Your famous tour begins and suddenly there is a loud rumble in the mountain, a thunderous boom occurs and collapses at the entrance of the cave. You have sixty minutes to find the exit and get yourselves and the tourist out so Santa can get back to the North Pole to deliver presents to all the little boys and girls around the world. You must help save Christmas."

Alex and I looked at each other with determination. We are both a little competitive by nature, so we raced each other towards the door and waited for the woman to let us in. When she opened the door, I pushed my nephew against the wall behind me and sprinted inside the cave. "Aunt Em, we are on the same team, you know."

I looked behind me. "Then keep up, water boy."

Alex shook his head and followed me. "You know I was the captain of my football team, not the water boy?" he said all serious like.

"Well, you're not the captain of this team, water boy. I am. Let's go." I slapped him on the shoulder.

We enter the room to see a magnificent display of ice crystals hanging from the ceiling. Fake snow filled all the corners, and the floor was glowing a soft blueish color that gave off the façade of slippery ice below our feet. Todd acted like he was losing his balance on the slippery ice, which made us all laugh.

Then, through the intercom system, came a voice welcoming our tour group while simultaneously a wall shot up into the ceiling, revealing a fake Santa in street clothes along with other touristy looking folks, including some of Santa's elves. No sooner did we all start walking towards our newcomers than we heard a thunderous boom, which we could only suspect was the avalanche we were told about a few minutes earlier.

Bella let out a loud scream, or maybe it was Alex. It was hard to tell the difference. They both sound similar in these situations. We all ducked as styrofoam ice blocks fell from the ceiling, blocking the front door. *Whoa...The game was on.*

At first, we all just stood there and looked at each other. Sawyer was the first to make a suggestion. "Well, obviously we have to save Christmas and get Santa back to the North Pole." We all turned to look at Santa, then back at Sawyer. "Don't look at me, that is all I got," she said.

Todd had the next suggestion. "Well, the whole point of these escape rooms is to find clues and then solve them one by one. The more clues we solve, the closer we get to getting out of here." He looked so proud of himself.

"Brilliant dad," Alex added.

I punched Alex playfully in the stomach. "Well, do you have any better ideas, water boy?" Alex rubbed his stomach. "Yes, I think we should first look at the tour guide brochure to see if there is a map that will at least tell us where the exit is."

I punched him again. "Excellent, nephew. I will grab Santa."

I jumped the rope where Santa and the other tourists were and grabbed the mannequin and headed towards the exit that was marked on the map when I heard a voice come over the intercom. "Please do not handle Santa Claus. Please return Santa to the tour group." I, of course, ignored this, as I knew very well the only way to save Christmas was to get Santa back to the North Pole.

Alex and Bella found a secret code on the map using a black light they found in a pair of ski boots on the ground. The code opened a locked toolbox, which provided us rope and a big hammer ice pick.

The kids were on a roll. They must have found at least four other types of code like puzzles while Santa and I discussed a Plan B in case we didn't get out of here.

Sawyer and Todd fought about if it was possible to get hypothermia in temperatures of fifty degrees but surrounded by ice. Doctors. Idiots. "Seriously people, Christmas was at risk, focus," I yelled at my team.

Another loud roll of thunder and a rush of cold blowing wind started swirling around us, which led to a piece of paper falling from the sky. Todd caught it and read it out loud to the group. "Get out of my cave." The wind stopped blowing, and we all had the same look on our faces. Fear.

Then out of nowhere the cave went pitch black, and Bella screamed, or Alex, I wasn't sure. Then a glow of red slowly brought the room back to life. When our eyes adjusted to the light, we found a skeleton sitting against a door that was locked with a backpack in his lap. I dragged Santa Claus over to the skeleton to grab the backpack and threw it over to Sawyer.

Sawyer opened it up and pulled out a puzzle box. "This box looks ancient. Do you think it's cursed?" Sawyer tried to open it. "I can't figure out how to open it. Maybe we should all sit down to conjure the spirit of the man who died, probably trying to save Christmas. I bet his spirit will know how to open this box," she suggested.

We all agreed this was a good idea, so we sat in a circle and joined hands. Sawyer started the chant. "Ohhhhhh spirit of the skeleton person, tell us how to manipulate this precious oak box. Do we turn, slide or shake it?" Then we heard a voice over the intercom. "You have twenty minutes to save Christmas."

I panicked and grabbed the box from the middle of the circle and threw it against the wall. It shattered into a million wooden splinters. Everyone gasped and just stared at me.

"What?" I stood up and grabbed the key from the splintered pieces of wood scattered across the floor.

We all ran to the door that the skeleton was sitting in front of on the floor. I kicked his bones out of our way and unlocked the door, which led us to another room where the exit was. Our final task. I knew we could do it. "No shame family, no shame in HOW we save Christmas. It's THAT we save Christmas. Alex, what's the next clue?"

Alex started frantically running all over the room, looking for the next clue. "I don't know. I don't see anything that looks like it could be a clue. Oh my god, there's nothing here, Dad. what are we going to do?"

I stopped him dead in his tracks and lightly slapped him across his chin. "Calm down, water boy, and think. This is Christmas we are talking about. We have got to get Santa back to the North Pole."

Sawyer grabbed my arm and swung me around. "Ember, lay off him. This is just a game." I pushed her off me and placed Santa between us. "Tell that to Santa."

Sawyer punched Santa in the face, and Bella started to cry. "What the hell are you doing, Sawyer?" I yelled.

Todd ran over to calm us down, but he was too late. Our sister brawl had already broken out. Sawyer's jaw dropped Santa again, and he flew out of my arms on to the floor. She turned to walk away, which made me so angry that I jumped on her back and pulled her chin back so hard it put her into a spinning motion. She tried to swing me off her, but it didn't work, instead we both fell to the ground, rolling in the fake snow, yelling obscenities at each other.

I finally got out of her grip and found a styrofoam ice block and wiped it at her head. The corner of the ice block hit her smack in the nose, which immediately created a pool of blood all over the floor. Sawyer threw one arm up at me to stop the fight and the other pinched her nose to stop the flow of blood.

All the lights suddenly came on and I looked around to see the entire place in shambles. Bella looked back and forth at both me and her mom and was now crying harder. "We didn't save Christmas. You and mom ruined Christmas!"

Before I knew it, we were all being asked to leave and never return, and Todd was signing a check for all the damages. The rest of us all packed ourselves into the van to go out for pizza, including Santa, who I just purchased for $275.

***

At the pizza place, Sawyer was holding a plastic baggie of ice on her nose. Two black eyes were beginning to form on each side of her swollen face. Todd was reading over the pizza menu and the kids were too embarrassed to sit at the same table as us, so they found a smaller booth as far away as possible.

"I am super sorry for ruining the escape room adventure. I sometimes get a little competitive, but in all fairness–" I stopped talking and just zoned out, as I looked between Todd and Sawyer's shoulders. I then turned my head and covered the side of my face with my menu, so Rayna wouldn't see me if she happened to turn around. I could only see the back of her head, but I was like ninety percent positive it was her.

Sawyer lowered the ice pack and looked over her own shoulder to see what I was looking at.

"What are you doing sis, don't look? I think it's Rayna," I said.

I regretted it as soon as the words came out of my mouth. Sawyer looked over at Todd, just as Todd looked at Sawyer. "Ember, are you okay? Seriously, you are scaring me."

Shaking my head and thinking about what an idiot I must sound like. "Yes, of course I am okay, sorry, sometimes I get all freaked out that I am going to you know, like run in to her, I mean, ugh oh my god, listen to me. I promise I am fine. It's so stupid, I know. Can we just forget about it and order pizza? I am starving."

Sawyer just kept staring at me and then looked at Todd, who also was staring at me. "Guys, I am fine, and if you don't quit staring at me, I am going to go sit at the kids' table." I threatened, then started to look over my menu.

Sawyer took a deep breath and put the ice back on her nose. "Fine, but I hope you are talking to your therapist about this, but you're right, this isn't the time or place. Let's talk about something else, like mom trying to kill dad. Is that still a thing?" I let her change the subject, letting the therapist comment slide, even though it was rude and uncalled for. Dr. Kayla and I had better things to talk about than my breakups.

Todd cleared his throat. "Well, um, apparently yes. I spoke with him recently and there have been a couple of incidents."

Sawyer and I both turned in a little closer. Todd was like our informant when it came to our parents' relationship. Sawyer and I were completely in the dark with all of this. They wouldn't tell us anything. Which was so odd, men were typically the ones who avoided talking about their relationships and women were the ones who talked about nothing else. But here we were, listening to Todd give us the down low on everything, Joyce and George.

Todd continued, "It's totally nuts. Both times dad overheard mom on the phone again. She was in the office, and he was in his recliner watching TV when he heard her say something to the effect of 'all the blood would be the first obvious sign.' Then the next week, he overheard her say, 'just one big bump to the back of the head and he's a goner.' Then he said she couldn't stop laughing."

We just sat there in shock. "Do we need to commit our mother, Sawyer?"

She looked at me and shook her head. "Maybe. I don't know what to do or think. My head hurts. Can I just call her tomorrow?"

Todd and I looked at each other and gave each other sympathetic smiles. We knew we had sucked every last bit of energy out of her today. "Sure sis, tomorrow is fine."

***

I walked down the street into the diner, instead of my apartment, after Todd dropped me off. It surprised me to find Jean acting happy to see me. "Well, look what the cat dragged in, and who's your new friend?" Referring to Santa.

I opened my arms for a hug, but she just pointed to the booth by the window and walked away. "Awe, are you still mad at me, Jean?"

She walked back over with a menu, water and silverware and sat it all in front of me and came in close to my face, "I wish I could hate you, I really do, but something keeps me coming back for more, I just don't know what it is."

I smiled and confirmed. "It must be my winning personality."

"What can I get you, and remember, you are still on a two drink limit here," she reminded me.

"Seriously, how can you dictate how many drinks I can have? I am a paying customer." I tapped the table with my pointer finger to remind her who had the upper hand.

"My diner, my rules, take them or leave them." She smirked, waiting for me to decide what to order.

"Fine, how about just a glass of wine?" I handed her my menu and winked. Jean took my menu, rolled her eyes, while smiling, and turned to walk away.

After Jean left me alone at my table, I retrieved my journal from my bag.

*63 hours until my next session*

*Oh, the holidays. When you are young, they make you feel so full of excitement. Santa, presents, making cookies and all the holiday music. Then you get older and start attaching all these adult emotions to everything, and suddenly they are just lonely and sad. They just don't make you feel as happy as they once did.*

*I remember Sawyer and I would go to bed and night, giggling until we were too tired to try to stay awake to see if we could catch Santa in the act of leaving our presents. We would end up waking up at 5:00 in the morning and run downstairs to see what Santa left for us. It was always something big, a dollhouse, a kitchen set, new bikes, one year mom and dad bought us both little girl office sets, with our own desk, chairs and blackboards. I loved having chalk to write on the blackboard. We had every color you could think of. We pretended we were at school all Christmas day. Sawyer was, of course, the teacher, and I was the student. By the end of the day, I was in detention and didn't get my afternoon snack. Thinking back now, Sawyer could be such a bitch to play with sometimes.*

*Ember*

Jean brought my wine and sat it down in front of me. "What are you writing about in that little book of yours?"

I shut my journal and moved it to the side. "Oh, just making a list of all the things I find wonderful about you."

Jean started to blush and sat down across from me. "You can suck up to me all you want, but you're still not getting more than two glasses of wine."

I took a small sip of my wine. "That's okay, I have a big week at work and can't afford to start it hung over."

Jean turned around when she heard the bell of the front door ding to see a couple walking in. "Be right with you folks, go ahead and sit where you like," she yelled from our booth. "Well, I should get back to it. Have a good night, hon." She winked at me.

"Holy shit, Jean, I think you are getting a little addicted to me," I teased her.

She grinned and shook her head. "Don't hold your breath." She slid the bill onto the table and walked away.

*62.5 hours until my next session*

*I was thinking last night as I laid in bed awake, that I picture myself as this brave person who goes out into the world and does all these amazing things, says all the things I am too shy, or too scared to say, this person who goes all the places I would never venture on my own. I would be strong and brave. I would never hurt or feel pain. I would love harder, I would...I would...I would...*

*But then this funny thing happens, the light of day happens, I am reminded I am not brave or strong at all, I won't say those things, or go to those places or feel those things. The fact is...I just make the most of the darkness, that is when I am the bravest, when everyone is sleeping, when I should be sleeping too...because the truth is, I am not brave in the light of day at all. What is it about the dark that makes me so much braver?*

*Ember*

# Chapter Twenty-Two

"Stormy, where is my other shoe? I know you know, buddy." I was tossing everything in the air, finding a bag, a shirt, everything but my damn shoe. I don't normally oversleep, but I forgot to set my alarm last night and now literally everything that could possibly go wrong to make me run even later for work was going wrong.

I crawled under the bed where sometimes Stormy likes to chew on his bones. "Ah, there it is." Grabbing my shoe, I crawled back out from under my bed.

Picking up my little man, I gave him a bunch of kisses on his snout, which he enthusiastically returned. "Stormy, I do find it adorable that you cuddle with my things, but could you start cuddling with them in pairs, please?"

I laid him on the bed, tickled his belly, then I rushed towards the door. "Love you buddy, I'll miss you."

Right as I was locking my apartment door, I felt this presence closing in on me. I looked over towards Isla's apartment and sure enough, there she was inching towards me. "Hi, Ember, I wasn't sure if I should bug you. You look like you are in a hurry."

I looked over at the elevator, which had just shut, and figured since I was already running late, what was another minute or two? "I am, but I can spare a couple of minutes. Is everything okay?"

Isla quickly walked over to me. "I will make it quick, promise. Some of us are going to one of those drive-thru Christmas lights in the park this weekend and I was wondering if maybe you wanted to go with us? We all plan to grab some dinner afterwards?"

I stood there, shocked for a moment. "Yes, I love lights in parks, especially Christmas lights, I mean."

Isla smiled. "Great." She genuinely sounded excited that I accepted her offer.

My heart started to pound with excitement. "Okay, let's do it. Should I meet you there?"

Isla turned around to go back to her apartment. "I will text you the details soon," she said as she disappeared into her apartment.

She was so nice to keep inviting me to things. *This would be the event that I redeemed myself for sure.* I thought to myself.

I arrived at work a half an hour late to find Bev with my coffee, along with a not so happy look on her face. "Your desk. No stops. Immediately."

I took my coffee from her hand and headed toward my desk. I was sipping my coffee when suddenly it spilled down my chin as I felt a slight push of Bev's hand on my lower back to hurry me along. "Bev, ease up. What could be so urgent that I can't even take a drink of my coffee? It's been a morning, if you can't tell."

Bev shoved me into my seat and spun my chair around to face my visitor's chair in which she sat herself in. "I don't want you to freak out, okay?"

I was starting to get worried now. "Bev, you're scaring me." Bev stood up and looked over my cubical walls, then sat back down. "She's here."

I looked at her with full on confusion. "Who is here?"

She spoke through her pursed lips. "She. Is. Here."

I nodded in agreement that I heard her the first time. "Yes, you already said that, but who is she?"

Bev took both my hands in hers and confirmed my worst fear. "The pots and pans, woman."

My mouth dropped. "For real?"

"Yep, and you have a meeting with her in twenty minutes," Bev said.

"Shit. Shit. Shit. I am not prepared for this. Okay, breathe, I will just, what, go in there and say hello? Ignore her? What am I supposed to do, Bev?" I was in full panic mode now.

Bev stood up again and looked over the cubical wall again. "Shit is right. Bethany is coming to get you. Ignore her, pretend like you only know her professionally. That's it, okay? Come find me at your first break. I will want all the details."

"Ember, our guests from 'Simmer and Sauces' are here. I am surprised you aren't already in the conference room greeting them." Bethany looked disappointed.

I rapidly gathered my things, dropping my folders on the floor, papers flying everywhere. Bev and I hit the floor, scurrying to pick them up off the floor and stuff them back into my folders. "I'm on my way now. I was just double checking the lunch order with Bev. We are all set with lunch, right Bev?" We crawled up to each other and met eye to eye.

Bev looked at me with that 'oh no, I forgot to order lunch' look and replied, "yep all set, lunch at noon, like always."

I hoisted myself up off the floor and sprinted down the hallway, making a quick stop at the restroom before heading into the conference room where I was about to confront my one-night stand.

Right before I arrived at the ladies' room, I saw her, Cara. She was exiting the bathroom and heading back down the hall to our meeting room. My heart sank, but it wasn't because I was nervous or scared, it was because she was beautiful, and I wanted her. This was going to be a long day of ignoring her, when all I wanted to do was kiss her again.

When I entered the conference room, I went to my normal corner of the room and set up my station to get ready to take notes for Bethany. I decided not to acknowledge Cara and just take my seat since the meeting was going to begin any minute. Cara had other plans, though. She walked up to me immediately before I could even sit down and held out her fist. I fist bumped her to be polite, but didn't do much more to acknowledge her.

"Hi Ember, interesting that we will be working together, huh?" She tried to play it cool.

I tried to play it even cooler. "Why is it interesting?" I was hell bent on making her squirm.

She shrugged her shoulders. "Oh, I don't know, maybe 'interesting' isn't the right word to use. Anyway, good to see you again. Hope you are doing well," she said before she went back to her seat.

I ran my hands through my hair and sat down. Wow, she is a pro at this. She was able to acknowledge our one-night stand, make it okay, then also confirm our current professional relationship, all while blowing me off all in one sentence. Where the hell was Bev when I needed her?

Bethany walked in and turned down the lights. When she turned on the projector, a picture of me standing at the Pots and Pans vendor stand came onto the screen. I was immediately embarrassed because I knew exactly what I was doing in that photo, and it wasn't trying to land Bethany a deal.

"Welcome everyone, we are so glad you are here. We have a very demanding agenda over the next few days, but before we review our schedule, I want to draw your attention to the photo I have on the screen. This one photo tells the story of how our journey and partnership began."

I had no idea where this was headed, but I slide a little further down in my seat hoping no one would notice I was the woman in that photo.

Bethany pointed to the back of the room. "Ember, please stand up and wave so everyone can put a face to the photo up here."

*Bitch.* I stood up, waved, and then immediately sat back down.

Bethany continued her story. "Our story begins in Vegas, Nevada, in sin city, as some people call it. They say what happens in Vegas stays in Vegas, but that's not true, is it, Ember? In fact, Ember and Cara made quite the impression on each other, which led to them sealing this deal."

I stood up and yelled, "Objection!"

Cara quickly came to the rescue. "I agree Ember, without objection, Simmer and Sauces knew that this partnership with SBTK Advertising was what we've been looking for all along. We are so excited to be here. Thank you, Bethany and Ember." Cara sat back down and looked back at me and smiled. She is good, really, really, good. A pro, in fact.

Bethany ended the meeting reminding everyone about the Christmas karaoke party at the bar next door starting at 7:00 p.m. Bev and I would go over early to set up and start drinking as soon as possible.

I gathered my things and left the conference room without even so much as looking at Cara. My intentions for the rest of the night were simple. Get drunk and try to avoid having to sing karaoke with Bev.

***

I danced around with the microphone in one hand and my beer in the other, taking in al

I danced around with the microphone in one hand and my beer in the other, taking in all the brightly colored lights shining down on us while we danced and sang on the stage. As we both landed our drunken spins, we shared the microphone to belt out the lyrics to rock songs, the crowd went wild, screaming our names, it was obvious our fans wanted more, so when we started our next set, which was a slower song I announced, "We're going to slow it down a bit, so grab your snuggle nugget, even if it's just for tonight and, hold them tight." I instructed our fans. It was then that Bev sang from the depths of her diaphragm, a melody that just blew everyone away.

I jumped off the stage to go over to the bar and grab a couple of beers, one for me and one for Bev. Not that I needed another beer, but I desperately wanted another beer. As I stood there waiting for our drinks, I saw Cara come into my peripheral vision. "I'll have what she's having."

"Ah, and here we meet again, at a bar." I teased.

"Yes, most likely for the last time as well. I typically only come for the kickoff meeting, and that is it. This will be my last trip and probably the last time we ever see each other." Cara said matter-of-factly.

"Well, I hope you are enjoying our company party?" I turned to face her.

"I would enjoy it more if we got out of here," she said boldly as she looked straight ahead at the bottles that line the wall behind the bar, then took a long pull off her beer.

I also took a drink of my beer and set the bottle back on the bar. I felt a familiar excitement in my body for Cara as I did in Vegas, so I leaned in and pulled her chin towards me with my finger. I paused and smiled at her, teasing her. Coming close to kissing her, but then slightly backing away. The way she let out a slow gasp of air and her head tilted to the side told me she was ready for me to take anywhere.

But instead, I said, "Just that night." I ached saying these words with how badly I wanted to take her hand and find somewhere to undress her so I could press my body against hers again, to hear the sounds she would make when my hands slid along her hips, to feel her body tremble when my lips met the hollow of her neck. But tonight, the only sound I needed to hear was of me walking away.

And that is exactly what I did. I grabbed my two beers and walked over to Bev and sat at the table with my back to the bar. I knew if I looked back at Cara, it was possible I might change my mind and I couldn't do that to myself again.

"I'm proud of you Em, I know how hard that must have been to walk away." Bev said. "Cause she's smoking hot."

"You're an asshole Bevie, but I love you."

"Gotta love your Bev-Bev, now let's go karaoke, Em." Bev took my hand and dragged me back on the stage.

# Chapter Twenty-Three

I walked in the therapy office today and waved to Lisa, who gave me an interesting look, which at first, I just blew off as Lisa being Lisa, until I was stopped dead in my tracks. There was a stranger sitting in my corner. I looked back at Lisa. She looked at me and shrugged her shoulders and went back to typing on her computer.

I decided to take the seat across from this person who stole my seat. I was completely flabbergasted. Who was this stranger that had zero respect for seat assignments? It was obvious I needed to assert my authority around these parts, but then again, maybe not. Maybe I would try to befriend this stranger instead.

I reached over to pick up a magazine and started to rapidly flip through page by page while keeping an eye on the woman across from me the whole time. She must have noticed, because she looked up at me and smiled. I took this as my cue to interact with her.

"So, what are you in for?" I nodded at her.

"Excuse me?" The woman cocked her head, looking confused and defiantly offended by my question.

Before I could respond, Lisa called me to her desk. "Ember, we encourage all our clients to keep to themselves in the waiting room and not interact with each other. We want this to be a safe place for everyone. So, if you could please respect everyone's privacy, that would be great."

"Lisa, she's in my seat." I pointed out.

"Technically, that is not your seat, Ember, this is a waiting room. People can sit wherever they want when they arrive," she stated sternly.

"I *will* be talking to Dr. Kayla about this." I pointed at her before walking away.

"I think that is a really good idea." I heard Lisa's voice trailing off as I was almost back to the other side of the waiting room.

"Dr. Kayla, I have two very important things to discuss today. One is seat assignments, and the other is I feel like we sit here every week, and you tell me nothing about yourself. Zero. I ask you questions, and you won't answer any of them. You expertly change the subject. Every. Single. Time. At first I didn't notice this, because you are a professional subject changer, but then last week when I asked you if you like hot or mild sauce on your tacos, I thought 'wow what if you are vegan and don't eat tacos,' so I asked you if you like meat and you asked me if I eat meat and I answered yes, then you asked me if anyone judges me for my choices, I realized it then. How are we supposed to build the true foundations of this relationship if won't tell me your favorite color?"

I looked down from the ceiling to see Dr. Kayla with her mouth slightly ajar, staring at me. "Um, well, I believe it is better for my clients if they are not clouded by what I believe or think about on any given topic. Our time together is about you and moving you forward in the therapeutic process. I believe it would be distracting and selfish to talk about myself. I am not sure my favorite color or choice of taco sauces would bring any value to your healing."

"I bet it's red." I guessed.

"What is red?"

"Your favorite color."

Dr. Kayla sat back in her chair, pinching the bridge of her nose.

"Okay, Ember, how about we discuss some things that are important to you? What are the things that you find are the foundational pieces of a relationship?"

"Is this from our conversation last week? Or like with my parents? Or my sister? Who are we talking about here?"

"Really, any relationship. There are basic needs we all have, no matter who we encounter. What are your needs? What is important to you? What do you want to receive from others?"

Then it hit me: no one has ever asked me what I needed before. What is important to me in a relationship? I didn't know what I needed or what was important to me. I started to bounce my leg and as soon as I looked up at Dr. Kayla, I realized she really wanted to know. For the first time, someone really wanted to know. I started to tell her that I didn't want to be scared anymore, but my voice was shaking, and I couldn't put my words together. I was getting dizzy and before I could even attempt to say anything else, I dropped my head in my hands and filled my palms with tears.

"Ember, it's okay to cry and talk at the same time."

I lifted my head and tried to tell her what I needed from a relationship, however what was in my head and what came out of my mouth were two different things. "I. Can't. See. Talk. Relationships. Touch. Needs. Receive. Receive. Hugs. Contact. Relationship. Talk. Receive," I cried hysterically.

"If I understood you correctly, you said you need to receive lots of physical contact and communication is important for your needs to be met. Did I get that right?"

I stopped crying a little and looked up at her. "Yes, that's right." *I love you*, I thought to myself.

She leaned back and breathed a sigh of relief, or maybe triumph. We were finally connecting, and I think we were both finally feeling it.

"Okay, that's great, Ember. If you find that communication is important to you, how do you see yourself as a communicator?"

"Rock star level communicator here." I said, pointing at myself. "I mean, I feel like I say what I mean, mean what I say, ya know?"

"What type of listener are you?"

This stopped me dead in my tracks. Oh my god, is that what happened? Did I not listen? Is this how I ended up alone, with a geriatric best friend, and in therapy?

***

The rest of the week slowly trickled by, so I was glad to receive Isla's text on Saturday telling me we should meet in the lobby of our apartment at 6:00 p.m. to catch the Uber to the park. I was there, ready and waiting, but Isla hadn't shown up yet. I guess I was about twenty minutes early, so I pulled out my journal and decided to scribe for a bit.

*63 hours until my next session*

*It was so nice to be with Dr. Kayla this week. I am starting to miss her more and more between sessions. I have got to tell her how I feel soon. Otherwise, I may never be able to get through a session without melting down.*

*Tonight, I am going out with Isla and her friends. They are such nice people. It is nice to have more distractions than sitting at home.*

*I thought about asking Isla out on a date to distract me from Dr. Kayla, but she is probably no more likely to say yes than Dr. Kayla is. There is no way someone like Isla would ever date someone like me, either. She's way out of my league too. She probably just feels sorry for me. Her pathetic neighbor, who sits on her balcony crying. She is turning out to be a good friend, though, which I will take. Can't have too many good friends, they say. I don't know if I am ready, anyway. I might be a little ready. How do I tell?*

*Ember*

"Hey stranger." I jumped a little when I heard Isla's voice come out of nowhere.

"Hi. How are you? It feels like forever since we've seen each other." I shut my journal and hid it in my bag.

"Let's go. I think you are really going to like what I have in store for us tonight." Isla held out her hand for me to take. I grabbed it and looked down at our hands interlocked, then up at her smiling back at me.

The Uber driver pulled up outside and stopped in front of our building. We walked out to the car holding hands like a couple, even though I knew we weren't. It felt like the most real thing I have felt in a long time, and I was on top of the world.

When we arrived at the park to find Isla's normal group of friends waiting for us to arrive. They all ran up to us, ready to start our adventure through the park. From the energy level of the group, it seemed like everyone was in the know of something more going on tonight than just a drive through the park to view some Christmas lights. Some were jumping up and down, others were pointing to the long lines of cars waiting to get in. Whatever was going on, I had a feeling that it had to do with Isla.

"Okay, everyone, quiet down. I rented a hayride for us tonight," Isla announced to our group. Everyone melted at her very words describing how the rest of our evening would go; Christmas music, blankets to snuggle under, and hot coco to indulge in as we traveled through the park enjoying every bit of a typical, over the top Isla gathering. I still don't understand why she keeps inviting me to these things.

We all grabbed a hot coco and a blanket before finding a hay bale to sit on. I sat near the back, figuring I would give her friends the better seats. After all, I kind of felt like the tagalong in the group. The tug of the horses taking off and the Christmas music filling the silence were the first signs that our holiday light display ride was about to begin.

We trotted under an arch of shimmering gold lights that welcomed us to the park. Turning the corner, we went under a long tunnel of rainbow lights. I don't know why, but I felt a bit overwhelmed with emotions. I was trying not to cry, but the tears slid down my cheeks anyway, which I quickly wiped away. I wasn't a mess, just sad. Here I was surrounded by all these gracious people, and I had never felt more alone in my entire life. Typical Ember Rue.

I glanced towards the front of the trailer and saw Isla looking back at me. I turned away because I didn't want her to know I was upset. Not when she was being so nice by inviting me on this outing.

Display after display, each flashing animation brought laughter and all sorts of different kinds of excitement to our little circle of friends. Chickens crossing the road, tiger cubs frolicking about, hockey players making goals, and Santa going down a chimney. *Too soon,* I thought to myself.

Just as I was starting to calm down and enjoy the evening, Isla stood up and asked for our attention. "Okay everyone, I invited you all here tonight not only because I thought it would be super fun so close to

Christmas, but also because I have something very special I want to share with you all."

Everyone quieted down and gave Isla their full attention. Because she's Isla and when Isla speaks, people naturally tend to listen. The horse went around the final corner of the park and there it was, Isla's special surprise. Isla stood up at the front of the trailer and asked the coachman to stop the trailer for a minute. It was one of Isla's more famous paintings in the form of a light display with an announcement that it would showcase her at the Los Angeles County Museum of Art.

Everyone started to clap and cheer, as it was obvious what this meant for Isla. She was breaking out of the Pacific Northwest and moving down the coast. Her work was being seen on a larger scale. It was just a matter of time before she would be a world-famous painter and I would be able to say that I once knew her. Damn, I was going to miss her so badly. *Why does everyone leave me?*

Bowing to the right, then to her left, she said, "Thank you, thank you. I am very excited. This is huge for my career. I have dreamt of this day since I was a teenager. But I want you all to know that I couldn't have done it without all your support over the years."

I shouldn't be here. I had known this woman for what two months. I felt so out of place. I had no right to be celebrating this moment with Isla and her friends. I just wanted to jump off the side of this rig and bolt through the park into the night. I could feel my body temperature rising, so I threw the blanket off my legs and tried to take a deep breath. I had to get off this ride.

My leg began bouncing rapidly. The deep breaths weren't helping. Since the trailer wasn't moving, I decided it was now or never. I couldn't do this. I couldn't breathe. I jumped up, spilling my coco on the ground, others quickly jumped up and back to avoid getting splattered with my drink.

Isla stretched out her arms to stop me from leaving. "Ember, wait. Where are you going?"

I nudged right past her. "I'm sorry, Isla, I, I just don't feel well. I have to go. Congratulations, I am so proud of you." And I did just what I planned to do. I ran off into the dark of the night.

I ran, and I ran until I tripped over my own feet and fell to the ground on my hands and knees. I was crying so hard that I started dry heaving, spitting up what little contents I had left in my stomach. I was finally able to capture a pocket of air when I finished getting sick, so I crawled back a couple of feet and rolled over to watch a completely different type of light display.

I probably stared up at the stars for an hour before rallying the strength to go find another Uber. I just needed to go home.

Yep, this would definitely be the last straw for Isla. I have officially fucked up this friendship. She would never want to see me again.

I arrived home so exhausted that I didn't even bother to take off my wet muddy clothes. I just fell onto the bed and shut my eyes. I had been asleep for a couple of hours when I heard Stormy barking at the door. "Stormy, come back to bed, buddy." But he so was relentless and kept barking.

I rolled over and picked up the clock. Eleven. Tossing the clock on the bed, I sat up and called Stormy again back to bed, but he decided either I would come to the door or listen to him howl the rest of the night.

"Okay, okay, Stormy, hush it. Who is it?" I called out as I shuffled to the door.

"It's Isla." Her voice stopped me dead in my tracks.

"Um, what's up? Now's not a good time. Can we talk tomorrow maybe?" I stood now on the opposite side of the door with my forehead resting on the frame.

"It's okay if you don't want to open the door. I understand, or at least I think I understand. We can just talk right here, like this. I just want you to know I'm not mad that you left tonight." I could hear her body slide down the outside of my front door to the hallway floor.

"You're not mad?" I also slide down the inside of my door to the floor. We were now sitting back-to-back with just a solid piece of wood between us. "But I just took off in the middle of your big announcement. I ruined your night. Your friends probably think I am such a loser or something."

"They don't, and you didn't ruin my announcement or the night. We just finished the hayride, then had dinner, and I came right back here to check on you." Isla sounded sincere, but I was skeptical. Being this was now my third fuck up with these people.

I leaned my head back against the door, wondering if Isla was matching my same body movements when she said something odd, "I know Ember. Larry, 'Larry the Landlord' told me." She tried to mimic the silly voice I used when I say his name. "And it all makes sense. I just want you to know I understand. I mean, I get it, I really do. I get it." I threw my head forward and looked back at the door, totally confused. *What the fuck.*

"Look Isla, I am tired. Can I text you tomorrow?" I got off the floor and hurried back into my bed. This time, I stripped down to my tank top and underwear and climbed into my bed. Isla must have left because Stormy jumped up into bed and curled up behind my legs. I laid there and stared into the kitchen. I doubt I will get any sleep tonight.

# Chapter Twenty-Four

I felt bad for how I left things with Isla over the weekend, so I sent her a text to apologize for my abrupt departure from our door conversation. I thought if I asked her if she'd be willing to watch Stormy when my family and I went on vacation over the Christmas holiday, hoping that might seem like we were still okay. I didn't mention her odd comment, and neither did she. Isla agreed to watch Stormy, so maybe our friendship could just be that. I would water her plants when she was traveling the world showing her art, and she could help me with Stormy occasionally if I traveled.

Stormy and I settled on two laps around the block and an unplanned stop at the bakery this morning. He deserved it. We haven't been going on as many walks lately. Maybe I was finally getting a life, or maybe it was something else, but I got to see Dr. Kayla this week and I felt so excited to see her. I felt safe with her, like nothing or no one could hurt me in her therapy room, and if anyone tried, she wouldn't let them, or at least I don't think she would let them. I wonder if she looked at her schedule and got excited when she saw my name on there, too.

I had an extra pep in my step today. I think between the walk and knowing that the weekend was over, and that with every new week meant I got to see Dr. Kayla, gave me a little more energy.

# THE NEXT 167 HOURS

The sun was shining through the windows throughout the main lobby, hitting the metal woman just right to send off a beam of light from her hand to the ceiling. I knew the artist positioned her this way, but it still amazed me every time it happened.

"Ember, good morning." Mr. Lee called out from behind his desk, so I thought I'd stop to chat for a second. Damn, I was in a good mood this morning.

"Good morning, Mr. Lee. How was your weekend?" I genuinely wanted to know as I threw my work bag on top of the counter.

"It was good. Me and Mrs. Lee brought our Christmas tree and decorated it." *And I'm done. Enough of the lovie-dovie, cuties, couple crap. I have work to do.* I thought to myself.

"Wonderful, glad you had a nice weekend, Mr. Lee." I grabbed my bag and headed towards the elevators, where I found Amy pushing the button to retrieve the elevator.

"Good morning, Amy. So nice to see the sun today, isn't it?" Not letting Mr. Lee's love fest of a weekend completely ruin my good mood.

"Hi, Ember. It is. We don't typically see the sun much in December around here." The elevator doors opened, and I walked in and scooted back to my corner.

"Looking forward to your shower next weekend." I called out from the back of the elevator. Amy looked slightly over her shoulder at me and smiled a little with a nod. I was glad to see she was excited as well.

The doors opened to our floor, and with a skip in my step, I popped out of the elevator to suddenly find myself just standing there dumbfounded. I looked around, confused. Where was Bev? Bev is always here with my coffee. I first walked over to her desk, but she wasn't there. Then I walked over to my desk and dropped off my work bag and then went back to her desk to see if her computer was turned on or her purse was on the floor where she typically kept it. Her computer hadn't been turned on and her purse was nowhere in sight.

My heart started to race as I could feel a panic start to rise inside me. This wasn't like Bev. In my eight years with this company, Bev has always been here. Every day. Where the hell was Bev? I ran over to Dan's desk. "Have you seen Bev this morning?"

Dan looked up and me, then got the same look on his face that I had on mine, concerned. "You know, Em, I haven't. That's odd. Bev never misses work."

I rushed from his desk. Surely her boss, Lydia, would know where she was. I swung around her office door. "Lydia, have you seen Bev this morning? No one has seen her yet and none of her stuff is at her desk."

Lydia looked at her watch, then up at me. "Calm down, Ember, it's only eight twenty. Maybe her bus is running late."

I completely ignored her ignorance and doubled back to my desk to grab my phone. *This is ridiculous, what boss doesn't know their own employee arrives at 6:00 a.m. every morning.*

It was now 8:20 a.m., Bev would be almost two and half hours late for work. Idiot. I grabbed my phone and saw two missed text messages, both from Bev. My heart sank, but was relieved at the same time.

> "I'm at the hospital with Ed. He had a heart attack."

> "Em, I'm scared. What will I do without my mole?"

> "I'm on my way."

I stopped by Lydia's office before going to meet Bev. "I am heading to the hospital to sit with Bev."

Lydia came around her desk. "Oh my god, why, what's wrong? Is she okay? You're right, she really should have been here hours ago." She looked at her watch.

Annoyed that she suddenly seemed to care, I said, "Bev is fine. It's Ed. He had a heart attack. I don't have any details, but I will have her call you when she knows something."

I raced into the hospital to find Bev sitting in the middle of the ER waiting area by herself. She looked so small, frail and...old. "Bev," I called to her from across the waiting room.

She stood up and hobbled towards me, and we embraced each other by the nurse's station.

Her words just started pouring out. "He's in surgery now. They said one of his arteries was ninety-nine percent blocked, but his prognosis looked good. They think he's going to make it." She took a deep breath of relief, as she could finally say those words out loud... "He's going to make it."

I led her back to the waiting room and sat her back down. "That is great news. I am so sorry you are going through this, though. You must have been terrified. What the hell happened?"

Bev grabbed a tissue from her purse and blew her nose. "Well, it was about four o'clock this morning. Ed woke me up and said that he was having some chest pains, but that they were coming and going. I said, maybe we should go to the ER. He said not unless they became closer together. I said, 'you're not in labor you idiot, you could be having a heart attack.' But he waited a whole hour before he let me call an ambulance. And here we are. The doctor said if we waited much longer, we'd be having a whole different conversation. I told the doctor when I get a hold of Ed, we still might be having that conversation."

"Oh Bev, that's just sounds awful. I was so scared when I came into the office, and you weren't there. I didn't know what to think." I surprised myself when I started to cry, but it didn't seem to surprise or bother Bev, because she just pulled me in close and we just held each other in our arms.

The doctor walked into the waiting room and sat next to Bev. "Ed did great. He'll be in recovery the next couple of hours, then you should be able to see him. Believe it or not, if everything goes as planned, he'll be able to go home tomorrow, but not without some serious restrictions. We'll talk a little more later, okay?" He patted Bev's leg a couple of times before getting up and walking away.

Bev drew a huge sigh of relief. "Thank goodness. Now my plan to kill the bastard myself one day is still on." She giggled as tears building up again.

I smiled at Bev. "Come on, let's go down to the cafeteria and I'll buy you some breakfast. It will kill some time until you can go see Ed." I put my hand out for her to take mine for once.

***

"My friend Bev almost lost her husband to a heart attack yesterday." I started my therapy session by telling Dr. Kayla about Ed.

"Oh no, I am sorry to hear that. Do you want to talk about what happened?" she asked.

"No, I just thought you might want to know. Like I said, a heart attack. But I don't think there is much to say about it. They are much older than us. In their late sixties. Anyway, we can move onto a different topic. He probably ate like crap, sat in his delivery truck all day, not exercising. Anyway, how are you? But hey, who cares if he leaves his wife behind, alone, scared without him? How has your week been? You know, at least he could have done was go to the doctor when he started to feel like crap, because he hadn't been feeling well, you know." I edged to the end of my chair.

For the first time ever in a therapy session, I stood up and started to pace the room. "What if he would have just been like hey, I don't feel good today, maybe I will make a doctor's appointment and they will check my heart and then maybe it won't attack me in the wee hours of the morning and make my wife think I am going to die. You know, be a little proactive. I really don't have anything I am coming into session with today." I sat back down in my chair.

I looked back up to Dr. Kayla staring at me for a moment, then she asked, "Why are you mad at your friend's husband?"

I just sat there. I didn't know how to answer that. I wasn't mad at Ed. I mean, I felt horrible for Ed. He was sick, he just had a heart attack. "I'm not mad at him, per se. I just think he could have taken better care of himself and maybe this could have been avoided."

Still staring at me, "What are you if not mad at him?"

I started to tear up. "I am reminded."

"Of what?" She leaned forward.

"Of how quickly everything can be taken from you. I walked into the office that morning, and Bev wasn't there. Bev is always there. But she wasn't there. Then I got to the hospital and told her how scared I was. She thought he was going to die and be left alone. She is not religious, we tend to have the same views about life and death."

"What are your views?" Dr. Kayla asked curiously.

"I think we are recycled."

"Recycled?" She repeated my words.

"Yeah, recycled."

"Okay, tell me more about that," she encouraged.

"Well, if you really want to know. I think we will come back after we die. I think we will keep coming back over and over again. We will come back to right our wrongs to become a better version of last selves. Then when we succeed, we come back as an animal, we get to come back as these beautiful creatures who will become one with the earth, as we were always intended to be. It will be then and only then that we will complete our last cycle."

I looked up from fidgeting with my fingers to see Dr. Kayla staring at me. "That sounds really nice, Ember."

I don't know why, but today I didn't cry. I think I surprised us both. Dr. Kayla was already in her crying position, sitting back ready to just sit with me, but it didn't happen. Instead, I looked up at her, then at the wall.

"Do you see me as a difficult? Last week, you asked me about my communication style. Is that because I am hard to talk to?"

"Do you think you are hard to talk to?" Dr. Kayla asked.

"I kind of don't like it when you do that. Answer my questions with another question."

Dr. Kayla smiled. "I do not find you hard to talk to. I am curious why you think I or others might, though?"

"Well, I am glad you don't. Then I will keep talking to you." I put my fist out for a bump before I left. Then instantly regretted it when she made it awkward by just smiling and shaking her head and walking me to the door.

\*\*\*

I stopped by the diner for dinner to find Jean wasn't there. *Why the hell is no one showing up for work today?* I thought to myself.

I stomped my feet on the dirty rug just inside the door. "Hey Timmy, where is Jean?"

He quickly responded. "Night off."

I guess I can't be mad at that.

"Sit where you like," he yelled back.

As always, I took my normal booth and waited for my menu, water and silverware, which weren't coming. "Hey Timmy, you going to bring me a menu?" He was either ignoring me or truly didn't hear me, so I waited patiently for another minute or two. After all, he was literally just standing at the counter reading a book.

"Timmy, a menu, please?" He finally grabbed a menu and brought it over to me and walked away. "Silverware and a water would be great too." I requested. "Seriously, are you new here?" I said under my breath.

Timmy returned with my water and silverware, and I guessed by the way he annoyingly held his pad of paper and pen. He was also ready to take my order.

"Okay, I will have a fried chicken sandwich, mayo on the side, sweet potato fires and a glass of red–"

Timmy interrupted me. "Two drink limit."

I was shocked. "What did you just say?"

Timmy lowered his pad of paper. "I said, two drink limit." He seemed irritated now.

I got a bit upset by his comment. "Why on earth would you say something like that to me?" I wanted to punch him.

Timmy flipped over his pad of paper so I could see the other side and there it was, a message from Jean, right on top. "Ember, you are on a two drink limit in my diner. Sorry hon. Hearts, Jean."

"Fine, I'll just have water." I said sharply and handed Timmy my menu.

*160 hours until my next session*

*I remember being a kid and playing in the rain. Jumping in puddles, pretending those same puddles were little oceans, making boats out of leaves and putting sticks on those leaves to see if they could make it across the treacherous seas. I would push the leaf and see how far it would float before it would just whirl in circles in the middle of the puddle. I kind of feel like that stick today.*

*Ember*

# Chapter Twenty-Five

The cars kept honking at each other to move out of the way so an ambulance could maneuver through the thick downtown traffic. The blaring sirens that kept beeping on, then off, on, then off, made both Bev and I jump every time we heard the noise. I quickly grabbed the door handle to the front entrance of the department store door to let Bev inside, so we didn't have to listen to that jolting sound anymore.

As soon as we got inside, we both relaxed enough to get on with our purpose for being at the store, which was to buy a wedding shower gift for our coworker, Amy.

"F," Bev said, "that shit is loud."

I giggled, ignoring her attempt at 'youthful' bonding with me. "So, how's Ed feeling?

Smelling the perfumes at the first counter we stopped at. "He's cranky, unfun, whining about everything. Hates his new diet, doesn't like to exercise and won't have anything to do with putting up the Christmas tree. He says I have enough plants around the house. My mole has always been kind of a killjoy, you know that." I agreed, and we moved on to the customer service department to find Amy's wedding registry.

Amy's gift registry was forty-two pages long, so it took a good ten minutes to print out. While we sat there waiting, I thought back to her comment about most of these places wrapping gifts for you. I wondered if they really did gift wrap the gift here like Amy said. "Excuse me, ma'am, do you all gift wrap here?"

The woman behind the counter, who was meticulously taking one piece of paper off the printer at a time, turned to me. "Yes, we do."

Nice. I wondered if it was free. "Excuse me, ma'am, is it free?"

She continued to take the next piece of paper off the printer. "Yes, for standard size gifts, it is free."

Excellent. I wondered what constitutes a standard size gift. "Hey, ma'am, what do you consider standard–"

Without giving me a chance to finish my question, the woman whipped around with all our printouts and handed them to us. "I am sure once you are done shopping we can answer the rest of your questions, okay, you good?"

Using both my hands, I took the papers from the woman and nodded that I was, in fact, good.

Before we got started, I saw the cutest shoes I wanted to try on. Bev didn't argue because she liked the same ones, so we ran over to the shoe department and asked the woman to get us both a pair to try on in each of our sizes. "We could be twins, Ember."

While we sat there waiting, we went through Amy's list. "This is a weird list. There are only pictures and prices. No descriptions or anything." I handed Bev half the sheets, and I kept the other half. "Wow, a two propane tank outdoor grill with four burners. That stove is bigger than the one I have in my apartment." I called out.

"Look at this," Bev said, stabbing her finger at one of the pictures on the sheet of paper. "A king size mahogany, hand carved bedroom set, including two nightstands, dresser, and an armoire. Look, Em, look at the little unicorns carved into the wood."

I looked closer at the picture Bev was showing me. "Oh yeah, those are unicorns and little gnomes. I think those are little gnomes. Are those gnomes, Bev?"

I dropped the top sheet to the bottom of the pile to expose the next sheet. "Oh, no way on god's green earth is she asking for her friends to buy her a ten-thousand-dollar ruby necklace shaped like an apple, with an emerald stem? Amy, who are you?" I looked over at Bev, shaking my head. "Do we even know this woman? I mean, you think you know someone, right? But do you really? What are we getting ourselves into later today at her wedding shower?" I was getting nervous that we might not fit in where we were about to go.

Bev nodded in agreement. "It's at her parents' country club, that's all I know. I can't see how we wouldn't fit in there. I mean, really, Em, how much could we stick out? Really?" I nodded in agreement.

We continued to look through each page and still could not believe the type of things Amy was asking for. "We really can't afford any of these things, Bevie."

Bev took the remainder of my list from me and finally came to something she thought we might be able to swing. "Here, this, we could go in on this together."

I grabbed the papers from her hand and looked at the picture. "Oh, it's a..." I turned the paper sideways to get a better view, "A..." I turned the paper upside down to get a different perspective.

Bev ripped the paper out of my hands. "Ember is just a back massager." I decided to just go along with that. "Okay, if you say so."

Bev threw her hands up as if she gave up on me and headed off to the intimate department to pick up the massager. "Hey Bev'er wait up. Would you consider that 'standard size' so we can get the free gift wrapping?" I asked innocently, while trying to catch up to her.

***

The Uber driver pulled up to the country club. "Wow, you want me to wait out here for you? Looks like a rough neighborhood." We all laughed as we collectively stared at the mansion that stood in front of the car. Was this a country club or Windsor Castle?

We paid the driver and got out of the car. We didn't move, even as the car's dust spun up behind us. Do we go in or stand out here? Would they even let us in? Who *was* Amy?

"Welp, I say we just go up to the door like we belong here. Like we would at any country club," I said as I took Bev's hand and made our way to the building.

"Have you ever been to a country club?" Bev asked.

"No, this will be my first time, but how different can it be than on TV. I am sure there is a restaurant, a golf course, a swimming pool, and probably some tennis courts. I am sure we are just going to some event room for cake and presents. In and out." I reassured her.

Before we even arrived at the entrance, Amy came running out like an excited teenager. "You both came. I am so glad you are here. Come inside. We are all in the gold room." Bev and I looked at each other cautiously, but followed Amy inside anyway.

The double doors magically opened, and we found ourselves standing in front of a freshly polished grand staircase that made us both feel like we were definitely in a mansion now. Bev and I looked at each other and shrugged our shoulders. "I feel like a princess," said

Bev sarcastically, before we continued to follow Amy down the hall to the gold room.

We suddenly stopped right behind Amy as we almost colliding into her back as she flung open the French doors to announce the arrival of her final guests, her coworkers, Ember and Beverly. The room silenced as everyone turned to size up these strange women who were apparently not made aware of the dress attire for the party.

I leaned over and whispered, "Amy, why didn't you tell me this was a formal affair?"

Amy leaned over and whispered sternly back to me, "Because it's not what I wanted, and mommy knew that. Oh, and I also told mommy you're a lesbian. She doesn't approve, but I told her you are my friend, and you are staying, so don't worry about her or her friends, okay?"

By looking around the room, it was no mystery who mommy and her friends were, as my eyes landed on the group of women standing in the corner glaring at me. I gave a quick little wave and smile, with nothing in return from the crotchety old ladies.

The crowd eased back into chit chatting, so I took the opportunity to grab Bev and drag her to the side. "Bev, do you see what is going on here?"

She looked confused, but took a stab at an answer, anyway. "Someone told them this was a Downton Abbey costume party instead of Amy's wedding shower?"

I thought about this for a second, but quickly got back on track. "No, Amy is using us to piss off her mom. She purposely didn't tell us what the dress attire would be, so we'd show up dressed like we always dress, and her mom hates lesbians."

Bev looked at me like I was crazy. "Em, nobody hates lesbians in this day and age. I mean, look at the women–"

We both looked over at Amy's mom, who was giving us a death glare. "Ember, did she just give us a 'get out' motion to leave?"

I clenched my fist to my sides. "Yes, Bev, that's what I am saying. I think we've been duped into coming here."

Bev took a deep breath. "Okay, let's just tell Amy we need to leave, then."

"You're not leaving, are you?" Amy appeared out of nowhere. "You two are like my only work friends that came. I would be so sad if you left after just getting here."

Before I could even make up an excuse, Bev started reassuring her we weren't going anywhere and would stay until the end.

Bev looked over at me and gave me her best sad face. "Well, we are her only work friends that showed up."

"F, Bev."

I went to get something to eat and drink from the mammoth buffet table that included everything from a chocolate fountain to an ice sculpture of a unicorn and gnome. *Doesn't anyone just make pigs in a blanket anymore?*

"Sorry we don't have beer and brats at this event. You'll have to go to a *lesbian* bar for that kind of food." I turned to see who had just said that to me, only to find it was Amy's mother.

"Hi, Amy's mom, I'm Ember. The food here is fantastic. I wouldn't take a beer or brat over this spread any day. I mean, one thing is missing. But I guess it is just a wedding shower, or maybe you couldn't swing it in time. I'm not sure what went wrong." I turned so I could continue loading my plate.

She looked at me curiously, maybe even a little challenged. "What? Um, I'm Cecilia, by the way. We have everything here. Every kind of fruit, meat, non-meat, seafoods, vegetable, dessert, my bartender can make any drink you could ever desire. How could you possibly be wanting for anything else?" She sounded a little panicked, and I was simply enjoying the moment.

"Well, in the lesbian culture, which I know you know very little about, we are actually very strict about the foods and drinks we consume, and I was admiring your table, and I found it to be a somewhat blah."

Cecilia's eyes pierced. "Blah, you say. Do tell me, lesbian Ember, what would make it less blah."

"Honestly, I was extremely disappointed not to see a cheese connoisseur to serve us fine cheeses onsite." I simply stated.

Cecilia said nothing more to me. She just turned around and hollered, "Edward, get me a cheese connoisseur down here immediately! Why in the hell is there no cheese on this goddamn table?" She stormed off, and I grabbed two brownies. One for me and one for Bev.

Sitting in a large circle, we watched Amy open her presents one at a time. Now that we were here and saw the 'real Amy,' I was not at all surprised when I saw her open a picture of the bedroom set. I was even less surprised when she held up the beautiful apple necklace and held it to her chest for the rest of us to ooh and ahh over. I wish I could say the same thing for everyone else's reaction when they saw Bev and my gift.

Amy opened the massager and there was a lot of "oh my lord have mercy" and "what is that thing" along with "dear god," but the best was from a little old lady in the back that said, "Mine is pink."

Amy's face was so red I thought she was having a hot flash. She spun around and glared at us. "What were you two thinking?"

Bev immediately went to defend us, pointing to the picture of the massager from the gift register. "It was on your list, it's the massager."

Amy went into Zen mode for a full twenty seconds, then came back to the present, speaking softly to us. "That is a picture of an immersion blender for my new kitchen set." She set the box aside and went on to the next gift.

Bev stared at the picture in silence for a good two minutes and finally said, "Ohhh, I see it now. Look Em, it's the tip that is different."

"Bev, just put the paper away." I said as I ripped the gift register from her hand.

We then sat in silence like two school children sitting outside the principal's office.

When the gift opening was complete, we thought it was time to leave, but nope, it was game time. "You have got to be fucking kidding me, Ember." Bev mumbled.

I looked sharply at her. "Bevie, language."

Amy's maid of honor, Cassidy announced there would be three games total.

The first game we would each try to bounce a small rubber ball on top of the opening of a champagne bottle.

Bev and I immediately jumped up and chest bumped, being the Ollie's Bar 2018 Beer Pong champions.

Sadly, we ended up losing the rubber ball game to Amy's grandma and her friend, who were surprisingly extremely patient with bouncing that little ball.

"The second game is called 'tie-the-knot,' the first person to tie a cherry with their tongue wins. Start now." Cassidy gave the signal by chopping the air with her hand.

"I'm done." I said two seconds later.

"Lesbians." I heard Amy's mom say with disgust from the back of the room.

Bev elbowed me. "You tied it with your fingers, didn't you?"

I laughed. "You know I did." Elbowing her back.

Cassidy handed me a gift bag and walked away. "Okay, the last game is called 'best of the best love stories.' Everyone will write, then read aloud, their own personal love story and then we all vote for the best one. Whoever gets the most votes will win a free weekend getaway in the mountains."

Everyone clapped but me. Not even a free weekend getaway could get me to tell my love story. Was it even a love story? I felt Bev's hand on my leg, which made me jump. "Ember, it's okay. You don't have to do this."

"No, I know. I think I am done here. Can we just go, Bev?" Bev knew what to do. She always knew what to do. Don't ask questions, just get me out of here.

Bev went over to Amy and said something, then came back over to me. "The bathroom is down the hall." Her eyes got big, telling me to just go along with her. I stood up and followed her out of the gold room, down the hall and out the front door. We walked to the street and called an Uber from there. Bev promised she would think of something to tell Amy on Monday.

We sat on the curb waiting for our driver. Bev wrapped her arm around my shoulder and just held me without saying a word.

# Chapter Twenty-Six

Sitting on the couch, I spun my journal around and around on the coffee table. Even writing in this book was starting to feel more like a task than a helpful healing process, like Dr. Kayla said it would be. This time between sessions was getting to be too much. Dr. Kayla never wants to read my journal, so why am I even writing in this damn thing, anyway? I stopped spinning it and threw it in a pile with the magazines I planned to recycle. Being the non-committal person I am, I quickly grabbed it out of the basket and tossed it back on the coffee table.

I walked over to the wine rack, grabbed a bottle of red, and popped the cork. Screw a glass, I went and sat back on the couch, fulling intending on drinking the entire bottle. I took a long draw off the bottle, swallowed hard, then leaned my head back on the cushions and closed my eyes. I imagined a day when I was happy. When I was really happy. Every day. I would come home and kiss my girlfriend. We would make dinner together and cuddle on the couch. We would travel and camp, make love, laugh. Jesus, we would laugh so hard. I felt the tears trickle down each side of my face as I grabbed my cell phone and hit 'call' on Rayna's number.

It rang...and rang...

"Hello?"

Panicked. I tapped 'end' on the call and dropped my phone. I ran into the bedroom and started going berserk, launching everything within arm's length against the wall. Every piece of clothing, furniture, I was breaking pictures, glasses, vases, and candles. Stormy was barking at me to stop, but I couldn't control myself. I couldn't stop until I literally only had the strength left to pick up a pillow off the bed and screamed into it until I dropped to the floor.

I was pulling air into my lungs so hard as I tried to catch my breath that I started to hyperventilate through my cries. I struggled to breathe, so I rolled onto my stomach and rose to my hands and knees. Stormy crawled under my belly and laid down as if he was trying to give me support. I rocked back and forth and back and forth until I could finally feel the air catch in lungs again. I was too weak to stay in that position much longer, so I rolled over to my side, pulled Stormy into me, curled my body around his, and just passed out.

I woke up a few hours later to Stormy licking my face. I sat up and surveyed the damage in my bedroom. "Shit, I'm so sorry, buddy. Mommy lost her shit a bit, didn't she?" I said as I picked him up to put him on the bed so he wouldn't cut himself on anything broken on the floor.

I swept up the broken glass and pick up all the different things I threw around the room. When I swept up some pieces of a black vase, I uncovered a part of a picture of Rayna and I that must have fallen on the floor.

The picture was from earlier in our relationship. Rayna was sitting in front of me, between my legs. It was one of our first dates. She invited me to one of her friend's birthday parties. I was so nervous about meeting her friends. In the picture, I had my arms wrapped around her chest and our cheeks were snuggled together. We had these huge, cheesy grins on our faces. The frame that held the picture said,

'*I will never let you go.*' "Bullshit, you had no problem letting me go," I said to the picture of us.

I laid back on the bed and started crying uncontrollably again. I held the picture so tight, "I didn't want you to go, Rayna. Someone please take away this pain. Please make it go away." I gave up on trying to wipe the tears off the frame, instead I just let them collect into a pool of water on the glass.

I laid there and sobbed until I fell asleep again, this time until the next morning.

\*\*\*

After sitting in silence for the first couple of minutes of our session, Dr. Kayla was the first to speak. "You seem a little off today, Ember. Anything you want to talk about today, we don't have to. We can do some relaxation exercises?" Dr. Kayla probed.

"Well, we seem to talk a lot about me in here," I observed.

Dr. Kayla nodded in agreement. "Go on."

"Maybe today we could talk about something else. Like not about me," I offered.

"We could do that. Why do you want to talk about something that is not about you or what is going on with you?" She continued probing.

I had a feeling she was going to fight me on this. "Well, Dr. Kayla, it's like this. I am only one person out of a billion people in this whole big world. Yet, I come here, week after week, and talk about myself. Kind of selfish, don't you think? So, I was thinking that maybe we could talk about something different. Like, do you have favorite clients? Am I your favorite client?"

Dr. Kayla looked like she didn't know whether or not to take me seriously. "Well, the easy answer is all my clients are my favorite."

"But that would be a lie?" I finished her answer for her.

"Not really a lie, but more of a hard question to answer. I have so much admiration and respect for all my clients and the strength it takes to come into this room and do the work they do. One day can be so hard for one of them, and at the same time another day they come in with so much joy. Sometimes they have really big, hard feelings, while on another day they celebrate something awesome in their life. Sometimes they are navigating through the pain while simultaneously making tremendous progress towards their goals."

She paused and smiled. "Most importantly, each of my clients allows me the privilege to sit here with them as they process all these emotions and traumas and that is such an honor for me. See, Ember, they put so much trust in me to be present for them and hold space and care. How could I ever begin to pick only one of them to be my favorite?"

This time it was me who leaned forward. "I promise I won't tell them it's me."

Dr. Kayla smiled and chose to move on. If you don't have a topic today, I was thinking we could talk about your ex-partner a little more. Dig into some of those feelings.

Suddenly feeling nauseous, I told her, "I am not feeling very well today. Would it be okay if we cut our session short? I am sorry, it just kind of hit me. Must be a bug or something going around. I don't want to make you sick. Dr. Kayla."

Taken off guard but compliant, "Oh yes, of course. I hope you feel better, and I will see you next week."

I started to walk towards the door but stopped just short of opening it. I turned around and looked at her. "It's getting really hard, you know. These hours between our sessions, the journaling is helping a little, but it's still hard waiting so long to see you again." I said nothing else.

"Ember..."

I just quietly left and shut the door behind me.

\*\*\*

The rest of the week was torturous while Bev was still on leave, taking care of Ed, so it was good to see her exactly where she should be when I arrived at the office on Friday morning. Holding my cup of coffee and waiting to greet me. "Oh my god, I could just hug you. It's so nice to see you back in the office. I would have waited to come back to work on a Monday, though."

I handed over my work bag in exchange for the cup of coffee and we started walking towards my desks. "Are you kidding me, dog and miss Friday night happy hour? Hell no." Bev exclaimed.

"I am certainly looking forward to that this week." I slumped in my chair.

"Well, I have a surprise for you. But you need to promise two things first." Bev looked serious.

"Bev, what are you up to? Okay, I promise, but only because I am desperate for some fun and need to kill about seventy-five hours."

"What? Why do you need to kill so many hours?"

"Never mind. What are we doing? This better be good, Bev."

# THE NEXT 167 HOURS

"Great, okay, the rules are simple. One, you have to say yes, and two, you can't say no." Bev smiled, proud of the rules she just made up.

I glared at her because these particular rules always came with something I was not going to like. "Fine." I begrudgingly agreed.

"We're going speed dating tonight." Bev was now jumping up and down like a kindergarten.

I shot up out of my chair. "The hell we are." I grabbed Bev by the arms to stop her from jumping.

Bev grabbed my arms back. "Yes, and to double your chances of winning, I am going to also do the speed dating to check out the lady lake for you."

"It's pool, Bev. It's called a dating pool, and this is a horrible idea. These things never work. I've heard absolute horror stories about these speed dating, including people ending up murdered," I lied.

Bev let go of my arms and turned away. "I will be back at five to get you. Tootles." She waved all her fingers individually over her shoulder.

We arrived at the bar that was hosting the speed dating event just in time to hear the rules. They seemed relatively easy to follow. Each person would have three minutes to ask whatever questions you wanted to ask the person across the table from you. The bell would ring once, then you switch, and the other person would ask their questions. At the end, if you want to exchange phone numbers, you can.

"Bev, I didn't come prepared with any questions. I didn't even know I was going to be speed dating tonight." I turned to her nervously.

She handed me a sheet of paper. "Go get 'em, tiger," she said, and pushed me towards the woman sitting at the first table.

I stumbled up to the table from the little shove by Bev and pulled out my chair to sit down. "Hi, my name is Ember." I held out my fist to bump.

"Hi, I'm Sandy. This is weird, huh? Speed dating."

"Did someone drag you along like my friend did to me tonight?" I tried to build camaraderie.

"No." She sounded irritated.

"Oh, sorry, it's just, you said this was weird, so I thought maybe you were in a similar situation." I tried to explain.

"You know, you don't have to be here. Some of us are trying to meet someone and want to be here. Some of us want to fall in love and meet the woman of our dreams. So, if you're not here for the same reason, don't waste our time." She went on for the next six minutes about how she believed in love at first sight, and when the love of her life sat in front of her, she would know she was the one, and that is why she was speed dating. This was her seventh event this month. Yes, I gladly gave her my three minutes as well.

*Ding.* The bell rang for us to move to the next date.

"It was nice to meet you, Sandy. Good luck."

I hurried to the next table. I sat down without looking up at the woman because I was trying to unfold my list of questions. "Hi, my name is Ember." When I finally got it unfolded, I looked up to see a woman looking disgustedly back at me.

"Not interested." She looked down at her manicured nails.

"Oh, okay, well, that saves me from asking you 'what animal do you most identify with?'" I looked away from her.

After a minute of pure silence, she replied with, "A poodle."

Maybe she had a change of heart. "Oh, that's interesting. Why a poodle?" I was genuinely curious.

"Still not interested. When is this damn bell going to ring?" She continued to look at her nails.

"Got it. We will just sit here and stare at the table then."

"Sounds good to me," she replied.

We sat there in silence for the remainder of the five minutes until the bell rang. It was the longest five minutes of my life.

*Ding.* The bell rang.

I scurried to the next seat, and to my relief, I found Bev sitting across from me. "Bev, this is a total disaster. I have been shunned and told I was ugly, well basically, I was told I'm ugly.

Bev gave me a confused look. "Really? I got two phone numbers."

I threw my hands in the air. "Well, I give up. This was a dumb idea. I have no idea why I am even doing this. I will tell you the same thing I told Sawyer. I am not ready to date. Can we please just leave now? Please."

Bev looked like she was about to cry. I obviously hurt her feelings. "Bevie, don't cry. I'm sorry. I didn't mean to upset you."

She put her hands up then gathered all her things, getting ready to leave. "No, you didn't upset me. It's fine. I was just trying to do something different and fun with you and maybe, just maybe, in the process, you might meet a nice girl. But I overstepped and I shouldn't have."

Pulling Bev back down in order not to make a scene to the other speed daters around us. "It really is okay. I know you were just trying to do something nice for me. But the truth is, I don't know if I will ever be ready to be date again."

I think this last comment hurt her even more. "I just wanted you to be happy again, like you used to be. You're different. I know it's normal, but what can I do to help you, Ember? You're my friend and I love you." She was full on crying now.

"Bev, I can't do this right now, okay?" I put my hand on hers. "I love you too, but I really can't do this right now. Let's get out of here. I think Ollie's is the happy hour where we belong. What do you think?" I grabbed Bev's hand and pulled her toward the door.

# Chapter Twenty-Seven

"Ember, did I put you on the calendar wrong, I thought your appointment with Dr. Kayla wasn't until two o'clock today?" Lisa said standing in front of me.

I looked up at her from my book. "Oh no, I just got here a little bit early is all, you didn't schedule me wrong."

Lisa suddenly connected the dots. "Ember, its noon, this isn't about the assigned seats thing, is it? You're not seriously here two hours early so another client wouldn't sit in your favorite seat?"

I sat my book down in my lap. "Look, I've been coming here for what, two months now, and every single time, I sit right here, in this seat–" Just as I was pleading my case, I saw the 'other client' walk in. "Oh shit, Lisa hide, go back to your desk." I shooed her away. "That woman is coming in the door." I slung my book back up in front of my face to pretend like I was reading it.

Lisa rolled her eyes at me, but smiled at the seat stealer and said, "Good afternoon, I will get you checked in, go ahead and take a seat anywhere you'd like." She stressed the *"anywhere."* Part.

*Oh, that was a dig if I ever felt one Lisa.* I peeked my eyes over my book to see that the woman was sitting across from me staring at me. I covered my eyes quickly. I waited a couple minutes before I lowered my book again to find her still staring at me.

"I know you are looking at me." She caught me.

"I'm not looking at you per se, I was looking around you," I retorted.

"Around me? What does that even mean?" She sounded really annoyed.

"Like to your side, then around you to the behind of you, obviously." I am pretty sure this woman wanted to fight me.

"You're making no sense lady." She laughed, but not in a "ha ha" way, more in she thought I was crazy way. Now I was pissed.

"Look seat stealer, you come in here all high and mighty like you own the place, like you can just sit in other people's seats when clearly, this seat doesn't belong to you–"

Before I could finish my rant the seat stealer totally interrupted me, "I knew it, I told my boyfriend that this crazy lady that went to my therapist's office thought she owned the corner seat, I even made my appointment an hour earlier to avoid you, but yet here you are."

I stood up to show my dominance which to be honest I almost never do because I am a lover not a fighter, but 'here I was', is right. "I am ready to go a round if you are seat stealer."

She stood up and got nose to nose with me. "You don't have the balls to fight me."

"You are actually right about that, I do not in fact have the balls to fight you, but I do have the balls to take my corner back." I grumbled in her face.

Suddenly, we found ourselves playing the part of musical chairs when the music stopped, and we were both trying to sit in the chair at the same time. She threw an elbow to my rib cage. "Ouch!" I yelled.

I threw my hips and butt out as far as I could to push her back from the seat as we circled the cushion, when we heard "Ladies, that is enough!"

We both stopped to find Lisa glaring at us with total disgust and disappointment. "What the hell is wrong with you two? Never in my career had I thought I would be offering two complete strangers in my waiting room couples therapy, but I think we need to think about how to resolve this once and for all. This is absolutely ridiculous.

"I'm sorry, Lisa, it's been a really long few weeks." I looked over at the other woman and said, "I am sorry seat stealer, I didn't mean to push you with my ass."

"I have a name, it's Mindy. I am sorry, even though I did mean to jab you in your ribs, I do hope you are okay. In all fairness, I am in therapy for anger management," she offered as a half-assed apology.

I nodded. "Makes sense, I may be in therapy for things related to loving that corner chair."

Mindy gave me a pathetic look. "Oh god, gross, you win, you can have the damn chair." She walked away and sat at the other end of the waiting room.

Lisa didn't even look at me, she just picked up the table we knocked over and put the magazines back on it, then went back to her desk.

I think I really upset Lisa this time. I would have to find a way to say I am sorry. I bet she really hated her job sometimes. I had another hour to kill before my appointment, so I used that time to figure out how I could make it up to here. I just went back to my corner to read my book and to think about my actions.

I heard the squealing of the door and looked up to see Dr. Kayla standing there with a big smile on her face. I got up and headed her way, I glanced over at Lisa, but she didn't acknowledge me. I felt super horrible. I slightly smiled at Dr. Kayla as I walked through the open door to my seat.

She sat across from me. I was nervous because I wasn't sure if Lisa told on me or not. I started to rub the center of my palm and bounce my leg. "So, sounds like rumors have been circling the waiting room about a fight over a chair." I thought I should just come clean.

"Oh yeah, I haven't heard anything," she responded with a pursed lipped smile and then looked down like she was trying not to laugh.

Was she letting me off the hook? Should I just move on? I think I will just move on.

"Oh, well in that case, what do you want to work on today?" I asked.

"I do have something I would like to discuss before we get started today, if that is alright?"

"Of course, it's kind of nice that I don't always have to be the one doing all the talking," I said, thinking this was a nice change of pace.

We shared a glance for a second then she went on. "Every year I take the last two weeks of the year off, so we will not be meeting for two weeks. How do you feel about this?"

My heart dropped into my stomach, the room started to spin, no not spin, wobble. Why would she do this, why would she leave me for two weeks? "Um, can I email you or call you if I need you?"

"No, Ember, but if there is an emergency, there are crisis hotlines. We also have other therapist that you can schedule time with to discuss whatever is on your mind."

"Really? Whatever is on my mind, but they don't know me though. How will they be able to navigate my insides? My feelings, thoughts, my fears, when they don't know me? I keep trying to tell you I can barely get through these one hundred sixty-seven hours between our sessions now you are asking me to go what, double that, three hundred and thirty-four hours? Seriously, please Dr. Kayla, don't do this to me."

"Ember, I didn't realize this would be so hard. What support do you think you need over these next two weeks to get through this? I really do want you to know that you are feeling supported is important to me while I am out."

"Support? You mean with you gone? Again, you are not an option?"

"I am sorry, I am not. For me to continue to be the best support for you when I am here, I also need to find time to recharge, just like you when you go on vacation. It doesn't mean I don't think about my client and are hoping the best for them while I am away. I am just taking the time to take care of me for a few days. How about we take the rest of our time together today to put together a plan in case you need something while I am out, that way no matter what happens you will feel supported." Dr. Kayla offered.

I thought about this for a minute. "I guess one of these weeks I will be in Hawaii with my family. Is there a one-eight-hundred number for 'quick tips on how to keep your parents from killing each other?' Or do you have a book on 'not taking your mom's insults personally?'"

Dr. Kayla giggled at this. "I don't have anything specific on those two topics, but there are support lines you can call, and I will supply you with those phone numbers. How else might you feel supported?

I picked up a little stone out of a dish that she had sitting on the table next to my seat. It didn't look like anything fancy. It was gray, with spots of darker grays blended through the rock. "Would it make you feel more connected to the therapy room if you borrowed one of those stones until we meet again?" she offered.

I rolled the stone between my pointer finger and my thumb, "Is that weird? That might make me feel safe? Better? To have it with me?" I asked.

"I don't think it's weird, I would like you to bring it back though. So, we can talk about what it meant to you while you had it with you over these next two weeks. How does that sound?"

"I think this all sounds like a solid plan." I said, although I still felt scared and sad.

"Hawaii, huh? How do you feel about this trip?" Dr. Kayla asked.

"I think I am excited." I kind of surprised myself with that answer.

"That's wonderful, Ember. You will have all the resources you need to get you through these two weeks that we don't see each other. I want to acknowledge that I hear you when you say that these hours between are sessions are hard for you."

"You do?"

"I do," she confirmed.

I held my rock a little tighter. "Thank you, Dr. Kayla."

\*\*\*

The work week flew by, so when Saturday arrived, I knew I had to get packed for Hawaii, but I was going to miss Stormy way too much to start that chore just yet. I just wanted a little more time with him first. We hadn't been back to the park in a while, so we decided this morning we'd pull ourselves together and get out there.

I laid in bed fumbling the stone from Dr. Kayla office between my fingers. It was soothing to feel the polished finish on the stone, first cool to the touch, but the more I moved it though my fingers the warmer it became. I loved having it, I really wish I didn't have to give it back. I set the stone back on my nightstand and sat up in my bed pulling the covers up to my chest because it was quite chilly in the apartment this morning.

I decided to playfully wake up Stormy. I began with a soft poke to his side with my toe. "Buddy, *park* time..." nothing. I poked a little harder, now I wiggled my toe to tickle his side. This got him panting. He was awake, but still wasn't coming to the surface. "Stormy, *bakery time...*"

I immediately covered my face in order not to get scratched when he *zoomed* out from under the covers in his flamboyant, bat-like fashion to fly down the hallway. He ran his typical four or five laps until he wrecked into the pillows beside me and decided to go back to sleep while I got up to get ready for our walk.

We were standing in front of the elevator, waiting for the door to open, when Isla showed up beside us. I might not have noticed if it wasn't for Stormy jumping up and down whining for her to pet him. I swear he was more in love with this woman then he was with me.

"Hi Ember," she said as if she was walking on eggshells.

"Good morning, how are you doing?" Trying to ease the tension.

"I'm good, where are you all headed?"

"Just to the bakery, then for a walk in the park, wanna tag along?"

"I would love that." Isla sounded genuinely excited.

We first stopped at the bakery, grabbing a peanut butter muffin for Stormy and two blueberry muffins for Isla and me. We certainly were not going to leave the bakery without two coffees either. Next stop was the park.

We walked a couple of laps around the lake before settling on the bench where Stormy and I typically sat to eat our muffins. Even though the weather was cold, and the skies were dreary the overall mood between us seemed nice and friendly.

Isla started our conversation about the weather and Stormy's care routine while she watched him when I was in Hawaii, but then she turned serious, "Ember, I just want to apologize for the other night. I had no right to say what I said about talking to Larry and knowing how you felt. Of course, I don't know how you feel. You don't have to say anything back, I just want to let you know if you ever want to talk, I am here for you, because I like you. I really like you."

I just sat there not knowing how to respond. "It's all good, really, let's just forget about it okay? I like you too and I really appreciate you watching Stormy for me. I think he is falling in love with you." I smiled at her.

Isla grabbed my hand. "I have to get back for a meeting that I have today, I am happy to watch Stormy this week, especially if it gets me in good with his mom." She winked at me. "I will see you both when you drop him off before you head to the airport in the morning."

My stomach did a swirl, a good swirl. "Okay. We'll probably hang out here a bit longer before we go home and pack. See you in the morning."

We waved goodbye.

Stormy whined as we watched her walk away. "I know buddy, but she's way out of our league."

\*\*\*

The work week flew by, so when Saturday arrived, I knew I had to get packed for Hawaii, but I was going to miss Stormy way too much to start that chore just yet. I just wanted a little more time with him first. We hadn't been back to the park in a while, so we decided this morning we'd pull ourselves together and get out there.

I laid in bed, fumbling with the stone from Dr. Kayla's office between my fingers. It was soothing to feel the polished finish on the stone, first cool to the touch, but the more I moved it through my fingers, the warmer it became. I loved having it. I really wish I didn't have to give it back. I set the stone back on my nightstand and sat up in my bed, pulling the covers up to my chest because it was quite chilly in the apartment this morning.

I decided to playfully wake up Stormy. I began with a soft poke to his side with my toe. "Buddy, *park* time..." nothing. I poked a little harder, now I wiggled my toe to tickle his side. This got him panting. He was awake, but still wasn't coming to the surface. "Stormy, *bakery* time..."

I immediately covered my face in order not to get scratched when he *zoomed* out from under the covers in his flamboyant, bat-like fashion to fly down the hallway. He ran his typical four or five laps until he wrecked into the pillows beside me and went back to sleep while I got up to get ready for our walk.

We were standing in front of the elevator, waiting for the door to open, when Isla showed up beside us. I might not have noticed if it wasn't for Stormy jumping up and down, whining for her to pet him. I swear he was more in love with this woman than he was with me.

"Hi Ember," she said, as if she was walking on eggshells.

"Good morning, how are you doing?" Trying to ease the tension.

"I'm good. Where are you all headed?"

"Just to the bakery, then for a walk in the park. Wanna tag along?"

"I would love that." Isla sounded genuinely excited.

We first stopped at the bakery, grabbing a peanut butter muffin for Stormy and two blueberry muffins for Isla and me. We certainly were not going to leave the bakery without two coffees, either. Next stop was the park.

We walked a couple of laps around the lake before settling on the bench where Stormy and I typically sat to eat our muffins. Even though the weather was cold and the skies were dreary, the overall mood between us seemed nice and friendly.

Isla started our conversation about the weather and Stormy's care routine while she watched him when I was in Hawaii, but then she turned serious. "Ember, I just want to apologize for the other night. I had no right to say what I said about talking to Larry and knowing how you felt. Of course, I don't know how you feel. You don't have to say anything back. I just want to let you know if you ever want to talk. I am here for you, because I like you. I really like you."

I just sat there, not knowing how to respond. "It's all good, really. Let's just forget about it, okay? I like you too and I really appreciate you watching Stormy for me. I think he is falling in love with you." I smiled at her.

Isla grabbed my hand. "I have to get back for a meeting that I have today. I am happy to watch Stormy this week, especially if it gets me in good with his mom." She winked at me. "I will see you both when you drop him off before you head to the airport in the morning."

My stomach did a swirl, a good swirl. "Okay. We'll probably hang out here a bit longer before we go home and pack. See you in the morning."

We waved goodbye.

Stormy whined as we watched her walk away. "I know, buddy, but she's way out of our league."

# Chapter Twenty-Eight

I dropped Stormy off to a half-awake Isla who wished me a good trip and shut the door as quickly as it was opened. I guess it was 6:00 in the morning. What artist ever gets up this early? Stormy didn't even look back. He just raced into her apartment like it was his second home.

Alex was downstairs waiting for me in the lobby when I came out of the elevator. "Hey, Aunt Em, you ready for our big Hawaiian adventure?"

I gave him my biggest smile. "I'm ready." But in all honesty, I was feeling scared of being so far away. Going to Vegas was one thing, but Hawaii was a whole different thing. What if I need Dr. Kayla? Wait, that wasn't an option. I felt my knees get weak as I walked towards the car.

Alex grabbed my suitcases. "Mom said you really needed this trip, and we should try to make it special for you. So, I thought we could go snorkeling or something." He headed off without my response.

Getting through security was a breeze. We located mom and dad at the gate wearing their matching bright red Hawaiian shirts and cargo pants. They looked very adorable and not like two people where one of them wanted the other one dead.

Waving frantically, dad yelled, "Over here! We're over here!" None of us wanted to acknowledge them, but thank god for our little fifth grader, who still loved her grandparents.

"Grandpa!" Bella raced up to dad, jumping into his arms.

Everyone seemed to be in a good mood so far, so I was hopeful that we were going to have a good trip to the island. Well, that was until mom decided I clearly needed to dress more appropriately to travel on an airplane to a tropical island. "Ember, dear, since when are jeans and a button down something a young woman wears to Hawaii?"

I looked down at what I was wearing. "Since, like, right now," I said, waving my arms all over my body.

Pointing at Sawyer. "Look at your sister. She has on a nice flowery sun dress with a beautiful straw hat." I glared at Sawyer, who just shrugged and looked away.

We landed in Hawaii around lunchtime, which was perfect since I hadn't eaten breakfast. After checking in at the resort, we headed straight for the restaurant, which was attached to the pool. I certainly wouldn't complain if we spent every Christmas like this.

"What are you going to order, Em?" Mom asked as she looked over her own menu.

I had just picked up my menu and started to glance at the drinks. "I think I am going to drink my lunch, mother." I smirked.

"Ember Rue, not in front of the children, seriously show some maturity like you, sister." Mom snapped at me.

"If this is how the whole vacation is going to be, mom, I am going to sit by the pool and talk to none of you."

Sawyer stepped in before we really started to argue. "Enough, both of you. We are here to have a good time and enjoy being together as a family. If we are going to do that, you both need to put aside your snide comments, learn to tell when each other is joking, and for god sakes drop the sister comparison comments, Mom."

"Yeah." I added.

"Ember, knock it off." Sawyer said.

"Grow up, Ember." Mom mumbled under her breath.

Sawyer took a deep breath and looked at Bella. "You just might be the most mature female in this family, Bell."

"I know." Bella agreed.

After an amazing lunch of coconut prawns and a salmon BLT, we went to our rooms and unpack before meeting at the pool. We booked two suites. Sawyer, Todd and the kids in one. Me and my parents are in another.

Walking into our suite, we found ourselves in a small kitchen. It was just the right size to have a snack or a cup of coffee in the morning. I skipped exploring the living room that was right off the kitchen and went straight out to the patio to find a dramatic view of the ocean that I imagined would accompany amazing sunsets in the evenings.

Going back inside, I saw that on either side of the living area, my parents and I would each have our own private bedroom and bathroom. I figured it couldn't be that bad sharing a suite with my parents with this kind of setup.

After getting settled into our rooms, we all put on our bathing suits and headed to the pool. Once there, we all jumped in. except for mom, who found a lounge chair and got herself all squared away with her book.

I was practicing my back float when I heard my dad screaming, "Cramp! Cramp!" I swam to the surface to see dad bobbing up and down in the water, inhaling water each time he went underwater.

Todd immediately swam like crazy towards dad, grabbed his arm, and pulled him to shallower water. We all gathered around dad to make sure he was okay. "I'm okay," he said, with each cough spitting up pool water.

When I looked over at mom, she was turning to the next page in her book, continuing to read, unphased by the fact that her husband almost drowned.

"Don't worry Mom, Dad is okay, he didn't die." I yelled from the side of the pool.

"I see that, honey. Good news," Mom replied, never looking up from her book.

Sawyer and I shared a disgusted look. "What the fuck?" Sawyer mouthed to me.

I threw my hands in the air, resolved to the fact that our mother did, in fact, want our father dead.

After we got dad comfortable in a chair next to mom, he fell asleep. Mom ignored him and kept reading her book. The kids seemed content swimming in the pool, so the three of us hit the tiki bar and discuss what to do with mom and dad, because clearly something had to change before someone got hurt.

I ordered three pina coladas at the bar and took them to the small table where we could keep an eye on the children, plus Alex and Bella. "I honestly think mom might have one of those brain tumors that is making her violent. Sawyer, you're a doctor. What do you think?" I asked.

Sawyer drink was halfway to her mouth when she stopped to consider this, then she continued to take a drink before answering my question. "No, I don't so, she wouldn't have any impulse control, and most likely would have tried something by now."

Sitting there, we all nodded our heads in agreement, then Todd made the next observation. "Don't you find it interesting though how your mom never did anything about the affairs? I mean, why do you think she stayed with him all these years if she hates him so much?"

We all continued to nod in agreement. Sawyer chimed with a brilliant plot twist. "Because she is waiting until we all go on a tropical vacation to make it look like an accident. Come on guys, you read all the time how elderly people die on these islands: shark attacks, drownings, heart attacks, and hiking accidents. She knew exactly what she was doing when she suggested this little 'family' vacation."

Now we were all aggressively nodding in agreement. "Sawyer, you just hit the nail on the head. We need to do an intervention. But when, how?"

Swallowing the last of her pina colada, Sawyer suggested, "We are here for eight days, seven nights. We don't want to bombard them with murder accusations, especially with the kids around."

"True story." I agreed.

Sawyer continued. "Okay, so tonight is Sunday. That leaves us with another seven days of babysitting our parents. We don't have any activities planned this whole week, so we should be safe, because they will never be left alone. Ember, you keep your eyes and ears open at night. Todd and I will take the day shift. Then on our last night, after the luau, we will sit them down and settle this nonsense once and for all. All in? Go Team Parents?"

We all put our hands in the middle over the table, one on top of the others, and shouted, "Go, Team Parents!"

Babysitting mom and dad in the evenings after dinner so far this week had been uneventful, but tonight after dinner something was definitely up. The three of us were sitting at the kitchen table talking about the luau the next night when dad said he wasn't going. Mom said she would stay back with dad and us kids should go and have a good time. This was weird, because after the luau, we were supposed to execute the intervention. I couldn't let down 'Team Parents.'

I put my foot down. "Everyone is going to the luau. No arguments from the two of you. Alex and Bella would be devastated if you didn't go." I had no problem using my niece and nephew as leverage.

"I just don't want to watch your mother drooling over some muscle-bound guys in grass skirts dancing around on stage." Dad expressed.

"Me? You George. You will probably try to dance with those ladies in the coconut bras." Mom snapped back.

"What the hell is wrong with you two? When did going to a traditional luau become a strip club? You are both going, and you will behave yourselves. For Christ's sakes. Now go to bed. It's past eleven." I dropped my head in my hands. I can't believe I just sent my parents to bed.

\*\*\*

The kids were back in their suite, where we set them up with popcorn and a movie. It was time for family intervention. We had been practicing all week. Being the family manager, Sawyer was going to kick us off with a small speech about love and acceptance. Then Todd was going to jump in about how important it was to come together as a family to support each other when things are tough and that we can get through anything as a family. My job was to take notes.

Mom and Dad sat down on the sofa, Todd and Sawyer took the two chairs. I brought a chair from the kitchen into the living room and sat it next to Todd.

Sawyer poised herself at the edge of her chair. "Mom, Dad, first we want to tell you how much we all love you–"

Mom knew exactly what was going on. "What the hell are you three up to? If you have something to say, just say it. Is someone sick? Are you getting a divorce? Are you pregnant Sawyer? What is it? Just say it?"

Todd jumped in, solely because he had a role to play and didn't know what else to do except to execute on said role. "Mom, Dad, as a family it is so important that we work through hard time–"

Dad had about enough of this as well. "Todd, what are you doing, son? You sound like one of the girls. What the hell is going on?"

Finally, I just jumped in, because obviously the only thing I had written down so far were two angry faces. "Mom, Dad seriously thinks you are trying to kill him, and we think he might be right. You have been acting super weird."

Mom burst out laughing. "What? Why?" She started laughing so hard that she got up and ran to the bathroom, holding her crotch. "I'm going to pee myself," she squealed, as she slammed the bathroom door shut.

Dad's eyes narrowed as he stared at the three of us. "What is wrong with you guys? Now I'm a dead man for sure."

Todd walked over to the couch and sat next to dad, putting his hand on his shoulder to show his support. "George, let's not overreact. We are going to get both of you through this. That is why we are having this conversation."

We heard the toilet flush, and mom walked out wiping the tears from her eyes with a tissue. "Oh my god, that is the funniest thing I've heard in a long time, girls."

Sawyer patted the chair where Todd was sitting. "Mom, please sit down, this is serious. Dad thinks you are plotting to kill him. He has heard you talking on the phone, saying things about covering up his murder."

"On the phone? When?" inquired Mom, still giggling and wiping her tears.

"It's been consistent Joyce, every Thursday you call your hitman and plan my murder. I can hear you from the living room. You think I am sleeping in my chair, but I'm not. I'm wide awake, Joyce, listening to every little detail."

Mom started laughing uncontrollably again. "Oh my god, this is killing me. The best, this really is the best. I cannot wait to tell the girls. They are going to get such a kick out of this."

"What girls?" I asked Mom confused.

"The girls in my murder mystery book club," replied mom, still laughing.

"Book club?" We all said simultaneously.

"Yes, what your dad is overhearing is my Thursday morning murder mystery book club. Sometimes we really get into it and do a little improv on Zoom, but it's just our book club. That is probably what your dad is hearing."

Sawyer was the first to bring it all together and ask the real question. "What is really going on here? I mean, Dad, why would you really think that Mom would ever want to murder you? What have you done so wrong that would push her to want to do something like that?"

Dad lowered his head and said, "Well girls, I haven't always been a great husband, or father, for that matter."

"George, stop, this is nor the time or the place to talk to our daughters about this," Mom said.

Dad waved mom off. "No, it's fine. They are old enough to know the truth about their father. Back when you girls were younger, I drank a lot and had some female friends. Your mom stayed with me for you girls. I quit drinking and have been faithful ever since. We went to therapy for many years and have a very loving relationship now, or so I thought. But then I started hearing these phone calls and with everything going on this year with you Ember, I guess I just started wonder if she was having regrets and wanted to leave me, or worse." He made a slitting motion at his throat with his finger.

"Oh, so this is my fault?" I asked, now completely pissed off.

"Ember, you didn't make your dad drink or cheat all those years ago, although sometimes I do wonder if you are even my biological daughter." She laughed.

"She's kidding, Ember. She's your mom. She would have had to be the one to cheat for your dad to not be your biological father," said Todd.

"Yes, thank you for the medical explanation, Dr. Todd. I get her very not funny joke."

"And George, I want to kill you for a lot of things, like leaving your underwear on the bathroom floor and your dentures on the kitchen counter, but I have forgiven you for your past affairs many years ago. You're stuck with me, you old goat. I love you."

"I love you too, honey. So you really don't want to kill me?" Dad looked at mom for any sort of reassurance.

Mom grabbed dad's hand and winked. "Are we done here? I am tired and want to go to bed. Sleep with one eye open, Georgie." Mom walked over to dad. "Boo!" She kissed him on the tip of his nose, then walked into the bedroom and started laughing hysterically again.

Sawyer, Todd and I all looked at each other and shook our heads.

"I guess they are okay, then," Todd chimed in.

"I'm done." I got up and walked out the front door, leaving my sister and Todd in the living room to deal with dad.

I reached the beach just in time to see the sun starting to set. I loved feeling the teeniest of pebbles push between my toes as I walked along the sandy beach, wondering how my life got to this point. This time last year looked completely different. I was truly happy. I had everything.

I wanted Rayna here with me. Walking hand in hand, stopping to pull her hips into mine, run my fingers through her hair, along her cheek, draw her chin towards my lips to feel her soft kisses...just one more time. I would give anything to just feel her soft lips on mine. I pulled my phone out of my pocket and selected Rayna's number to call her.

"Hello. Hello. HELLO!"

I tapped 'end' on the call as I sucked in a deep breath and continued my stroll down the shore. I stopped and sat down on the edge of the water so I could feel the waves wash under my legs. It felt calming to have the warmth of the saltiness on my skin, so I moved further in to let more of the water rush over my body. I wasn't happy, I wasn't sad. In this moment, I just was. I laid back in the water in awe as the color of the sky went from soft pinks to deep reds while the sun graciously gave center stage to the moon. I witnessed this beautiful transition for the next twenty minutes, it was enough...for now.

# Chapter Twenty-Nine

*39 hours until my next session*

*Being back home from Hawaii is a relief. I missed Stormy so much. I thought I wanted this vacation, but it ended up being one of the loneliest trips I've ever taken. I tried to hide the pain, but I think everyone could see that the food, the family bonding, the beautiful scenery didn't just make everything better. I need to be the one who makes everything better. I think I am starting to realize that. I just have no idea how. This trip wasn't the easy fix we were all hoping for.*

*So, here we are, 'new year, new me,' I think that's what they say, anyway. I am going to start this year off by telling Dr. Kayla how I feel about her. How these 167 hours between sessions are more than unbearable, they have been physically painful. That I write in this journal with no relief. I tried to fill my time socializing with new people, but no one has been able to fill this dead space in my heart. I've worked harder at my job, but it's brought me no joy. I've tried new adventures, traveled, attempted romances, and become more numb with every interaction. I need to tell her I really like her, and I don't know how not to feel this way, or even if I want to not feel this way. She makes me feel more cared about than anyone has made me feel in a long time.*

*Ember*

***

I sat in Dr. Kayla's office dreading the conversation I was about to have with her, but I knew if I didn't have it, I would not be able to keep coming to therapy.

I heard the familiar squeal of the door and looked up to see Dr. Kayla standing there with a smile on her face. My stomach started to twirl, not the nervous twirl, but excited to see her twirl. I smiled back. Oh *my, Ember, you flirt.* Then I snapped twice into the air to show I was present. *Jesus Ember, pull yourself together.*

"Take a seat, Ember. I would like to talk with you about something today if that is, okay?" Dr. Kayla said as she took her own seat.

I sat down in my seat and leaned back. "Of course, what's up? Am I in trouble?" I really was curious if I broke any therapy rules.

She leaned forwarded, looking very serious, and asked, "What do you want to get out of therapy, besides not feeling broken? I only ask because we have been seeing each other for a couple of months now and I want to make sure that you feel you are making progress here. It would be helpful for me to understand a little more about what, 'not feeling broken,'" she did air quotes, "looks like to you. Maybe over the next few sessions we could start to explore this more? Go another layer deeper? What do you think?"

I leaned forward and looked Dr. Kayla directly in the eyes. "I like you."

She tilted her head with a confused look on her face, "Well I like you too, Ember. I think we work well together."

I felt a little frustrated as I shifted in my seat. "No, what I mean is, I really like you. I have, like, romantic feelings for you. I think about you when I am trying to go to sleep, I think about you when I am not trying to go to sleep, I want to hold your hand, I want to take you out for pizza and a beer, do you like beer?" I shook my head to have her dismiss that question.

"Sometimes I think about calling you, but then I don't because that would be weird, right? That would be weird to call your therapist out of the blue. I think about how when you smile, how those little creases next to your eyes smile too, and there's your laugh. It makes my stomach spin, but in a good way. The way you always stared at me, at first, I hated the way you would stare at me. Now I never want you to stop. I love the way you lean in to get closer to me when I talk to you. I like the way you say big words that I have to look up when I get home. I should probably stop talking now, huh?" I lowered my head, but kept my eyes focused on her reaction.

For once, Dr. Kayla didn't hesitate to respond. "Thank you for being so vulnerable, Ember. I am sure it wasn't easy to share your feelings, especially not knowing how I would react. A lot of times when a client comes into the therapy room with romantic feelings, I want to honor and give them space to talk through them to see where the root of these feelings might come from. You are very brave to share such special feelings with me, and I feel honored you felt safe to do so."

I pondered her words for a few seconds before I asked. "So, do you like beer, then?" Dr. Kayla laughed.

"I do like beer, yes, but we should focus on what is important here, and that is you and what you are experiencing right now."

I nodded my head and sat back. "How do I stop? Stop thinking about you...us?" I didn't even realize I was crying until I felt a tear drop on my hand, so I grabbed a tissue so I wouldn't be a blubbering mess.

"Do you want to stop thinking about these things right now? Do you find comfort in these thoughts?" she asked.

"I do. Is that weird?"

She smiled, "It's completely normal, Ember and together I think we'll be able to work through this."

"I think I need to leave." I stood up and just walked out without saying another word.

I flew out of Dr. Kayla's office, devastated. This was not the reaction I wanted. I felt so stupid. She was so nice and professional about it, but I don't think I could ever go back. I will never go back. I felt so embarrassed. I had been having these ridiculous fantasies that she might actually like me too.

"I'm such a fucking idiot." I mumbled to no one as I opened the front door to the liquor store. I certainly wasn't going back to work today. I had already called Bev and told her I would meet her at Ollie's for happy hour later, but I needed something now and while looking down the tequila aisle, I knew exactly what that something was.

Hours later, I wobbled down the street, using the building as my support to not fall over. I hit send on Rayna's name on my cell phone.

"Hello. Who is this? Why do you keep calling me? Stop calling me." The call ended.

I stared at the blank screen on my phone. "Rayna..." I muttered.

I was either late or Bev was early because the pitcher of beer was half gone and so was I. "Bev. Bev'er. Beveragely. How are you, my best friend?" I called out as I was swaying towards the table. Bev noticed I was a bit unsteady on my feet, so she hurried around the table and caught me before I lost my balance, then helped me up onto the bar stool.

"Ember, you're completely shit faced. What the hell is wrong with you? It's barely fucking dinner time." Bev sounded pissed.

I patted Bev's hand like she always did to me. "Bevie, language. I'm fine, I'm an asshole, but I am totally one hundred percent fine."

"Honey, I don't think you are fine." She sounded increasingly agitated.

"Hey Bev, do you want to hear a ghost story?"

Bev's anger quickly turned to concern as she shook her head no. "Ember, please don't do this. You're drunk. I can see you are obviously upset about something. I'm here for you, honey. Whatever it is, it's going to be okay. Is there someone I can call? Your sister, or maybe your mom?"

I threw my head back and laughed. "Someone to call, oh Bevie. I love you. But no. There is no one left to call anymore. I've tried to call Rayna, you know, a hundred times, but she won't answer. Do you know why?" I slammed my hand on the table.

Bev jumped at the vibration of my hand hitting the wood. She just stared at me with tears in her eyes. "Yes, Ember, I know why."

"You know, when I left for work that morning, she was sitting at the kitchen table drinking her coffee. She pulled me on to her lap and said, 'I'm going to miss you so much.' She kissed me and held me so tight. I didn't even think anything was wrong. I had no idea anything was even wrong. I just went to work feeling like the most loved woman in the world."

Bev grabbed my arm. "You were the most loved woman in the world."

"Hmm. Really? Then why was it when I came home, Rayna still in that same chair, still in her pajamas? I asked her, Bev, I said, 'Rayna, what are you doing, honey? You look like you haven't moved all day?' Then I touched her, and she fell over, limp, into my arms. She was so cold, like her skin was freezing when I touched her. My god, her eyes were so empty, and I couldn't get them to connect to my mine. I kept trying to hold her head up to make our eyes connect. I thought if I could get our eyes to connect, she would start to breathe, but they just kept looking right through me. I tried to get her to breathe. I tried everything I could think of to get her to take just one breath. I swear I did."

I stopped talking for a second and noticed Bev was crying, wondering if she even knew any of this. I thought she needed to know. Bev needed to know this, so I kept going. "I pulled Rayna to the floor, but she was so heavy that she just fell on top of me and all I could do was just hold her and scream. I screamed and screamed for her to just take one breath, but she wouldn't. I screamed at her for ignoring me, Bev, I thought she was ignoring me and that is why she wouldn't breathe. I did everything to warm her back up. I wrapped her in my coat and held her as tight as I could and kept screaming at her to stop ignoring me, that if she would just fucking listen to me, she would be able to start to breathe again. I wouldn't leave her, so I screamed at the door until finally someone came to help us. Larry was the only person who came, but when he saw us, he left again. Stormy ran out from under the table where he was curled up in Rayna's slippers. He was just a baby, a little puppy Bev. He didn't understand. He came over to her and kept licking the back of her arm. He was trying so hard to make her better, too. We both tried so fucking hard."

"Ember, it's okay to stop. You don't have to tell me all of this. I know she's gone. I was there with you at her funeral. I know how you lost her." Bev said, reaching across the table to grab my hand.

"Really, so you know, when the police and paramedics arrived, they kept trying to take Rayna out of my arms, but I wouldn't let them. No one was going to take her from me. The police had to pull me out from under her body, they had to drag me out of the kitchen screaming as I begged them to let me go, so I could go lay back down with my her. I just wanted to keep holding her. That was the last time I saw her, Bev. They took my Rayna."

I started crying so hard, and Bev came over to my side of the table to hold me. I looked up at Bev and finished. "The paramedics gave me a shot to calm me down. The last thing I remember that night was Sawyer lying in bed with me. She told me Rayna took two bottles of pills, that she killed herself. They didn't even try to help her. 'She's gone,' they said. 'She died sometime between nine and eleven in the morning, they said. An hour or so after I left for work."

"Ember." I looked over, and Sawyer was standing behind me with tears rolling down her face. "Let's go home, okay? I will drive you home, honey."

The tears were spilling down my face too. "I called her phone tonight, Sawyer, somebody else answered. It's not her phone anymore."

"I know. The police department called me and asked that you quit calling that number. It's reassigned to someone else. I am so sorry, honey." She stroked my hair.

I knocked her hand away from my head. "No, they can't do that. Then I can't hear her voicemail anymore. I need to be able to hear her voice. Please, no, don't let them do that, Sawyer. Please." I clenched her coat and begged her not to let them take away the one thing I still had left of Rayna.

I pushed past Sawyer and ran out of the bar and up the street to my office. I wasn't there long before they found me, and Sawyer took me home. She spent the night with me. She laid next to me in bed and held me like when we were kids, and when Rayna died. She stroked my hair and squeezed me tighter every time I started to cry.

***

When I woke up in the morning, I was drained, but ready to talk, ready to heal. I knew I couldn't live like this anymore. It was time to find a way to not let go, but to move on.

There was a knock at the door, but I wasn't in the mood to answer it, so I let Sawyer go see who it was. "Ember, you have a guest. I am going to run out to get us coffee."

I glanced up and saw Isla standing inside the door with flowers and a stuffed puppy. "Hi," she said.

I slowly moved towards the door and took the flowers and stuffed puppy. "Awe, thank you so much. I am not sure what I did to deserve this, but you are very sweet for the thought."

Turning around to go get a vase to put the flowers in, I felt Isla grab my elbow and turn me back to face her. She pulled me into her arms and brushed my hair away from my forehead. "Hi," she said again.

A smile crept across my lips as I stared into her eyes. "Hi."

She pulled me in close to her, our hips softly touching. After a gentle kiss, she said. "I talked to your sister last night."

I started to pull away, but she pulled me in closer. "It's okay, I have been waiting for the right moment to tell you how I feel since the day I locked myself out of my apartment. It's just every time I tried to, or got close enough, you ran away. I like you. I more than like you. I know about Rayna. I have for a while, and it's okay if we take things super slow. I will be as patient as you need me to be. I just don't want to lose the opportunity to be with you, Ember."

I had no idea Isla felt this way about me. I was in utter shock. "But you're out of my league."

Isla laughed. "I have no idea what that even means in the context of love."

My heart fluttered. "I really like you too. I just never in a million years thought you would ever be interested in someone like me. I appreciate you being willing to be patient with me. I have some work to do, as you can probably tell, but I am ready to take a first step, and I would love that first step to be with you. I can't promise when I will be ready for the second step, or what that might look like, but if you are willing to stick around to find out, we might end up being something pretty damn amazing."

I wrapped my arms around her waist and nuzzled my head into her chest. God, it felt good to be this close to her.

Isla lifted my chin and kissed me so tenderly that even Stormy started barking and jumping on us to show his approval. "I think Stormy would rip me apart if I didn't wait around to see what was in store for us. I don't want to be with anyone else but you, Ember."

"I don't want to be with anyone else either. Thank you for waiting for me, Isla."

# Chapter Thirty

Riding up the elevator, I knew it was going to be awkward seeing Bev for the first time since my breakdown a month ago. Sawyer had called my work to explain everything. They all knew the circumstances of Rayna's death and everything I had been through, so they were happy to support my time to heal.

I had a few things to do before going back to work officially next week. I was only here today to sign some paperwork before my leave of absence ended. I never took any time off after Rayna's suicide. I just buried myself in my work and holed up in my apartment with Stormy, so HR highly recommended that I take a few weeks to rest.

I couldn't bring myself to move out of the apartment after Rayna died. We found that place together; we made it our home. I felt like her spirit was still there in some ways. Isla and I talked about getting another place together one of these days. I think it will help me move on.

We were taking it slow, but every day I spent with Isla made me realize I was glad I was doing the work to become a healthier me, so I could eventually be a better us. Her patience with me was truly impressive.

The elevator doors opened to a crowd of people cheering and clapping. Bev walked towards me. "Fucking awkward Bevie." We hugged each other so damn tight. "What is going on?"

I looked around the room to see everyone wearing the same shirts, just in a different color of the rainbow. "What's up with the shirts?" I asked.

Bethany walked up to me and gave me a hug, which I squirmed out of. "Remember our campaign for the New York fashion designer? You were supposed to help come up with the 'You are' slogan..."

I genuinely felt bad that I dropped that ball on that. "I know Bethany, I am really sorry–"

Bethany put her hand up to stop me from continuing to talk. "Well, after the evening you broke into the office, during your, well, 'episode,' I came into my office the next morning to find this." She turned around to show me the easel that said 'You Are...'

I looked at the easel, perplexed. "Okay, what exactly does this mean?"

Bethany gave me an emphatic look. "Ember, that night you came here from the bar. You broke into my office and wrote this on the easel. We sent it to the Fashion Designers, and they loved it.

I looked at the easel and saw that I had finished the 'You Are' phrase with "Needed" in my handwriting.

"Your one word is taking us to the next level. We told them your story and they want to start a suicide prevention campaign in Rayna's honor, of course, with your permission. For every article of clothing sold, a portion of the profits will go towards suicide prevention education. You are needed, Ember. Thank you!"

"Technically, I didn't break into the office building or your office. I have a key to both." I defended myself.

Bev grabbed my arm to stop me from digging myself into a hole and handed me a cup of coffee. We walked into my cubicle for a little privacy. "Wow, I didn't expect any of that. I'm taken a little off guard by all of this. I don't even remember coming in here that night, let alone writing on that easel."

Bev put her hand to her chest. "Well, it's certainly not a night I will forget anytime soon." Bev leaned on the edge of my desk to continue telling me about the events of the next day. "Monday morning, Bethany was racing around the office asking who wrote on the easel. We finally narrowed it down to you, but you were off work with strict instructions from HR that no one was to bother you, so we just got to work." I just stared lovingly at Bev.

"Why are you looking at me like that Ember? Did you get in my top drawer?"

"Shut up, I'm having a moment. I love you, Bev. You truly are my best friend. I don't know what I'd ever do without you."

We hugged again. "So what are doing with your last few days off?" Bev asked.

"Well, Isla and I are going to the cemetery to visit Rayna's grave. I think I am finally ready to say goodbye in person. She said she would stay in the car and give me all the time I needed. I am nervous, Bev, but it's time. Then I have an appointment with Dr. Kayla for my first in-person session since that night at Ollie's, so that should be interesting. We've only talked on the phone to get me through a few hard moments. I am starting regular sessions again. I am looking forward to really getting better, starting the healing process.

"You call me if you need anything, you hear me? I mean it. Especially if you need a little a little giggle green to make you smile," Bev said, looking over the cubicle wall to make sure no one was listening.

Shaking my head. "I'm fine Bev, I look forward to coming back to work on Monday though. A little normalcy sounds nice. I miss the hell out of you."

"I miss you too, dog." We hugged each other so damn tight.

\*\*\*

Walking into my apartment, I tossed my keys on the side table by the door, but they hit the floor instead. I knelt over to pick them up only to see Stormy trotting out of the bedroom with his little tuxedo on and a rose in his mouth. "Well, don't you look handsome, little man?"

My eyes rose to see Isla standing there in nothing but a T-shirt, the same T-shirt I saw her wearing in the hallway just a few weeks ago. Next to Isla was the painting of Stormy and I in the park. It was breathtaking.

My eyes slowly shut, then I opened back up to see her walking towards me. This wasn't a dream. I could tell she had just gotten out of the shower by the look of her wet hair and the smell of her coconut milk body wash in the air.

"Ember, I know we said we would take things slow, but I want you. I don't think I can wait any longer. Will you have me?"

I reached for the bottom of my shirt and pulled it over my head as I walked towards Isla. I grabbed her by the waist and walked her backwards until she fell onto my bed. I inched on top of her and slid my leg between her thighs while I loosened her lips with my tongue. "I want to be with you too, Isla." I whispered softly in her ear as I moved lower to kiss her neck.

I was eager to feel how much she wanted me. I slipped my hand into her panties. I could feel the heat of her wetness as I undressed her. I started to trace the inside of her thigh ever so lightly with the tips of my fingers. I wanted to take in every inch of the softness of her skin. I finished undressing us both, and crawled back into bed, where I lay flat on my stomach. I closed my eyes as my breathing started to speed up. I was quickly losing control as I felt Isla's hard nipples graze my skin with each of her kisses, which started at my lower back and moved up to between my shoulder blades. "I love the way your skin tastes," said Isla. The heat from her breath made me shiver as the goose bumps grew across my body.

I loved hearing the words she whispered, feeling the warmth of her skin as her body pressed against mine, the way her lips never left my body while her fingers softly brushed down the sides of my ribs and over my hips. I was going insane, just wanting her to make me scream.

Then she flipped me over, lowered her kisses from my neck to my chest, rolling her tongue around my nipples and down my stomach until she found her mouth between my thighs. Isla pulled my hips towards her, bringing me inside her mouth, where I started to throb. The pressure continued to build until I couldn't handle it any longer and I exploded with a loud moan, begging her not to stop. I literally had left my body.

I pulled Isla up to me. I kissed her eyelids, then her lips. I then flipped her on her back, where I saw she had tears in her eyes. "I love you, Ember."

"I love you too, Isla." She pulled me to her shoulder, and she held me so tightly. We spent the rest of the night exploring every inch of each other's bodies, laughing, talking, dreaming, falling asleep in each other's arms, waking up, and pleasing each other all over again. I eventually laid in her arms and let the softness of my breath flow across her chest as I fell into a deep sleep after hours of making love.

I woke up the next morning to find a note on my nightstand from Isla. "I will be back at ten to get you. I love you baby, -Isla," with the cutest little heart. My second Isla original piece. I will cherish it forever.

I sat up slowly, feeling the most well-rested I had in months. Stormy jumped up on the bed and stretched out his little body, and then fell next to my side. I twirled his ears between my fingers. "What do you think, buddy? Do you like Isla? Should we keep her around?" Stormy's head popped up, and he sprung out of bed and ran to the door like he expected her to be there. I took that as a yes.

Isla showed up at 10:00 a.m. on the dot and we walked down to the diner to grab some breakfast. Strolling down the street, I felt Isla's hand ease in mine, and I looked over at her glowing face. I was so happy, but it was a bit confusing to go from losing Rayna and still processing her being gone and moving on with Isla. I suddenly got a pit in my stomach. Was it too soon to move on? What if Rayna knew and could see me like this with Isla? I removed my hand from Isla's and slipped it into my pocket, then opened the diner door with my other hand.

"Sit wherever you ladies like," Jean yelled from the counter.

I told Isla to go grab the booth in the corner by the window so I could go talk to Jean for a second. I watched her walk over to sit down, oddly enough on the opposite side of the table that I typically sat at. *Hmmm, maybe we are meant to be together.* I thought to myself.

I turned around quickly to nab Jean before she got to our booth. "Jean, I need to talk to you for a minute." I said urgently.

"Sure hon, what's going on? Who's the woman? She's cute." Jean noted with a smirk.

I sat her down on one of the bar stools at the counter. "That's what I want to talk to you about. Jean, we had a good run, but I've moved on. I met a woman, she's great, her name is Isla. I don't want her to know about us, what we had between us. You and I had something special that I will never forget. Please don't be jealous. I think you are really going to like her."

Jean smiled. "Look, baby girl, what you went through with Rayna, no one should ever go through. I am so happy that you found someone who makes you happy. I think I will be okay. No, I know I will be okay. Now go sit down with your date and I will bring you two some menu's."

I slid off the bar stool. "I'd hug you, but, you know." I nodded towards Isla.

"Of course, sweetie." Jean winked at me.

# Chapter Thirty-One

We were both quiet as we entered the cemetery where Rayna was buried. Every now and then, our car would drive through the patches of fog hanging in the middle of the road and dissipate the mist into nothingness. I sat in the passenger seat, staring out the window, waiting for Rayna's headstone to come into view. When it finally did, I just pointed in the general direction, but said nothing. Isla understood this cue and simply pulled over.

She took my hand in hers. "Are you sure you want to do this alone?"

I squeezed her hand. "No, but I think I need to," I answered with a shaky voice.

They say it's disrespectful to walk on top of someone's grave. I imagine it was in principle. I mean, they are dead, so they don't know it was happening. But just in case their spirits were hanging out here watching me, I didn't want to piss anyone off by trampling on top of their graves, so I took my time, being very careful where I stepped until I reached Rayna's headstone.

I hadn't been here since the funeral. Everything looked different. This was the first time I had seen the bench her parents had installed in her memory and her headstone was now in place. I sat down on the center of the bench. It was a stone bench, cold and damp from the weeks of rain we've had. I didn't expect to find comfort where I sat, that's not why I was there. I was there to find some resemblance of closure.

The headstone had a picture of Rayna, one I would have never picked for her. It was almost like her parents wanted to remember a person she was long before her suicide. Maybe from a time they felt she wasn't broken, or they thought she was happy. It was her college graduation picture. She hated that picture.

The headstone said, "Rayna - loving daughter, sister, and friend." I wonder if I was the 'friend' they were referring to? Everyone knew we were a couple, including her family. It was all fine. We all got along, although we never kept in touch. They had so many questions that I just couldn't answer. In the absence of any suicide note, we all had the same questions. Why did she do it?

Rayna and I were happy. We had plans. We loved each other deeper than I ever thought I could possibly love anything on this earth.

"What the fuck happened, Rayna!" I yelled at her picture. "Why did you do this to us? I could have made it better, you know? I swear if you would have just let me try, I would have made it better. I swear, I would have done anything to make it better. For fuck's sake." I kicked the gravel at my feet, knowing some of the rocks would hit her headstone.

I tried to just breathe, so I wouldn't end up having a panic attack in the middle of this place. I kept trying to focus on my breathing. I sucked in a nice, deep breath through my nose and pushed it slowly through my lips. I continued this for a few seconds. "I am never going to know why you did this to us, to yourself, am I? I am just trying to figure this all out, Rayna. Trying to understand what to do next, how to live without you, how to live with myself, how to move on, how not to blame myself for not seeing the signs, or how to maybe fucking love someone again."

I pulled my journal out of my bag. I held it in the air at Rayna's picture. "Fun fact, I am in therapy. She told me to write in this journal. It's supposed to be what gets me through the crippling hours between each therapy session. Sometimes I want to write to you, but I don't know what to say. I don't know what to do. But I do know I don't want to end up like you. There, I said it. I love you completely, with my whole being. I will never love anyone like I loved you, but I have to keep going, it's just…it's not my time. I have more to do here."

I closed my eyes and rested my journal against my chest. I then put it back in my bag. "I probably won't come back here again. But I want you to know that I will always love you, god, I will always love you so fucking bad. I need to be honest with you. I met a woman. Her name is Isla. She is sweet and nice. I think you'd like her. Maybe you could give me a sign that you're cool with me, you know, moving on?"

I took another deep breath and gathered my things. I stood up from the stone bench and put my hand on the top of Rayna's headstone. "I guess this is it. Goodbye Rayna."

I stood there for a few more minutes and started to brush away the pines needles that had collected around her headstone when I heard some branches cracking. I tried to make out the image through the thick fog, then I saw movement from behind one of the large tombstones. My throat thickened, and I whispered, "Rayna?"

There she was, the same spotted deer from the mountains. I didn't dare move, and neither of us broke our gaze. I started to weep and reached out my hand towards her, but she made no effort to move towards me. She just stared.

I lowered my hand. "Be free, baby girl, be free. Your cycle ends here." Without looking back at the deer or Rayna's headstone, I turned and walked back to the car.

***

Lisa looked genuinely happy to see me when I walked into the therapy office. "It's so good to see you, Ember. How have you—"

I held up my hand to stop her from making a big deal about my return and went straight to my corner. I like to be consistent.

I only sat there for maybe thirty seconds before I heard the familiar squeal of the door and looked up to see Dr. Kayla standing there, smiling at me.

I walked past her without making eye contact. We weren't there yet. A lot had happened since we last saw each other and looking at her directly in the face scared the hell out of me.

I sat in my seat, Dr. Kayla in hers. I took the stone she let me borrow out of my pocket and rolled it between my fingers. I hesitated for a moment before deciding to place it back in the bowl.

I released a long exhale as I looked over at Dr. Kayla, who was sitting there waiting for me to speak, which I decided not to do. I just lowered my gaze to the floor. *This room is too damn quiet,* I thought to myself.

I looked again over to find Dr. Kayla with the same look on her face that she always had. I could tell she wasn't judging me for the way I acted the last time I was here, or for the things I admitted to her. She just looked at me with love. The same look I mistook for mutual attraction. The look I now understood as something completely different. It was simple, really. It was just the love that only a therapist has for their client. It's a 'unique' kind of love. That 'I have your back' kind of love. 'I will stop at nothing to help you heal' kind of love. 'You are safe here' kind of love. It's an 'unspoken' kind of love that you always feel, but words you will never hear.

I reached into my bag and brought out my journal. At this point, it had coffee stains all over it, maybe a few drops of wine as well. Stormy had chewed off the little leather string that was sewn into the binding, serving as a bookmark. I set the journal on my lap, wrapping my finger around the edge of the book. I sighed and smiled at Dr. Kayla.

"I don't know if you want to read this or not, but I think it is a good way to help you understand how I have been spending my time between sessions. For better or worse." I blushed. "It's what has kept me together when I didn't think I would make it through each week. I would literally count every one of the 167 hours until I could come here again. Writing in this book is what kept me going. Made me feel connected to you and this space. I imagine this is something that might be helpful to me even after I leave here someday. I mean, not today. I am way too fucked up to leave therapy today. Way too fucked up. Like super fucked up. Who's fucked up? Me." I whistled and pointed to myself.

Dr. Kayla smiled, shaking her head slightly, "I don't think you are fucked up. I think you've had some big experiences. Is there anything you want to share from your journal or if you are okay if we get started?" Dr. Kayla asked.

I thought about what I might share from my journal but decided for today's session I wanted to see where she was going to take us. "Nope, nothing from my journal. I am totally into this, full on ready for today. Let's do this." *I think I am going to puke.*

"Okay then, I want you to know that I have spoken with your sister and although I did listen to everything she had to say, whatever we have discussed in our sessions has remained confidential. She told me about Rayna and what happened. A lot of things make more sense now, so if and when you are ready, we can start working through some of those feelings. It must have been such a traumatic experience for you."

"Yes, I guess I just figured if I just kept telling myself that she broke up with me that maybe she would come back. That it wasn't as final as her being gone, you know, dead. God, it's still so hard to say that word. I miss her terribly. I am ready to accept Rayna being gone, that her suicide was her choice, her very painful choice. I also believed she loved me with all her heart and that her leaving me the way she did had nothing to do with me. I will forever love her, but I need to move on. And that is the work I need us to do. I need your help to rebuild and move on. I am ready, Dr. Kayla."

"I am glad to hear you say that, Ember. We can start at whatever pace feels right for you. Sawyer shared a lot of details with me, so I don't expect you to share anything you don't want to. We can navigate this in whatever way makes sense to you."

"Yeah, Sawyer told me you two talked. I am okay that she reached out to you. I want to apologize for being all over the place, and not just being honest with why I was coming into therapy. If I was honest, maybe I could have avoided the 'Ember's Big Meltdown.' But I want you to know I am here to do the work and get better. I want to get better. So, no more crying."

"You can cry," Dr. Kayla replied.

"I don't want to cry."

"But you can."

"Nope. No more crying."

She smiled at me, deciding not to argue.

"Can we start over, like this is my first session?" I requested.

"Would that be helpful?"

"Yes, I think it will make me feel like I am coming in here fresh, like a brand new me, a stronger me. So, Hi Dr. Kayla, my name is Ember." I held out my hand for her to shake.

"How about we drop the Doctor part okay? Hi Ember, my name is Kayla." She took my hand and shook it.

"It really is nice to have a friend like you, Kayla." I leaned forward and whispered, "Best friends." I smiled so big at her.

Kayla, as I was now calling her, looked at me with a worried expression. That at first confused me, but then it hit me.

"Oh my god, wait, what...we aren't...friends, are we?" My heart sank, and I felt that familiar pounding in my chest as my lower lip started to quiver. With one blink, a single tear fell down my cheek and Kayla placed a hand over her heart, like she genuinely felt mine breaking.

She went to speak, but she knew no words would stop the well of emotions that were about to flood onto her floor. Then, like so many times before, she sat back in her chair and held that same warm, loving space for me while I completely lost my shit.

I walked out of Kayla's office. "See you next week, Lisa." I waved as I slowly passed her desk, looking at the ground.

With a small wave back, Lisa's shoulders dropped. "See you next week, Ember."

# Acknowledgements

A big thank you to my editor, Sarah French who spent many hours fine tuning my manuscript until we got it just right. I learned so much from you that will forever make me a better writer. I am honored to have you as the editor of my first novel.

To my early readers, Leslie Westphal, Jessie Hall, and Susan Brunow. I am so grateful for the love that you had for Ember. You kept me on point and held me accountable from my first draft. Not an easy task!

My cover artist Sarah Earnhart is probably the most talented artist I have ever had the pleasure of working with. The way you were able to bring Ember's pain to picture and the soulful connection that you created between Stormy and Ember from words alone was so beautiful. I am so thankful you chose to go on this journey with me. Thank you!

To my readers, without you, authors would not have a platform to share our stories. Without you, our dreams of our books in your hand would always remain just that...a dream. Thank you! Thank you! Thank you! I hope you enjoyed reading this novel.

# About the Author

Moving from her Midwestern roots to the Pacific Northwest over a decade ago, Christa now lives with her wife, two Golden Retrievers and their Pug. Enjoying everything the Seattle area has to offer from the culture to the coffee, there is never a lack of inspiration for her writing. When not writing, Christa enjoys supporting women's sports, nature, rock hunting, reading, and traveling. This is her first novel.

Made in the USA
Columbia, SC
25 January 2024